BURNSIDE:
THE SECRET FILES

K. M. Lock was born in Oxford and began her
career as a journalist on the *Oxford Star*.
She has written extensively about television for *Radio Times*
and has published six TV novelisations and one non-fiction book.
She lives in York with her husband, Stephen, and daughter, Isis.

Other books by K. M. Lock:

Jimmy McGovern's The Lakes

Writing as Kate Lock:

Where the Heart Is: Home

Where the Heart is: Relative Values

EastEnders: Blood Ties: The Life and Loves of Grant Mitchell

Tiffany's Secret Diary

Bianca's Secret Diary

Who's Who in EastEnders

BURNSIDE:
THE SECRET FILES

K. M. LOCK

HarperCollins*Entertainment*
An Imprint of HarperCollins*Publishers*

HarperCollins*Entertainment*
An imprint of HarperCollins*Publishers*
77–85 Fulham Palace Road,
Hammersmith, London W6 8JB

www.fireandwater.com

A paperback original 2000
1 3 5 7 9 8 6 4 2

A catalogue record for this book
is available from the British Library

ISBN 0 00 710719 6

Set in Sabon, Letter Gothic, Grotesque,
Caflisch Script, Frutiger, American Typewriter

Printed and bound in Great Britain by
Clays Ltd, St Ives plc

For Stephen

With thanks for all the advice, support and childminding

Dear Frank,

The documentary goes out tomorrow night. Maybe you can still get an injunction. There's time. I tried to reason with Tony, but he wouldn't listen – his head on the block and all that. I told him yours was, too. He says I'm 'too close to the subject'. Ironic, isn't it?

I'm sorry about filming you, and pinching your tapes. Despite what you think, I have got a heart. I don't know any other way to prove it than by turning all the evidence over to you. So here it is. It's your call now.

Stay safe.

Pauline

P.S. There's one tape Tony never saw. That was between you and me. It'll never go any further.

DICTAPHONE TRANSCRIPT, TAPE 1A/92,
29.02.00, 13.15

BURNSIDE *[a car engine can be heard in the background]*: '29 Feb. Now there's a date for keeping a low profile. According to Janice in ASU, it ain't a proper leap year and by the time the next one comes round I'll be past my sell-by date. So that's me off the hook...' *[Continues louder]* 'Looks like we've picked up another one. Young girl, probably Croatian. She had a flyer in her pocket for something, had a Zagreb number on it. Otherwise, no ID, no bags, no nothing. Wouldn't say how old she was, but she don't look more than fourteen or fifteen. Interpreter couldn't get much out of her but she obviously ain't here on her holidays. Apparently she was attacked, possibly raped and dumped in bushes at Maidstone Services. Sounds as if she could have been hitching.

'It's not the usual MO, but there might be a link. What we're dealing with is organised: someone's importing these Eastern European kids for the ponces in Soho. They ain't gypsies, so we don't think the begging racket's branching out. The set-up's too sophisticated and they're coming in from all over – Bosnia, Serbia, Croatia, Russia, Bulgaria... It looks like they're being rounded up out there, smuggled in as a job lot and then auctioned off to the trade. They ain't asylum seekers; they're skipping off into the night and avoiding paperwork like the plague.

'What we do know is, they're all very young and they're all very scared – too scared to talk about how they got here, anyway. Someone's put the fear of God into them. The ones our lot are picking up are usually out of their heads on the hard stuff, so they ain't being bribed with sweeties, neither. We've got Vice checking the pimps. They ain't exactly being co-operative. Which means Mr Big runs a very tight outfit or he has extraordinary powers of persuasion. Probably both.

'Reminder: get Hedges onto that flyer, find out what it's advertising.' *[Rustling of paper]* 'Could be anything. My guess is it ain't a car-boot sale or she'd have left it at home.' *[Sound of sudden braking and horn blaring, followed by the hum of an electric window being opened]* 'Oi! You blind or what, pal? You ever heard of indicators?' *[Inaudible shouting]* 'No it ain't a bloody mobile! And if you don't get out of my way I'll have you for driving without due care and attention.' *[Window buzzes closed]* 'Dickhead...'

E-mail

From: Gary Hedges
To: frank.burnside@crimeocu.gov.uk
Subject: Operation Playmates

Sent: 2 March

Guv,

Have been in touch with Interpol (and you thought dealing with overtime claims was bureaucratic). I spoke to someone called Zvonimir Juric at NCB Zagreb about that name on the flyer. They checked it out and got back to me this morning: it's an employment agency that specialises in recruitment for entertainment, conference and leisure industries. Quite a set-up by the sound of it: seven full-time staff and over two hundred on their books. Apparently, Zagreb's big on international trade fairs and exhibitions and they supply mainly for that – waitresses, bar staff, cleaners, chambermaids, guides, etc. Could be our smugglers are channelling the girls through it? Brings a whole new meaning to on-the-job experience...

It doesn't appear to have form – certainly nothing to connect it with illegal immigration. Local police files log several instances of vandalism, two burglaries, one report of assault on premises (withdrawn). Registered address is: Petrinjska 23, 10000 Zagreb. The managing director is Davor Tomasic.

What's interesting is that its head office is in London, plus it has sister agencies in Budapest and Moscow. Terri rang the London number and got an agency called 'Xsecs' in Queensway. They're not in Yellow Pages but we found their ad in the back of a listings magazine. Looks pretty downmarket.

Do you want me to follow through on this?

E-mail
From: Frank Burnside   Sent: 2 March
To: gary.hedges@crimeocu.gov.uk
Subject: Your Message.

No.

TRANSCRIPT OF FILM, TAPE 16V/404; ADDITIONAL COMMENTARY BY REPORTER. XSECS EMPLOYMENT AGENCY, QUEENSWAY, LONDON. 02.03.00, 16.10

PAULINE'S VOICEOVER: 'The Xsecs Employment Agency is never going to recruit the *crème de la crème*. If you're looking for a top-notch PA's post, work as a legal secretary or even a humble receptionist's job, don't bother applying here. Experience in word-processing or knowledge of spreadsheets won't get you far. Forget formal qualifications: the only figures you need to be good at are 36-24-36 or thereabouts. As to letters after your name, think DD or larger.'

The camera pans round a spartan waiting area. It's wall-to-wall with glamour shots, a montage of breasts and bums. Two black leather sofas face each other across a coffee table bearing a cruddy ashtray and a selection of top-shelf men's glossies. Leafing idly through one is Burnside. A girl with spiky hair, panda eyes and multiple piercings is seated at a desk in the far corner, chatting on the phone. Burnside squints at a picture, raises his eyebrows, then cuts in.

'Oi, Miss November, or whatever your name is. I'd like a word.' The girl throws him a malevolent stare. She is stick-thin and unremarkable beneath her make-up. She continues to talk. 'Now.' He flashes his warrant card.

'Gotta go, some geezer's hassling me. See ya later.' She puts down the receiver and folds her arms. 'Yeah?'

'DCI Burnside. I'd like to see the boss.'

'She's out.'

'Who's "she"? The cat's mother?'

'Miss Miller.'

'Well, when Miss Miller returns, give her this and tell her I want to speak to her.' He hands over a card.

The receptionist studies it. 'Why?'

'I'll discuss that with her. What is this place, anyway? Centrefolds Anonymous?'

'It's a promotions agency.'

'And what exactly do you promote? As if I couldn't guess.'

'All sorts.' She picks up a paperclip and makes a show of cleaning her nails.

'They pick you for your natural charm, did they?' Burnside throws down the magazine. 'You tell your boss to call me – pronto.'

He turns to leave the office and cannons into two girls coming in through the door. One is a blonde, the other a brunette; both are revealingly clad. They're also gauchely young. Burnside backs off, apologetic.

'Sorry, ladies. Didn't see you coming. Bet you don't get many blokes saying that to you.' He eyeballs their skimpy clothes. 'Dressed for work, are we?'

'That's right.' The blonde strikes a pose, hands on hip. 'So?' She bats him a challenging look.

'Very nice. Do you get to wear it long?'

'We're not slags,' the brunette interrupts. The receptionist gestures a warning, finger across throat, which they both fail to notice.

'I can tell. You've obviously got style. Models, I'd say. Am I right?'

'Are you a booker?' The blonde thaws rapidly.

Burnside smiles genially. 'You could say that.' He motions to the walls. 'So, which ones are yours? It's a bit hard to pick out faces.'

The brunette snorts. 'We don't do this stuff. Runways, that's what we do.'

Burnside looks puzzled. The blonde enlightens him. 'Fashion shows – you know, the catwalks. Designer labels.'

'Oh.' He nods.

She droops. 'You're not a booker, are you?'

'No, sweetheart. And you ain't Naomi Campbell, are you? '

'We've done two charity events. And an auction.' The brunette is indignant.

'Yeah, and the motor show.'

The receptionist intervenes. 'They're working on their portfolios. We give them contacts and get them work; they get to raise their profiles and meet the right people.' She gets up and walks over to the door, holding it open. 'It's standard practice.'

'And what work do you provide them with, specifically?' Burnside ignores the hint.

'You've got to be intelligent to do what we do.' The brunette

13

sounds as if she's trying to convince herself. 'We're classy. It's not whipping your tits out.'

'That's right,' her friend chips in. 'We have to read the papers and talk about movies and all sorts.'

'You keep your clothes on and you discuss films. What are you, critics?'

They giggle. 'You're cute.' The blonde kisses his cheek. 'You can sit at my table anytime.'

'Carole! Jacqui!' the receptionist barks. 'If you want to work any more, you'd better remember the terms of your contract.' They shut up.

Burnside steps through the doorway, then turns back to her. 'Shouldn't you have said, "If you want any more work"?'

She slams the door in his face.

DICTAPHONE TRANSCRIPT, TAPE 8A/92, 02.03.00, 16.55

BURNSIDE [in his car again]: 'Xsecs Agency, Queensway: tarts' drop-in centre; tossers' paradise. Looks like they provide girls for all eventualities, some of which probably ain't on their books. Not the ones they show the taxman, anyway. They could be exploiting underage girls, conning them about becoming models. Not exactly original. No sign of any exotic Eastern Europeans, but then they'd have to keep them for behind-the-scenes stuff, being illegals. Might be a front for a knocking shop or something dodgy. The girls have obviously been told to keep their mouths shut, if nothing else – ' [He is interrupted by his mobile going off] 'Burnside... Yeah?... Well get a bloody warrant... On my authorisation! Look, while you're here, Gary, get hold of Vice, too. Brief them about this agency, Xsecs... Bayswater, that's right. See if the owner's got form. Miller... female... and anything else they've got on it. I think they supply escorts or hostesses, probably to a club. They're a bit secretive about it. Get a list of all known associates. They do photographic modelling, too... well, I couldn't bloody miss it. Talk about eyes following you round the room... Very funny. One more thing... don't let that lot get any ideas. This is our investigation. I don't want Vice queering our pitch... well put it into official jargon, that's what I rely on you for... Yeah, OK. See you back at the factory.' [*There is a beep as the phone is switched off. Burnside's obviously forgotten the dictaphone's still on. He switches on the car radio and gets Capital Radio. The newsreader is talking about Labour's selection campaign for the Lord Mayor of London. Burnside snorts, unimpressed with a soundbite from Frank Dobson*]

NEWSREADER: 'Other news: the Commissioner of the Metropolitan Police has revealed that its internal inquiry into corruption is stepping up apace. Over two hundred Metropolitan police officers were originally thought to have been uncovered by Operation Pepper; now it seems as if the figure could be even higher. An investigation team, which has been combing officers' backgrounds going back twenty years, has discovered shocking levels of criminality among Scotland Yard's most experienced detectives. Corrupt officers are said to have made fortunes from major drug deals and armed robberies, and some have even been implicated in contract killings. It's thought a catalogue of wrongful convictions may also come to light. So serious are the findings that the operation has been widened to cover the entire criminal justice system. Lawyers, judges, CPS officers and court staff are all having their case histories scrutinised.

'In the City today, shares rose sharply – '[*Sound of the radio being switched off*]
BURNSIDE: 'Jesus H Christ. That's all we bloody need.'

CHAMBERS: 'For the record, you are – were – a colleague of Frank Burnside's?'

HEDGES: 'He was my guvnor in Crime OCU. We worked together since he joined in December 1998.'

CHAMBERS: 'And would you say he was a good boss?'

HEDGES: 'Depends what you mean by "good". I never had any complaints. He could be tough. He demanded a lot of you. But he gave a lot of himself, too, so you never felt you was being hard done by. He had a reputation for being a bit evil, know what I mean? But me and Frank used to get along, we had a laugh.'

CHAMBERS: '"A bit evil"? Can you elaborate?'

HEDGES: 'Well, Frank's an old-style copper. When he was earning his stripes, detectives was all like *The Sweeney*. I'm not saying he's like that now. I never saw him stuff no one's head down the bog. But he can talk the talk, know what I mean? Walk the walk. He's been around.'

CHAMBERS: 'With criminals?'

HEDGES: 'How else d'you think he's nicked 'em! Look, I ain't saying Frank's bent. Not what I know of him. He may have been a bit fly in the past, who knows? He's a risk-taker; that's how he operates. He gets the bodies. Look at what he's pulled off undercover. Speaks for itself.'

CHAMBERS: 'Working undercover – that's one of Frank's – Burnside's – specialities, isn't it?'

HEDGES: 'Yeah. He's a cool customer, is Frank. Al Pacino, Robert de Niro, you think they're tough? It's acting, but the setting's fake. They've got stunt men and blank cartridges and some director yelling "cut". Going undercover's acting for real. You get found out by some of the types Frank's been mixed up with and the bullets leave brains on the wall, not ketchup.'

CHAMBERS: 'Have you been on any undercover operations with him?'

HEDGES: 'We done a few together.'

CHAMBERS: 'What about this one? It's had far-reaching repercussions, not least for Burnside. Were you involved in it at all?'

HEDGES: 'I did a lot of the legwork. Frank got the leg-over work.' [*He laughs uproariously at his joke*]

CHAMBERS [*Unamused*]: 'That's... speculation.'

HEDGES [*Still chortling*]: 'Yeah. Well. Letting Frank loose in a bar full of gorgeous birds with a brief to chat 'em up sounds like an open invitation to me. Though he did include me in that obbo, as it happens. He can be generous.

'We had this list of hostess clubs see, to cross-check against Xsecs. Six of 'em. So he says, "Right, Gary, you take three and I'll take three. Go home, put on some of your designer clobber – 'cos he knows I'm into Paul Smith, see? – and meet me at The Feathers at half-six; we'll have a swift one before we hit the town."

'Course, all the others was taking the mick something rotten – couldn't we pull without paying? That sort of thing. Jealous as hell, really. And the plonks was complaining it was discrimination and why couldn't they do it. As if! Sutton seemed to think it was a bit of a long shot, but I reckon he was worried about our exes.'

CHAMBERS: 'So what did you find?'

HEDGES: 'Me? I drew the short straws, didn't I? Burnside's got a knack for landing the big ones. But then I ain't telling you nothing you don't know, am I?'

CHAMBERS: 'No.'

A montage of shots showing interiors. Silks is decked out like the lounge of a cruise liner, with gilded mirrors, ostentatious chandeliers, round tables and a veneered bar with brass rails. Seating is in high-backed booths upholstered in plush red velvet. It's intimate and clubby, old-fashioned even. There are no poles or platforms here, though there is a small stage with a dance floor in front of it. Currently, the stage is occupied by the resident band, a three-piece combo churning out cover numbers in the interlude before the next cabaret. The sex theme is muted but pervasive: erotic prints and photographs adorn the walls, while nude statuettes occupy alcoves or are displayed on plinths. Scantily-clad table dancers, the mainstay of other such clubs, are conspicuous by their absence. In the muted glow cast by the Art Deco table lamps, the beautiful hostesses and smartly dressed men people an artfully accessorised fantasy. It's a bordello with a *Titanic*-themed makeover.

PAULINE'S VOICEOVER: 'Silks is a so-called "Gentlemen's Club", that is, a club where rich men pay to be "entertained" by attractive young women. And they pay handsomely for the privilege. They're expected to wine if not dine their "companion" lavishly: champagne – hostesses profess to drink nothing else – starts at £250 a bottle.

'The girls work on commission, taking a percentage of the total spent by each customer. All they are required to do is talk. Dancing is permitted, indeed encouraged, but sexual contact, other than kissing and cuddling, is forbidden inside the club. Off the premises, the official line is that whatever the girls do with their customers is their own business. The reality is rather different.

'None of the hostesses see themselves as prostitutes, yet sex is what the men come for, and sex is what the girls expect ultimately to provide. It's the invisible item writ large alongside the inflated prices of drinks; a commodity wrapped in euphemisms and slipped under the counter. This might look and sound like an exclusive club, but the truth is, it's King's Cross with class.

'So, what kind of men come to Silks? Foreign businessmen, typically Japanese and Korean. Thrill-seeking tourists. Arab princes. A surprising number of celebrities, media folk and politicians. A clutch of independently wealthy regulars. Many are just ordinary men with generous expense accounts, who simply put in a claim for "entertaining clients". Sometimes this is a genuine claim – corporate hospitality is big business here – and sometimes it is not. So long as your credit's good, no one asks or cares.'

Another camera shows a scene in a booth, where a man with receding iron-grey hair and a tan is talking to a young girl. Although the picture quality is not great, it's obviously Burnside. He pours champagne into two flutes and they drink, looking into each other's eyes. They appear intimate and relaxed and sit with their heads close together, laughing and joking.

The shot switches to another camera by the bar, which shows several beautiful but expressionless girls perched on bar stools. An older woman in a backless gown enters the frame, and introduces one of them to a customer. The girl's face becomes suddenly animated, as if someone had just switched her from 'vacant' to 'engaged', but the smile doesn't reach her eyes.

Standing next to the hostesses is a man whose flamboyant appearance contrasts sharply with the formally attired customers. The image – fringed white suit, black T-shirt and snakeskin cowboy boots – suggests an ageing pop star, and one with no intention of growing old gracefully. The seams on his face have been ironed out by cosmetic surgery, giving a creased-linen effect, and the hairline of his receding grey-blond mane sprouts obvious follicular implants. He wears his wealth like a dowry: fistfuls of rings, a gold chain on one wrist, Rolex on the other. Glistening conspicuously in his left ear are three diamond studs. A larger, teardrop-shaped diamond dangles from his lobe.

PAULINE'S VOICEOVER: 'This is Peter Dawson, the owner of Silks. Dawson, fifty-two, is said to be one of Britain's top five hundred richest men, a fact he refuses to confirm or deny. A self-made man, he was born in Hackney but made his fortune in South Africa. He took over the premises fifteen years ago and succeeded in raising its profile from downmarket clip joint to respectable gentlemen's club, a reputation it has managed to hang on to, despite competition from newer, more fashionable venues. Dawson's recipe for success is, he says, "giving the punter what he wants" – although this customer is clearly far from happy.'

The next clip of film shows Burnside walking up to Dawson and addressing him. It's obviously not a friendly greeting and the two men do not shake hands. Instead, Dawson leans back against the bar and, propping himself on his elbows, crosses his legs. He appears to be admiring his boots. His expression, as far as one can tell from his bland face, is one of amusement. Burnside, hands in pockets, looks less amused. Their discussion becomes animated and after a heated exchange, Burnside puts his face close to Dawson's and appears to issue a warning or threat. Dawson signals to two heavies, who have been hovering in the background, but Burnside brushes them off and stalks away. Dawson turns round and leans on the bar, ordering a large Cognac. A scowl furrows his artificially smooth brow, completely ruining the effect.

PAULINE'S VOICEOVER: 'The man you've just seen is a detective, DCI Frank Burnside. It was his visits to Silks, posing as an ordinary customer, that led me to discover the chain of vice and corruption that runs right to the very heart of the Metropolitan Police...'

DICTAPHONE TRANSCRIPT, TAPE 13A/92, 04.03.00, 00.25

BURNSIDE: 'Silks hostess club, off Piccadilly – bingo! Didn't think I was going to get lucky at first. Not in the criminal investigation department, anyway...' [*Laughs*] 'Hostess there, Emma, confirmed the deal with Xsecs; she's on their books, so are half a dozen others. It's not the way these places usually recruit: most of them do it through ads. So why use an agency when they could cut out the middleman? Or woman, in this case. It doesn't make business sense. I thought the set-up was iffy, and that was before the ghost of Christmas past put in an appearance.

'I was going to order another drink, 'cos this bird was well worth putting half a grand on expenses for, when I clocked this face at the bar. Something about it rang a bell and I went over for a gander. It's only an old lag called Dawson pretending he's Peter bloody Stringfellow! He's had plastic surgery so I wasn't sure at first, but they can never disguise the eyes. Question is, has he had it done to look pretty, or is it because he doesn't want to be recognised? Since it's given him a mug like a monkey's arse, I'm inclined to think he don't like the climate in Rio. Then again, he's obviously got the readies. Could just be he's got more money than sense – though where it came from, I don't know. Even if he's been running knocking shops for years, it wouldn't be making him enough to start up a West End club.' [*Long pause follows. Sound of Burnside drawing back curtains. Faint traffic noise from outside.*]

'He's up to something. Slags like Dawson don't change. Told

me he'd "gone legit", said he had been for years. I said, "Have I got 'stupid' tattooed on my forehead or what?" I mean, what does he take me for? OK, he stitched me up years ago, but he ain't pulling the wool over my eyes again. It's too much of a coincidence that Croatian girl turning up and the next thing I'm running into Dawson. I've got a feeling about this one...'

[*Another long pause. A siren wails in the distance. Burnside sips a drink. The tape runs for five more minutes, during which Burnside says nothing, then clicks off.*]

TRANSCRIPT OF TELEPHONE CALL, TAPE 72T/998.
SILKS HOSTESS CLUB.
03.03.00, 23.45

DAWSON: 'It's Pete – '

MALE VOICE: 'I told you never to phone me at home. What if Elizabeth had answered? Or one of the boys?'

DAWSON: 'Then I'd have said wrong number. Listen, this ain't a social call. You'll never guess who I've just had here.'

MALE VOICE [*dryly*]: 'Judging from the tremor in your voice, I'd say the Chancellor, Richard Branson or Prince Andrew.'

DAWSON: 'Frank Burnside.'

MALE VOICE [*taken aback*]: 'Burnside? What did he want?'

DAWSON: 'You tell me.'

MALE VOICE: 'What did he say?'

DAWSON: 'That he'd got a long memory and it weren't over between us. "I know your game and I'll be back." That sort of thing.'

MALE VOICE: 'Impossible. There's nothing to go on.'

DAWSON [*getting angry*]: 'Well you tell me why he was sniffing around then. He was talking to one of my girls, asking a load of questions, then he came over and started hassling me.'

MALE VOICE: 'What did she tell him?'

DAWSON: 'Nothing! She don't know anything. She's just a tart. Look, I know we're covered this end. It ain't the pussy trade I'm worried about.'

MALE VOICE: 'I'm sure Frank Burnside's not going to start raking up the past. It's not in his interests.'

DAWSON: 'It ain't in ours, either.'

MALE VOICE: 'Believe me, he's got more sense. Especially in the present climate. Don't you read the papers, man?'

DAWSON: 'Yeah. Gotta keep up with who's shagging who, the circles I move in.'

MALE VOICE: 'Try reading a broadsheet once in a while. There's a major internal investigation going on. Every officer who's served twenty years or more is watching his back.'

DAWSON: 'You think Burnside's just sounding off, then? All mouth and no trousers?'

MALE VOICE: 'In a nutshell, yes. He's winding you up. So keep your cool if he comes round again. Burnside's smart.'

DAWSON: 'Not that friggin' smart.'

MALE VOICE: 'A lot of water's gone under the bridge since then, Peter. Don't underestimate him.'

DAWSON: 'I called you, didn't I? You gonna keep your side of the bargain, or what?'

MALE VOICE [*curt*]: 'I'll be in touch.' [*Louder*] 'Coming, darling.' [*Lowering his tone again*] 'Just remember: don't call me. Got that?' [*The conversation is terminated abruptly.*]

Diary, 3 March.

This is OK. Not what I ever thought I'd wind up doing, but it's only temporary. Anyway, it's a real buzz, living a double life. I like having an alter ego, being this sexy chick. It lets me play out my fantasies, indulge my wild side.

It's not like I'm actually going with the punters, although they ask me to. I tell them my boyfriend's the jealous type and he comes from this big East End 'family'. If they don't get it, I say the last punter I went with got both his legs broken. That puts them off. I give Carole my tricks; she's up for most things. Sure, I'll take risks, it's why they gave me the job, but that's a line I'm not crossing. Nothing to do with ethics (I mean, who would know?); it's a power thing. I'm the one in control. As soon as you have sex with a bloke, you lose that. Besides which, getting rid of the kit each time would be a total nightmare!

Wearing the equipment still freaks me out. It's not as if I can get away with lots of layers. Fortunately, I've had help from a surveillance nut (he calls himself 'Data' but I happen to know his name's Stan). He claims to have been a spy, which I take with a pinch of salt, but he certainly knows his gear. I've got the latest wireless pinhole micro-video camera – the viewing hole is only a sixteenth of an inch, so it's invisible to anyone looking at it. Because it has a built-in wireless video sender, there's no problem with trailing wires, and the whole thing's less than 3cm long. It runs for 12 hours on a single 9V battery, which is a real boon, it's got a range of up to a thousand feet and automatically compensates for low lighting conditions – essential for the club. It transmits to a receiver, which I keep in my handbag. There's also a mike, which is equally tiny, although that has to be connected to a minidisc player, so it does have a wire.

After much experimenting with different undergarments – the most intimate Data's been with a woman, I'm pretty sure of that – I bought a couple of designer corsets, took out the padding from the bra cups and sewed a camera and a mike into the lining of each one. The advantage of the corsets is that they're boned – horribly uncomfortable to wear, but brilliant for disguising wires. And needless to say, Posh Spice has been snapped wearing them, so they're dead trendy. The look suits me, because I look quite like her with my spiky hair, and Dawson even calls me 'Posh', so it's become my nickname.

As for the minidisc player, it's flat enough to tuck it into the top of my stocking hold-ups on the inside of my thigh (I have to thread the wire under my knickers – no indignity spared in the surveillance game). Hold-ups are perfect because, unlike stockings, they grip your leg like an iron band. Luckily, I'm a size 8–10, so my legs are slim enough to get away with it. I have perfected walking with a sexy wiggle, à la Marilyn Monroe, to disguise what this does to my gait! I avoid really short skirts, but anything on or just above the knee is safe.

I also have another camera in my handbag and my mobile and personal organiser are both disguised cameras. The spying business is amazing: you can hide cameras in virtually anything. The other cameras are useful backup if I have a groper: sometimes I just ditch the covert kit in my locker and rely on them instead.

The other girls are pretty bitchy. They think I'm weird because I don't turn tricks. Most of them have got boyfriends, but they don't tell them what they do – their blokes all think they're doing bar jobs, not blow jobs. In a way, we're all leading secret lives, here. It's been an eye-opener finding out why these girls get into it. Some of them have a drug habit. Anna, Judi and Bridget get seriously coked up before the evening's even started. Quite a few have got kids. There's lots of students, too: only yesterday I discovered Vicky was doing a PhD in Chemistry.

Then there's the younger girls, who think they're going to be 'discovered'. Course, the blokes tell them that; I've lost count of how many so-called film producers and talent-spotters I've met. And Clare encourages them, makes them think they're going to end up like Julia Roberts in Pretty Woman. Sad, really. At best they'll make trophy girlfriends for a season. At worst – well, that's what I'm here to find out.

One of the things I get a kick out of is sussing out the punters, sifting through all the bullshit and trying to work out what their lives are really like. Had one this evening that was interesting. Most of them are pretty tame: bankers or businessmen who think going to a hostess club is kicking over the traces. This guy, he wasn't looking for an ego-boost; he was so together and assured. He said his name was Frank, but that's about all I got out of him. I did my usual 'Tell me all about yourself' routine and he said there was nothing to tell and kept asking me questions instead: how long had I been working there, how did I get into it, did they treat me well...

I told him I was Emma and stuck to my cover story about being a model-cum-actress, but it got tricky at times. Something about the way he was asking, the way he kept looking at me, made me want to open up. I don't mean blow my cover, I mean tell him what I really think about this place, the whole sexual politics thing. But I didn't think Mr Dawson would be too happy hearing one of his girlies sounding off like they're on Newsnight, so I just flannelled and played with my hair a lot.

It obviously didn't impress him because he got up to go after one bottle of champagne (my average is three!) Angie noticed and said I'd better get my act together, the old cow. To tell the truth, though, I was a bit disappointed myself. That was the first punter I've actually liked. NB: I think he's probably an entrepreneur of some sort. Definitely a risk-taker. I suppose that was why I got on with him. Ah, well...

CONFIDENTIAL PROGRESS REPORT: 'HIDDEN CHAMBERS' (TRANSMISSION TBC). DATE: 6 MARCH

PRESENT: RAY DUNTHORNE (PRODUCER), PAULINE CHAMBERS (REPORTER), TONY DILLON (DIRECTOR),

IAN DI MICHELE (ASSISTANT DIRECTOR), SAMANTHA GWILLIAM (RESEARCHER)

Eye Witnesses

Two confirmed: Catherine O'Leary (14) and Suzanne Kelly (15). Both have agreed to do interviews about how Xsecs set them up with modelling jobs that turned out to be making porn movies. One more possible, Kristina Tomasic (15). Very nervous but may be persuaded to speak on camera if her identity is disguised. Ray thinks she might be an illegal immigrant. If so, could this be relevant?

ACTION: Samantha to arrange times of interviews with Ian. (NOTE: Catherine is still very distressed so handle with care.) Ian to make further inquiries about Kristina's background.

Talking Heads

1. Rachel Coleman, psycho-sexual counsellor, Leeds University. Primed to talk about effect on girls, how this might affect their future relationships, self-image, personal development, etc.

ACTION: Interview arranged for 23 March, 11.00 am at Leeds.

2. Dr Paul Robertson (profiler, has written extensively about paedophiles & porn). Lecturer, based in Cambridge but currently at conference in San Diego. Should be back by 15th. Secretary sounded hopeful.

ACTION: Sam to follow up.

3. Helen Campbell, London League of Prostitutes. Against exploitation of minors but supports prostitutes working in 'specialist areas', so long as they are willing participants and are not coerced.

ACTION: Interview in can. Possible follow up, depending on what Pauline gets.

4. Vice Squad.

ACTION: Ian to pursue gay contact for quote, but only close to transmission.

5. New Mayor (whoever!): what is he going to do about cleaning up sleazy London?

ACTION: Tony to approach office for interview nearer transmission.

Silks

Pauline has been on the rota at Silks for three weeks. No problem with Dawson but credibility becoming an issue with other girls. Angie, the greeter, is also asking questions. Secret cameras and mikes are all in situ now (two behind bar, one in each private suite and one in Dawson's office) but checking and changing tapes and batteries is proving difficult. Pauline is going in early and switching them when the bar staff are in the cellar/on a break, but is finding it hard to do this regularly.

ACTION: Time to wheel on Tony doing 'jealous boyfriend' act? Pauline to monitor situation. Ray has reminded her not to compromise her personal safety, regarding the tapes.

Xsecs

Two cameras in place: one in reception, the other in Clare Miller's office. Pauline hasn't had the opportunity to check tapes yet. Phone tap likely to be more useful here. Receptionist Joanne Bennet is dissatisfied with her job – would be valuable if we could get her on side.

ACTION: Samantha to chat Joanne up, tell her she's researching a documentary on body piercing! Pauline to visit agency again soon.

Progress of investigation

Evidence is still mostly circumstantial. There are private suites at

Silks, but they're for entertaining VIPs. No sex goes on there; Dawson has a deal with the Hotel Rosetta across the road. He told Pauline he has a standing arrangement for half a dozen rooms at a discounted rate. This means he can sting the punters for the tab plus 'administration costs', which they're happy to pay because it saves embarrassment and hassle. The girls are allowed to leave with punters after midnight and are often back and working again within the hour.

It seems unlikely this is where the hardcore stuff takes place: too public, plus Dawson wouldn't risk taking underage girls there. All three eyewitnesses were drugged and disorientated, but describe white rooms with high ceilings, cornices, ceiling roses, etc. Possibly a private house? Dawson has made references to his 'day job' at 'the palace' in conversation with Angie. We need to find this place!

ACTION: Pauline to film Dawson's every move and generally keep her ear to the ground. Tony and Ian to tail Dawson to and from the club. Ray to visit club as punter and ask for the full menu? (But could be problem with entrapment.)

NOTE: Pauline's cover is OK at the moment but she thinks Silks might drop her if punters complain she's not putting out. Ray says upstairs are querying budget and we need to get a result soon.

TRANSCRIPT OF TELEPHONE CALL, TAPE 302T/998.
XSECS EMPLOYMENT AGENCY, QUEENSWAY, LONDON.
06.03.00, 09.30

MILLER'S VOICE: 'Clare Miller is out of the office. Please leave your message and number after the tone and your call will be returned.' [*Beeping noise*]

CALLER: 'Sod it. Clare, if you're there, pick up. It's – ' [*crackle of interference; the caller is on a mobile*]

MILLER [*breathless*]: 'Give me a chance. I haven't even got my coat off. What's up?'

CALLER: 'Bad news. The filth picked our girl up a week last Friday. My relief driver just called me from the services.'

MILLER: 'Jesus.'

CALLER: 'I know.'

MILLER: 'This is all your fault.'

CALLER: 'Don't start that again. How was I to know she was going to do a runner? I mean, it ain't in their interests, is it?'

MILLER: 'Maybe you gave her good cause.'

CALLER: 'I told you, I went in the wagon to see what was happening, 'cos one of them was crying and making a racket. This Sandra must've sneaked out behind my back.'

MILLER: 'I don't believe you. You were helping yourself to the cakes again. Pinching a cherry off the top. Weren't you?'

CALLER: 'What do you take me for?'

MILLER: 'Don't ask if you don't want to know. Christ, Pete's going to go mental.'

CALLER: 'Come on, Clare. We don't need to tell him nothing. He never sussed you slotted in a different one, did he?'

MILLER: 'For which you still owe me four grand.'

CALLER: 'We said two.'

MILLER: 'Yeah, well I want double that. Joanne's already had some detective leaving messages. I need frigging danger money.'

CALLER: 'The police? How could they have anything? The girls don't know zilch. Davor makes sure of that. No names, no addresses, no phone numbers. We keep 'em in the dark – literally. That way, we're all protected.'

MILLER: 'Let's hope he was just after my outstanding parking fines, then. Because if that girl's started blabbing, you're on your own.'

CALLER: 'I'd take you with me, Clare, and you know it.'

MILLER [*short pause*]: 'You've got to find her.'

CALLER: 'She could be anywhere.'

MILLER: 'Not without a passport. She'll be in one of those detention centres.'

CALLER: 'Do you think she'll talk?'

MILLER: 'Probably not – to the police, anyway. But if she confides in any of her new little roommates and word gets around...'

CALLER: 'So we've got to shut her up.'

MILLER: 'Correction: you've got to shut her up. Or get someone on the inside to do it for you.'

CALLER: 'Give me a break. Those places are like prisons. It's impossible.'

MILLER: 'What kind of a break do you think Pete'll give you if this all goes belly up? I'd say your skull would be his first choice.'

CALLER: 'You're a bitch, Clare. A right nasty piece of work.'

MILLER: 'Ooh, I just love it when you talk dirty. Now sod off and sort this mess out.'

Statement by Sanja Gregovic, Dover Police Station. 6 March 2000, 10.00 hrs.

'I am hitching across Europe. That is how I go to England. Hitching, working, sleeping rough many times. I come because I want a better life for myself, not just a waitress or a dumb shop girl in Zagreb. I am still young. People say I am very pretty. They tell me I can be a model and earn much money! And I have no family any more to make me stay. My parents and sister are killed by the Serbs. Many of my friends, too. So there is nothing for me in Croatia. It take me one month to go to Calais. I am very tired. I take a lift in a car with a British man. It is a white car with a big trunk full of boxes. He say he is a salesman. He say his name is

John. He is short and has no hair and a big stomach. He is wearing Gap T-shirt and jeans. We go on the ferry to Dover. We do not get stopped. He leave me at the motorway place but he buy me food first. He is a nice man, he does not hurt me. I am raped by a lorry driver when I ask to hitch a ride. He too has a big stomach but he is tall and strong. He has tattoos on his arms – a snake and a cross – but I do not read the writing. He has brown hair and blue eyes and his face is pitted. He tell me get in, then he beat me and force me to make sex with him. I fight back but I am weak. He throw me out of his lorry and I run away. I am frightened he chase me, so I hide in the bushes. He drive off in his lorry with all my things. That is why I have no papers, no passport, no clothes. I am cold and bleeding and very scared. When another man find me, I think he will rape me too. That is why I speak no English to him. When I see policeman, I do not know how to say what has happened because I am ashamed.'

DICTAPHONE TRANSCRIPT, TAPE 36A/92
06.03.00, 12.00

BURNSIDE: 'Update on Operation Playmates. I've just interviewed the girl they picked up at Maidstone Services. As I suspected, she does speak English, she was just being a bit shy the other day. She says she was raped, but I think she's telling porkies. FME's report suggests sex was consensual, thought she was obviously knocked about by someone. My guess is she was turning tricks in the lorry park and one of her punters turned nasty.' [*A car can be heard as it goes past. It sounds as though Burnside is in his car but the engine is turned off. It's not a busy road. He is eating what sounds like a packet of crisps.*]

'Traffic is looking out for the driver of the white car. It's likely he was smuggling beer or cigarettes from France. The tapes from the security cameras at the Maidstone Services will be sent on to our lot for checking. I'll get Gary on to Interpol again, see what the ASF can throw up about our little Sanja. Something about her story doesn't feel right. It's too tidy. Her passport being nicked, for starters. Very convenient. If she's lying and she was smuggled in with a load of illegals, she'll be shit-scared of reprisals. One little orphaned Croat ain't gonna be missed. She'll swear black's white to save her skin... She *claims* she was given the flyer for the Zagreb employment agency by someone in the street but says she never went in there. She also claims she doesn't know anything about their office in Queensway. Personally, I have my doubts. She wants to be a model: Xsecs hires models. Not the sort that'll ever give Kate Moss a run for her money but I don't suppose Sanja's fussy how she starts out. Even if she did get here on her tod, she's probably slept her way from Zagreb to Calais. I can't see how else she did it; it ain't exactly the season for grape-picking. Posing for mucky pictures would be a piece of cake.

'Either way, she could be the bait we need to land the big fish. If Immigration lets Sanja go, there's a chance she'll contact Miller if she thinks the heat's off. Depends how desperate she is for a catwalk career. All we need to do is keep tabs on her.'

E-mail

From: Commander David Webster, Operation Pepper   Sent: 6 March
To: roger.sutton@crimeocu.gov.uk
Subject: DCI Frank Burnside

Information has come to my attention regarding DCI Frank Burnside that I wish to discuss with you as his commanding officer as a matter of urgency. Please telephone my secretary to make an appointment. At this preliminary stage, my preferred option is to keep interviews informal. If there is evidence warranting further investigation, DCI Burnside will be called for interview by our inquiry panel. Should charges subsequently be brought, he will be suspended from duty in compliance with the usual disciplinary procedures.

I am sure I do not need to emphasise the gravity of this situation to you. The operation is highly confidential and all interviewees are under instruction not to disclose information about their involvement to any other person, particularly the subject of an investigation.

TRANSCRIPT OF FILM, TAPE 221V/404; SILKS. 06.03.00, 21.30

Burnside is seated at a table, a bottle of champagne in an ice bucket in front of him. He is impeccably dressed in a dark grey suit and navy silk shirt and appears relaxed. He looks up and smiles as 'Emma' joins him at the table.

'I was hoping you'd be here.'

'Angie said you asked for me personally. I'm flattered. I didn't think I'd made much of an impression, you left so quickly last time.'

'Business.' He gestures expansively. 'My life ain't my own any more, what with the mobile going off morning, noon and night.'

'You must have sharp ears. I didn't hear it ring.'

'That's because it was vibrating in my pocket.' He takes it out and lays it on the table. She strokes it with a polished fingernail. 'Are you sure that's what it was?'

Burnside gives her a full-on smile. 'Now you come to mention it... here, have a drink.' He pours them both a glass, then holds the bottle up and reads the label. 'Not what I'd call vintage stuff.'

'I know, it's rubbish. I call it Appellation out-of-contrôlée.'

He laughs heartily. 'Do you say that to all the punters?'

'I wouldn't last long if I did.'

'So what do you prefer to drink?'

'Guinness or whisky. Pimms in summer. Ice-cold Russian vodka when I'm feeling reckless. Oh, and proper martinis.'

Burnside starts to gesture to a waitress, but Emma puts a hand on his arm. 'No, it's OK. I'll stick with this. Club policy and all that. It gets more bearable by the second bottle.'

He regards her curiously. 'You don't strike me as your average hostess girl.'

'Why? Because I've got taste? It's not a bad way to make a living, you know. Some girls would give their eye teeth for this job, sitting around being chatted up and drinking champagne.'

'But not you.' He makes it sound like a statement of fact. Emma bristles. 'I like it.'

'So tell me why. What's so special about playing the patsy for blokes like me? You're young, you're bright, you're drop-dead gorgeous. You could do much better for yourself. Why work in this place?'

'Because... because it's easy money. And before you ask, no I don't. It means I'm free during the day to go to castings and auditions, and as soon as my modelling career takes off that's what I'll do. Meanwhile, I've got to pay the mortgage.'

'Doesn't your boyfriend mind?'

'I don't bother with boyfriends. They're a waste of space.'

'Does that apply to all men?'

She flushes. 'No, of course not. It's just that boys my own age bore me. I prefer older men. They're more appreciative.' She reaches over and covers his hand, pouring them both more champagne with the other, acting the nightclub hostess again. 'Now, Frank, would you like to show how much you appreciate me by buying another bottle of this?'

Burnside regards her steadily. He turns her hand over and strokes the palm with his thumb. 'How old are you?'

'Old enough to know what I want out of life.'

'Twenty-one.'

'Twenty-five, actually. A gentleman wouldn't ask.'

'Did I say I was a gentleman?'

'You're all gentlemen here, according to my boss, regardless of what suggestions I get whispered in my ears.'

Burnside gestures for more champagne. 'And make it a decent one, this time.' He turns back to Emma. 'Does he sanction it then, your boss, if a punter wants something – "special"?'

She gives him a suspicious look. 'I told you, I – '

'I believe you. But there are other girls that do?'

'Yes. No. I don't know. It depends what you mean.'

'I mean things you wouldn't see in top-shelf magazines at your local newsagent.'

Emma gets up abruptly. 'I really can't help you.'

Burnside's expression is unreadable. 'If I said I was asking for a friend, would you believe me?'

'Do you know how many men here have friends like that? Enough to start a whole other club.' Emma spits out the insult through a fake smile. 'Excuse me, I'll go and make enquiries for you.'

TRANSCRIPT OF FILM, TAPE 225V/404; SILKS.
06.03.00, 21.45

A private suite. Dawson is reclining on a plush sofa with his arms around two of the hostesses, watching an erotic video on a massive, widescreen television. He is wearing his white suit again and a black shirt, which is half unbuttoned. The door opens and Burnside is escorted in by Emma, who is still maintaining a rigid smile. She announces him and leaves without bidding him goodbye. Dawson does not deign to look up. Burnside strolls over to the group, hands in pockets, and blocks their view.

'Oi, you two, hop it. I want a word with Travolta here.'

Dawson flicks him a glance and makes a judgement. He squeezes the two girls, kisses them wetly on the lips and dispatches them with smacks on their bottoms. Burnside studies the video, where a threesome is climaxing noisily.

'That the kind of thing you want?' Dawson hits the remote, blanking the screen. 'Sorry, strictly private usage. Don't want to lose my licence, do I?'

'I'm surprised you've held on to it for so long. In fact, I'm surprised you've got one at all.'

Dawson crosses his legs and admires his boots, a different pair this time, in silver-coloured leather embossed with angels. 'I take it your request for a bit of specialist rumpy pumpy was a front.'

'I don't need excuses to interview you, you piece of filth. I'm here to find out just what kind of establishment you really run.'

'Take a look, feel free. I'll give you the tour.' Dawson grins. 'This is where we entertain our VIPs, of which we have many. There's another one on the next floor. Some of our customers are a bit publicity-shy, so we let them in through the back and take 'em straight up there. It's all legit, like I told you. We have regular inspections. I don't know what you think you're gonna find, Frank.'

'Evidence of your dodgy dealings.'

'You're beginning to upset me, Frank. I'm offering you hospitality. It's not like a bent copper to turn that down. Scotch? You'll like this one, it's ten years old. Limited edition. They only made two hundred bottles of it.' He reaches for a crystal decanter on the table next to him.

'What did you just call me?' Burnside's face is thunderous.

Dawson looks up from pouring. 'Come on, Frank, it's no secret. Everyone knows your reputation.'

'Which is?' Burnside's eyes glint dangerously, but Dawson is enjoying himself too much. He proffers a glass, which Burnside ignores; Dawson shrugs and drinks some himself. 'You do things your way. And your way ain't got a rule book, know what I mean?'

'If you're talking about what happened with Mal – '

'Forget it, Frank. Move on. I have – as you can see. And I'm grateful to you. Really. Without your little intervention… well, let's just say my life would have taken a different turning.'

'Don't thank me, pal. I ain't finished with you yet.'

Dawson waves a dismissive hand. 'I know you've gotta make noises, be seen to be doing your job. But don't take it too far, eh? You keep shooting your mouth off about my club, and business'll suffer.'

Burnside takes a step forward and yanks Dawson off the sofa by his lapels. 'Don't jerk me around, you slag. You don't fool me. I know this lot didn't come from a government enterprise grant. You were just a thieving little toerag when I last saw you and now you're wearing more rocks than Elizabeth Taylor.' Dawson flails as Burnside thrusts his face inches from his nose. 'Did you think I wouldn't suss you out? Soon as I saw your ugly mug again, I knew you was behind it all. You may think you're clean, but there's a trail. There always is. So I'm warning you. Next time I come back, it'll be to arrest you. Got that?' He lets go of the jacket and Dawson staggers backwards, falling onto the cushions in an undignified heap and spilling whisky all over his white suit. Burnside flicks the video on again and throws Dawson the remote. 'I always said you were a tosser. Why don't you get back to what you're good at?'

Diary, 6 March.

That guy Frank came in again this evening. Turns out he's a real sleaze. And I thought I could spot them by now. How wrong can you be?

We were getting on well at first, though I was worried he'd cracked my cover. He's got this knack of getting under my skin and I kept forgetting to be 'Emma' and started talking to him as myself. He was very flattering, telling me I was beautiful and too good to be working as a hostess. Stupidly, I fell for it. I ended up getting hugely defensive about why I was there, which isn't the way you're supposed to react. 'Never let it get personal', that's what Angie says. We're not supposed to argue or get into debates, either. I don't think we're supposed to have feelings at all.

So far that hasn't been a problem – I haven't respected anyone enough to care – but Frank's different. Or I thought he was. I respected him. He reminds me a bit of my dad, actually. Same penetrating eyes. Same dry understatement. Handsome, too. He's got what I call a 'lived-in' face – there's a couple of white scars to prove it. He's suave without being yukkily smooth. And he knows how to make you feel special. I told him I preferred older men, and it's true. Yeah, I'm admitting it, I fancy him. Correction: fancied him. I was taken in for a few minutes. The fact is, Frank's nothing like my dad, he's just the same as all the rest: a dirty, disgusting PERVERT.

And it doesn't stop there, either. I told Dawson a punter was asking for something 'special' (God, I hate these euphemisms) and he said to show him in. Frank was with him for about ten minutes and then left. I thought I was going to get into trouble for suggesting it, especially when Dawson called me into his office later, but he was OK. He asked me to tell him everything Frank had said – I gave him the edited version – and then he said he thought he should put me 'in the picture' about him. It turns out he's a policeman. Not only that, but a corrupt one: 'Bent as a nine-bob note', to quote Dawson exactly. That explains a lot of things. I asked what a bent copper was doing at Silks (other than the obvious) and he said, 'Me and Burnside go back a long way. He had a little proposition to put to me. I told him I'd think about it.'

I was seriously hacked off about the Frank thing to start with – if I'm honest, I'd glamorised him in my mind – but it occurred to me later that this could be the break I've been looking for. Too tired to think it all through now – it's 3.00 in the morning and I'm exhausted. I'll talk it over it with Tony tomorrow.

CONFIDENTIAL PROGRESS REPORT: 'HIDDEN CHAMBERS' (TRANSMISSION TBC). DATE: 7 MARCH

PRESENT: PAULINE CHAMBERS (REPORTER), TONY DILLON (DIRECTOR)
CC: RAY DUNTHORNE (PRODUCER), IAN DI MICHELE (ASSISTANT DIRECTOR), SAMANTHA GWILLIAM (RESEARCHER)

Silks
Possible progress here. A punter asked Pauline for (unspecified) hardcore action and when this was relayed to Dawson he invited him into the private suite. Punter's name is Frank Burnside. According to Dawson he's a corrupt police officer (detective? What rank?) They've obviously known each other a long time and Burnside seems to have put some sort of deal to Dawson. Q: Is he part of the porn ring? Seems unlikely, otherwise why would he go through Pauline? The team agrees he could have

got wind of Dawson's unofficial enterprise and be blackmailing him.

ACTION: Pauline to report back immediately if Burnside returns. Tony and Ian to have cars on standby outside the club: he may lead us to Dawson's other premises.

Xsecs Promotions Agency

No developments. Pauline has made appointment to go there tomorrow.

Progress of Investigation

Looking more promising, especially the Burnside angle. Tony is very excited: this could be potentially explosive. Even if Burnside doesn't lead us to Dawson's hideaway, he could be worth pursuing in his own right. Also, it's very topical. It would mean changing the focus of the investigation, but at least we'd salvage something from the budget/time expended so far.

ACTION: Pauline to go to the microfiche archives and trawl Burnside's background, plus pursue journalist contacts informally. Ian to sound out Vice contact, see if he's heard anything. Ray to make final decision by end of week.

Sun Hill Star   **4 April 1988**

'DETECTIVE BLOWS WHISTLE ON SOCCER THUGS'

By Steve Falla

Senior detective Frank Burnside shocked police colleagues by being arrested in a crime crackdown – on his first day at work. Unknown to officers taking part in the raid, Sun Hill's new head of CID was posing as a football hooligan in an undercover operation to infiltrate a gang of soccer thugs.

Burnside and another detective, whose identity remains secret, had spent a month with the notorious group, known as the Sun Hill Saboteurs or 'the Sabs'. Members are thought to be responsible for widespread hooliganism and violence on and off the terraces throughout South London.

Inspector Christine Frazer, who headed up the investigation – known as 'Operation Red Card' – said: 'I am delighted with our success in arresting this gang. The violence they instigate is deliberate and organised. A significant arsenal of weapons was discovered on the premises, including canisters of CS gas, machetes and knives.

'Our intelligence was that the Sabs had planned to use these at a forthcoming match between two rival South London football teams. I'm sure I don't need to spell out the consequences had that situation occurred.'

Inspector Frazer applauded the courage of the two undercover detectives, saying they had 'put their lives on the line' for the job. Officers had not been informed who the undercover operatives were in advance of the early-morning raid, leading to DI Burnside's cover being blown by a former CID colleague. DI Burnside, who returns to Sun Hill on promotion after two years at Stafford Row Police Station, said: 'The incident was unfortunate, but I can't blame DS Roach for reacting the way he did. I was only dressed in my underpants at the time! I suppose you could say I made a bit of an entrance. He was expecting to see me down the nick, not in a thugs' flophouse.'

Burnside, 36, is seen as a controversial appointment by some officers, due to his unconventional approach to policing. One officer, who wished to remain anonymous, called it 'a sad day for the Met'. Inspector Frazer, who has worked with Burnside on a previous occasion, countered this, saying, 'Frank Burnside is a first-class copper with a proven track record. He isn't here to win popularity contests. He's here because he gets results.'

Sun Hill Star   **26 April 1990**

'CORRUPT COPPER IN CRACK FACTORY SCANDAL'

By Steve Falla

Shamed sergeant Terry Cole was arrested today after a successful surveillance operation by Sun Hill CID. The bent Barton Street officer was caught on video when he stabbed an informant with a concealed knife.

Senior officers at Sun Hill were alerted to the possibility of a leak after a tip-off about a drugs drop left detectives with red faces. When police raided a suspected crack 'factory' on Ironbridge Road, they unearthed not drugs – but talcum powder.

An internal inquiry was set up under Inspector Gordon Wrae of the Drugs Liaison Squad, while DI Frank Burnside, who had led the raid, was taken off the case. Rumours that Burnside was the source of the leak were quashed when his suspicions about Cole were confirmed by the informant. He was reinstated and went on to ensnare the corrupt copper in a sting at Waterloo Station.

Sgt Cole was arrested and charged with various drugs offences as well as attempted murder. The informant, a man aged 23, is recovering in hospital.

Inspector Wrae has since been promoted to Detective Chief Inspector and appointed new head of Sun Hill CID. Celebrating his move, he told the Star: 'I am delighted to be taking over such a proactive and resourceful team and look forward to working closely with Inspector Burnside.'

Inspector Burnside was unavailable for comment.

Sun Hill Star   **27 October 1998**

'DISGRACED DETECTIVE IN CHAINS'

By Steve Falla

Frank Burnside, Sun Hill's once-celebrated detective, made an ignominious return to his old police station today – handcuffed to a former colleague.

Officers who had worked alongside Burnside in his heyday gazed open-mouthed as the rumpled and weary-looking figure was led inside to a cell. Burnside, who left Sun Hill five years ago under mysterious circumstances, was discovered in Manchester, where he was working as right-hand man for local mobster Phil Ryan.

The controversial ex-inspector conned DC Jim Carver and DS John Boulton, who came across him while pursuing another investigation, into believing he could help them. The officers were sceptical about his story and contacted the National Crime Squad, who confirmed they had Burnside under investigation.

He was arrested after the crack crime squad's officers stormed a meeting between Ryan, Burnside and Michael Hyde, head of a rival Mancunian firm. Ryan was shot in an exchange of gunfire and Hyde, who is wanted for abduction, attempting to pervert the course of justice and drugs offences, was arrested.

In a related incident, Burnside, who was brought back to London by DC Carver and DS Boulton, was almost killed after hitmen loyal to Hyde tried to assassinate him at Euston Station. DC Carver, a former protégé of Burnside's, dived to save him, risking his own life in the process. Police chiefs say he will be recommended for a commendation.

Sun Hill CID is keeping tight-lipped about what charges Burnside has been arrested on. A spokesman for DCI Meadows confirmed Burnside was being questioned, but refused to comment further.

Sun Hill Star   **29 October 1998**

'BURNSIDE VINDICATED BY INTERNATIONAL DRUGS BUST'

By Steve Falla

Frank Burnside, the ex-Sun Hill detective brought home in chains yesterday, has cleared his reputation after police chiefs revealed his role in a sensational undercover operation.

The news about Burnside was released following the arrest of Croatian drugs trafficker Yuri Kovich and his men. They were caught arranging to ship heroin into Britain through a gang headed by Michael Hyde, who is being held in prison in Manchester. Burnside, who has been posing as a fellow gangster, set up the deal and then tipped off police officers, who raided the meeting at the Victoria Hotel.

Mark Hyde, who is thought to have taken over from his brother, Michael, was arrested later at a penthouse flat in Docklands. Armed officers were called to the flat after reports that Hyde was holding Burnside hostage with a gun. A shot was fired before they could gain entry and the victim, a young woman, was pronounced dead at the scene. She was later revealed to be Michael Hyde's wife, Kim. Her sister, Linda, was also arrested and has been charged with manslaughter.

Burnside, who is rumoured to have been conducting an affair with Mrs Hyde, was said by one insider to be 'devastated'. Covert photographs of him kissing the mobster's wife were taken by National Crime Squad detectives, who were convinced Burnside had become part of Manchester's criminal fraternity.

Even Burnside's own colleagues were taken in by the way he appeared to have 'crossed over'. In fact, Burnside was involved in a sting, five years in the making, working directly for Assistant Commissioner Lom-Pierre at Scotland Yard. He has since been promoted and is now a detective chief inspector with the Met.'s Crime Operational Command Unit.

Sun Hill Star   **29 October 1998**

Star Editorial

So the knight in shining armour has returned to Sun Hill another notch up his career ladder – and, if rumour is to believed, another notch on his bedpost. Frank Burnside has a reputation for courting controversy and, while we applaud his dedication to duty, taxpayers are entitled to ask: is their money being spent wisely?

Five years is a long time to achieve results in any organisation and, it seems, Chief Inspector Burnside has been interpreting his 'undercover' duties a little too literally. While we sympathise with his loss, the revelation that he was sleeping with a villain's wife surely implies he was getting very cosy in the role – too cosy, even. Clearly, the powers that be think so too: it has been reported that he has received a severe reprimand from the assistant commissioner about his involvement with Hyde's wife.

When the blunt-speaking detective first arrived at Sun Hill it was on a wave of speculation and rumour. Officers even questioned how he had been missed by Operation Countryman, the investigation into police corruption in the seventies. Since then, Burnside has been accused of corruption on several occasions. Nine years ago, he was arrested in Operation Backwoods, when it was alleged he took a 'backhander' for a job. He has also been investigated by the Serious Crime Squad and the Complaints Investigation Bureau. Each time he has succeeded in clearing his name but, as one sergeant put it, 'Mud sticks – and Burnside's got a pretty thick layer of it'.

He is, of course, to be congratulated for helping to arrest the Hydes and their drug-dealing cronies. However, the time for maverick police officers is past. All too often, rogue detectives are just that. Tax payers are entitled to public servants who can be relied on not just to do the job, but to uphold moral standards too.

EXTRACT FROM TAPED INTERVIEW WITH SUPERINTENDENT ROGER SUTTON,

TAPE 87A/92, 19.07.00

CHAMBERS: 'Superintendent Sutton, were you surprised to learn that DCI Frank Burnside was under investigation by Operation Pepper?'

SUTTON: 'Yes – and no. Frank's always been a law unto himself, but I was convinced of his allegiance to the police force. I'm not saying he's any kind of role model – Frank's way of doing things is very much frowned upon these days – but he's essentially a good copper.'

CHAMBERS: 'Yet you sound an ambivalent note.'

SUTTON: 'Because it was inevitable that Pepper would catch up with him. Frank's got a lot of history and he's been under investigation before. Pepper's looking back over twenty years of case histories. You've got to have been a model policeman to survive scrutiny like that.'

CHAMBERS: 'I believe you yourself issued him with a written warning on one occasion?'

SUTTON: 'Yes. That was following an undercover operation he did on Tyneside. He got a first-class result, but we received complaints afterwards that he had headbutted another police officer. The man needed stitches.'

CHAMBERS: 'And there were also allegations that he had taken cocaine at an illegal gambling club?'

SUTTON: 'There were, but they were never upheld.'

CHAMBERS: 'So you've always known he's a man who – at the very least – takes risks. A man who might be provoked into acting violently?'

SUTTON: 'Frank's abrasive. He can fight his corner. I wouldn't call him violent.'

CHAMBERS: 'Or corrupt? It's an issue that seems to have dogged his career right from the start.'

SUTTON: 'Ultimately, you don't know, do you? As a police officer, you have to trust the men and women who work with you. Without trust you can't operate as a team. And if you can't do that, then you might as well pack it all in. I trusted Burnside.'

CHAMBERS: 'Let's go back to Commander Webster's interview with you about Burnside. What was his role in Operation Pepper?'

SUTTON: 'Operation Co-ordinator. He was in charge of the day-to-day running of the enquiry.'

CHAMBERS: 'I see. Was the interview recorded?'

SUTTON: 'No, it was just a preliminary meeting, fairly informal.'

CHAMBERS: 'What sort of things did Commander Webster ask?'

SUTTON: 'The kind of things that you're asking now.'

CHAMBERS: 'And do you think you gave a good account of Burnside?'

SUTTON [*Pause*]: 'That was certainly my intention.'

CHAMBERS: 'Did you succeed in convincing Commander Webster?'

SUTTON: 'No.'

CHAMBERS: 'Why not?'

SUTTON: 'Because he knew things about Frank that I didn't. His team had had a good old trawl through Frank's past, turned over every stone. I'd have called a lot of it minor stuff, but that's not the way Operation Pepper works. It was a pretty damning catalogue. One incident in particular.'

CHAMBERS: 'The case regarding Burnside's brother Malcolm and Peter Dawson?'

SUTTON: 'Yes.'

CHAMBERS: 'Had you heard about that before?'

SUTTON: 'No.'

CHAMBERS: 'Did it shock you?'

SUTTON: 'The evidence did not look … very good. It made me stop and think. I realised why a few of the longer-serving uniforms at Sun Hill didn't think too highly of him.'

CHAMBERS: 'Was that what made Webster come to you about Burnside?'

SUTTON: 'No. He said they'd received information that Frank had been blackmailing Peter Dawson.'

CHAMBERS: 'Why would he do that?'

SUTTON: 'To get revenge? I don't know.'

CHAMBERS: 'Is he the sort to exact retribution?'

SUTTON: 'Frank's got a long memory. He bears grudges. That's one of his failings. He never forgets. If someone crosses Frank, he wants payback. He's been warned about it often in the past.'

CHAMBERS: 'Have you personally come across this side of his character?'

SUTTON [*Pause*]: 'There is one instance I recall, though I think most of us would have had sympathy with what Frank did. Most of us would have liked to have done the same.'

CHAMBERS: 'Tell me about it.'

SUTTON: 'It was a case concerning a convinced paedophile, Carl Jones. They let him out of prison because he was supposed to be helping us track down the body of a murdered boy. Nasty business. Burnside was there to help Jones 'remember'. Jones kept stringing him along, acting smug and playing mind games with him. He said something to Frank that really got to him – I don't know what it was.

'Burnside broke him in the end, though, got him face to face with the lad's parents, made him see what he'd done. He took them to the grave. Afterwards, Burnside put him in a cell and let the boy's uncle pay him a visit. He was absolutely steaming, mad with anger and grief. He was also six-foot-four and built like a brick sh– well, you know what I mean. He nearly ripped Jones's arms off.'

CHAMBERS: 'What happened to the uncle? Was he arrested?'

SUTTON: 'No. Jones said he didn't want to press charges. When he could speak again.'

CHAMBERS: 'But he could have been arrested, surely? What does that say about Frank Burnside? He's pretty ruthless, isn't he?'

SUTTON: 'He takes no prisoners.'

CHAMBERS: 'An odd turn of phrase! Is that what they call a Freudian slip?'

SUTTON [*Coughs*]: 'I didn't mean it quite like that. Frank's attitude is, he doesn't care what people think of him. He uses people and he upsets people and he rubs people up the wrong way. That means he makes enemies. Ted Roach, Gordon Wrae, Kim Reid, Jack Meadows – they've all had their run-ins with him. And they're the good guys. As to the villains, tarts and snouts he's crossed – well, their memories tend to be as long as his. Frank doesn't do himself any favours.'

CHAMBERS: 'Life must be quieter now, without him around.'

SUTTON: 'We don't have so many fireworks, that's true. But the briefing meetings are bloody boring.'

TRANSCRIPT OF FILM, TAPE 39V/404. XSECS. 08.03.00, 09.48

Joanne, the receptionist, is on the phone. A leggy teenager in a micro-skirt perches on the edge of one of the black leather sofas, clutching a portfolio case. An older girl, absorbed in examining her split ends, sits facing her, champing gum. She flicks Burnside a cursory glance as he enters, then returns to her bleached hair. He walks over to the desk. Joanne ignores him.

'Yeah, we've got three like that available as of this moment. Shall I send them over? Just a minute, there's – hey, what d'you think you're doing?'

Burnside wrests the receiver from her and says into it, 'She'll call you back. Personally, I'd look elsewhere.' He slams the phone down and glares at Joanne. 'I don't like having my calling cards ignored.'

'You can't just come barging in here – '

'Oh yes I can. Remember?' He holds his warrant card in her face. 'Not only can I come barging in, I can make life extremely unpleasant for you and your boss. So go get her.'

'She's – '

'And show her this.' He reaches into his jacket and brings out

51

a photocopy of Sanja's flyer. 'Tell "Miss Miller" I'd like to have a little chat with her about it.'

Joanne studies the flyer. 'It's all foreign. She won't understand it.'

'I think she'll get the gist.' He holds her eye. She retreats, sullen.

'I'll see if she's free.'

'You do that.'

Joanne stomps off down a corridor and knocks on a door.

Burnside turns round and addresses the two girls. 'You realise you've got more chance of being spotted in Woolworth's than you have here?' The younger one leaps up and scuttles out, looking tearful. The other girl curls her lip, revealing a wad of grey gum. Burnside shrugs. 'Then again, maybe not.'

Joanne reappears. 'You can go in. Straight through there, it's on the right.'

'She read it?' A nod. 'Bet you didn't know Miss Miller was such a cunning linguist, did you?'

TRANSCRIPT OF FILM, TAPE 40V/404. XSECS. 08.03.00, 09.50

In contrast to the flesh-fest adorning reception, Clare Miller's office is fussily feminine and has peach-coloured walls decorated with pastel prints. She is at a coffee machine in the far corner as Burnside enters, and turns round with a bright smile. 'Good morning, Detective Chief Inspector. It won't be a minute. I hope you like Colombian.'

'We are talking coffee, here, aren't we?'

She puts her head on one side, coquettishly. 'Naturally.'

Burnside looks slightly thrown, as if unsure how to reconcile Miller's mumsy appearance with her flirtatiousness, let alone her alleged criminality. She has short brown hair, big teeth and protruding eyes, and her petite, plumpish figure is squeezed into a powder blue suit that does nothing for her thick ankles. A pink, frilly-necked blouse and pearls complete the look, which is more bank clerk than brothel-keeper.

'I thought Croatian was more your thing.'

'Take a seat.' She indicates a chair. 'Black, white, sugar? Choccy biccie?'

'Look, I didn't come for a chit-chat. I want to know what your connection is with this.' He indicates the flyer.

Miller pours herself a cup, fastidiously wiping a spill off the saucer, and sits down at her desk. She dons a pair of gold-rimmed glasses and smoothes out the sheet of paper. 'As it happens, I do recognise it. It's an advertisement for our Zagreb office. We have several outlets in other countries. Xsecs is an international concern, you know.'

'So how do you operate?'

'What do you mean?'

'Do you have some sort of arrangement with them?'

'Oh, no. We're all run independently.'

'They don't send girls over for you? You know, pile 'em high, sell 'em cheap.' He gives her a sardonic smile.

'I'm sorry.' Her tone is frosty. 'I really don't have any idea what you're referring to.'

'Come on. Those ain't photo spreads from *Country Life* out there.'

'DCI Burnside.' Clare Miller sets her mouth primly. 'I can assure you *our* girls are all professional models. That applies to any we employ from overseas, too. We do have a couple from Croatia on our books. We also have models from other Eastern European countries. That look is very 'in' at the moment, as I'm sure you'd realise if you read the fashion press. Which, clearly, you don't.' She looks him up and down witheringly.

'So you'll have their paperwork, then?'

She picks up the phone. 'Joanne. Bring in the personnel files, please. Davor's girls. Thank you.'

'That would be Davor Tomasic, would it?' Burnside leans back and crosses his arms. Clare Miller scarcely misses a beat. 'That's correct. Out of curiosity, how did you...?'

'Let's just say it dropped off the back of a lorry. Along with a fifteen-year-old illegal immigrant. And that's what led me to you.'

She sips her coffee daintily. 'Davor gives those things out all over the place. I can't be held responsible if some wretched asylum seeker turns up with one. It doesn't prove a thing.'

'I haven't said I'm accusing you of anything. Yet.'

The door opens and Joanne enters bearing files, which she places in front of Clare Miller. 'Shall I cancel your ten o'clock?'

Miller shoots Burnside a poisonous look. 'No, I won't be long.'

He picks up the files uninvited and leafs through them. 'I thought you said you had two. There's three here.'

'One's left.'

'Kristina Tomasic? Daddy's girl, I assume?'

'Yes.' She clears her throat. 'I'm afraid Kristina didn't work out. She didn't have the... strength of character for modelling. It can be a very soul-destroying business, all those rejections.'

'So where is she now?'

'I believe she got a job as an au pair.'

'Do you have an address?'

Clare Miller smiles sweetly. 'Sorry.'

'And these other two? Made of sterner stuff, are they?'

'Ah, the twins. Very professional. They're at a shoot today, in fact.' She makes a show of consulting her desk diary. 'Some new moisturiser. They've got *lovely* skin.'

'Then I'll send my sergeant to interview them. He could do with a few tips.'

'That won't be possible. It's a closed set.' Burnside's eyebrows shoot up. 'Body moisturiser. Shower scene,' she explains, giving him a butter-wouldn't-melt look.

'Tomorrow, then.'

'Talk to Joanne. She'll arrange a time. Now, is that all?' She rises to her feet and holds out a hand. 'It's been a – '

'Peter Dawson.' Burnside doesn't move.

'I beg your pardon?'

'Got a club, Silks. You supply escorts to him.'

'Well, I – '

'No need to be coy, Miss Miller. It ain't exactly a secret, is it?' He gets up, still holding the files. 'I'll have these for now.'

'But – '

'Though I can't understand it myself. I mean, must put his costs up, hiring through an agency. Unless you give him some sort of special deal?'

Clare Miller draws herself up to her full five-foot-two. 'Our arrangement with Mr Dawson is completely above board. We provide quality and reliability, and that's what he pays for. His customers are very discerning, and so is he.'

Burnside grimaces. 'Who else does your agency supply to, Miss Miller? I'd like a list of all your clients.' He heads for the door, then stops. 'In fact, why don't you just give me all your books? I like a juicy read.'

'On what grounds?'

'Call it moral. Or should that be "immoral"?' Burnside gives her a twinkle and looks almost as if he might nudge her. Clare Miller's mouth is set in a hard line.

'I can get a search warrant within the hour.'

'That won't be necessary.' She stalks off ahead of him. 'I've got nothing to hide.'

TRANSCRIPT OF TELEPHONE CALL, TAPE 359T/998.
XSECS.
08.03.00, 10.25

DAWSON: ''Ello?'

MILLER [*gushing*]: 'Peter! How are you?'

DAWSON: 'Knackered. You know what time it is?'

MILLER: 'Look, I'm sorry, I know you sleep late, but this is important.'

DAWSON: 'It'd bloody better be.'

MILLER: 'Since I've got you up, why don't we do lunch? Get up to speed on everything.'

DAWSON: 'Did I say I was up? Just spit it out, then I can get me head down again.'

MILLER [*crisp*]: 'There's no time for that, Peter. Take a cold shower, make some black coffee and pop whatever you need to get going, then ring me back. We need to talk.'

DAWSON: 'Alright, alright, Miss Bossy Boots. You got me fired up now. Spill.'

MILLER: 'Are you alone?'

DAWSON: 'Am I 'eck.'

MILLER: 'Get rid of her.'

DAWSON: 'Them.' [*He chortles*]

MILLER: 'Now.'

DAWSON: 'Give us a chance.' [*Rustling of bedclothes*] 'Wakey, wakey, girlies. Off you go. Daddy needs to do some business.' [*Sound of sharp smacks, squeals and protests*] 'I'll see you two later.' [*He gulps a drink*] 'Cor, that's done it. Ugh, foul.'

MILLER: 'Are you quite ready?'

DAWSON: 'I'm all yours, baby. What's the drama for?'

MILLER: 'I've had a visit.' [*Pause*] 'From the police.'

DAWSON: 'And?'

MILLER: 'They haven't got much, just a lot of conjecture, really, but they're piecing it together, Peter. And they've got my books.'

DAWSON: 'Bloody 'ell. Not – '

MILLER: 'No, not them. But they'll be back and looking for the rest if we don't do something.'

DAWSON [*cursing under his breath*]: 'I've been having grief an' all. Bigfoot said he'd sort it. How'd they get on to you?'

MILLER: 'They've picked up one of the girls. Must be one you got shot of. She had something on her – just an advertising leaflet – but it was enough for them to make the connection.'

DAWSON: 'Has she coughed?'

MILLER: 'I couldn't tell. I don't think so. That's why they're making noises. Trying to put the wind up us.'

DAWSON: '"Us"?'

MILLER: 'He mentioned your name. Asked what kind of deal we had going.'

DAWSON: 'Don't tell me: Frank Burnside.'

MILLER: 'Correct.'

DAWSON: 'This is serious.'

MILLER: 'That's what I've been trying to tell you.'

DAWSON: 'No, you don't know. This is… Jesus. [*Shouting*] 'I warned him – '

MILLER: 'But they haven't got any evidence.'

DAWSON [*grim*]: 'And they ain't gonna, neither. I ain't letting that lot jerk me around.'

MILLER: 'So what are you going to do?'

DAWSON: 'I'm going to send Jonno on a little errand. It's time he put that special training of his into practice again.'

MILLER: 'And what about me?'

DAWSON: 'You just sit tight, babe, and do what Daddy tells you.'

Diary, 8 March

Had a close call today. This horrible bloke – fat, sweaty, B.O., the works – was coming on to me, hands everywhere. I'd ditched the kit earlier on, thank goodness, 'cos he stuck his hand right up my skirt. Not seductively or anything, just – wham. I squeaked and jumped a mile in the air and then he accused me of being a 'frigid little bitch'. Angie came swanning over to see what all the fuss was about, and he started complaining. His actual words were, 'what sort of a hostess was I if I couldn't take a friendly tickle'! Of course, the customer is always right at Silks, however revolting or unpleasant, so he got offered Cara instead. As Angie put it, 'she's warm, outgoing and has a delightful sense of humour'. For which read, 'she's a bombed out coke-head who'll put up with anything to get her next fix'.

Afterwards, Angie pulled me to one side and gave me a lecture. She made it clear what she thought of girls who promise but don't deliver and told me I was jeopardising not only my own job but hers as the greeter, as she was copping all the flak from my disaffected tricks (or non-tricks). Ergo, I was endangering Silks' reputation by being a monumental prick-teaser. I felt like saying it's a topsy-turvy world when you acquire a bad reputation for not sleeping with men, but I let it pass. Instead I kept my cool and told her Dawson had made it clear that sexual contact wasn't allowed in the club, and that having some punter shove his hands in my knickers counted as sexual to me. She said I had to 'learn to go with the flow'! I reiterated my spiel about the jealous boyfriend, but since no one's actually seen him yet, it's beginning to lose its credibility. That was when I decided it was time to wheel on Tony.

He was waiting round the corner in case Burnside turned up, so it was simple to arrange. I called him on my mobile and he swaggered in a couple of hours later with Ian in tow as his East-

End buddy. I was praying Ian would keep his mouth shut, because he wouldn't fool anyone as a hard man. Fortunately, he did. Tony was really getting into the role: he kept shooting these viscous looks at the poor bloke sitting with me – a harmless old widower who wanted to talk about his wife – and practically exploded when the bloke gave me a kiss on the cheek. I made a big show of telling Tony to calm down and let me get on with my job, but he sat there glowering like a guard dog. Eventually I 'persuaded' Tony to go, then got Steve from security to have a peek and check if he was outside, which of course he was. It made the point, but I was worried Tony was the one who'd end up getting his legs broken. I've seen Steve in action.

Tony gave me a lift home – I thought he'd better, after all that – and we discussed tactics on the way. I'm concerned we've overplayed it and that I might get sacked because my boyfriend's a liability. Tony thinks it'll be OK so long as he sticks to making his presence felt outside. The theory is, while he's hanging about watching for Burnside, Steve'll think he's waiting for me. I suppose it might buy us a few more days, but Angie's not going to put up with much more, she made that clear. The pressure's really on me now.

To make matters worse, Tony got carried away playing the boyfriend and came on to me on the journey home. He's not seen me 'at work' before and he obviously found it a turn-on. When we got to my flat he invited himself in for coffee, even though it was late. He was drooling over my corset, asking if he could help loosen my stays, etc, etc. I thought he was joking, but then he started caressing my shoulders and kissing the back of my neck. I told him he could drop the method acting, but he didn't get the message. He was breathing into my ear, going, 'Don't you get frustrated, leading all those men on?' He might as well have said, 'Come on, you know you want it', because that's what he meant.

It made me feel incredibly insulted. It's like Tony sees me in a different way now, because of what I'm doing. Instead of treating me like a fellow professional, he's treating me like I'm a tart. I told him that, and we ended up having a blazing row. Then he had the nerve to say, 'Why do you think I picked you for the job?' That was when I threw my coffee over him. I thought he was going to hit me, he looked so mad, but he stormed off into the night and rang me twenty minutes later on his mobile to apologise. He said he'd been completely out of order and didn't mean any of it, but I'm not so sure. If hostessing's taught me anything, it's that men, whatever their background, have double standards when it comes to sex.

It's going to be dead embarrassing facing Tony tomorrow, but we've got to meet up to talk about Burnside. There's been progress on that front, thank God, otherwise I'd seriously consider jacking in the entire investigation.

E-mail

From: Frank Burnside   Sent: 8 March
To: gary.hedges@crimeocu.gov.uk
Subject: Operation Playmates

Re. Xsecs. We're on to something. Call NCIS, and tell them to pull Tomasic in for questioning. He has a daughter, Kristina, aged fifteen, who worked for Miller for a couple of weeks, then took off. Apparently she didn't make the grade — whatever that was. See what Tomasic has to say and whether he's got an address. If you don't get any joy, try au pair agencies here. She could be our best shot at cracking this.

There's two other Croats working for Xsecs London. Suspect they're token. Get Terri to talk to them, find out what they know. The books are clean, but that doesn't

60

mean anything. I'd bet Miller's running a clandestine hardcore operation alongside the cheesecake stuff and Tomasic's sending her the girls. Leave Miller to me; I've already got feelers out.

I've twisted arms in Immigration and they're letting Sanja Gregovic go, pending the usual. It's risky, so we need to keep full-time surveillance on her: DI Wright's got some of his mob doing the legwork; they'll keep you informed of her movements. If she does go to the agency, we've got them.

E-mail
From: Gary Hedges   Sent: 8 March
To: frank.burnside@crimeocu.gov.uk
Subject: Re. Your Message

Terri gets sixteen-year-old twin models filming a shower scene? What's she got that I haven't? Or do they want her as an extra?

E-mail
From: Frank Burnside   Sent: 8 March
To: gary.hedges@crimeocu.gov.uk
Subject: Re. Shower Girls

Congratulations sergeant — you've proved my point.

DICTAPHONE TRANSCRIPT, TAPE 38A/92
08.03.00, 20.22
[*The muted sounds of a radio can be heard in the background — light, easy-listening music, with occasional chatter from announcer*]
BURNSIDE: 'Miss Miller. Well, well... looks like Miss Whiplash

from where I'm sitting. It's always the quiet ones.' [*Sound of Burnside shuffling through photographs*] 'Must've been a while ago. Then again... blimey... that's put me right off me pizza – if it ever turns up.' [*He gulps a drink*] 'Obviously a game girl. Underneath that Tory matron's gear beats a heart of pure PVC. She's no stranger to handcuffs, anyway.' [*He snorts*] 'Nice one, Lonnie mate, I owe you. Now let's see: two charges of living off immoral earnings, both dropped, and several offences under the obscene publications act, ditto. She's either been a lucky lady or she's more than good friends with someone influential. Which takes me to Peter Dawson...' [*Sound of door knocker*] 'At long bloody last.' [*He gets up and opens a door. There's a smash followed by a roar and crackle of flames*].

BURNSIDE: 'What the... aargh!' [*He stumbles back into the room, spluttering and coughing. Frantic beating and Burnside cursing. His footsteps retreat. The roar and whoosh of flames gets closer. We hear Burnside again. His breathing is laboured. He is struggling to do something.*]

BURNSIDE: 'Come on!' [*He coughs and gasps. There's a 'clang', like a heavy metal object being dropped, followed by a thud. Somewhere in the house, a pane of glass shatters. The backdraught bursts open the living-room door. Instantly, the noise of the fire is louder. It's impossible to tell what's happened to Burnside. At first, the explosive hissing of a fire extinguisher isn't audible above the blaze, but gradually the sound of a high-pressure jet of foam drowns out the flames. The fire spits and pops, but recedes. Within a few minutes it's out. Now the house is eerily quiet, except for a steady drip, drip, drip onto the sodden carpet. In the background, the radio continues to play soothing music.*]

CONFIDENTIAL PROGRESS REPORT: HIDDEN CHAMBERS (TRANSMISSION TBC). DATE 9 MARCH

PRESENT: PAULINE CHAMBERS (REPORTER), TONY
DILLON (DIRECTOR), RAY DUNTHORNE (PRODUCER),
IAN DI MICHELE (ASSISTANT DIRECTOR)
CC: SAMANTHA GWILLIAM (RESEARCHER)

Eye witnesses

Suzanne Kelly: interview done. Headline-grabbing stuff but too graphic for usual slot? Detailed descriptions of what she was subjected to. The gang-rape scene is a stand-out: use in (post-watershed) trailer? Suzanne comes across as articulate and together, which lessens impact slightly. Tony commented she's not emotional enough to hold audience sympathy. Ian says this won't matter: Catherine O'Leary is weepy, so likely to be a good contrast. (Catherine interview scheduled for Monday 13th.)

Kristina Tomasic: Has agreed to be interviewed in silhouette if her words are spoken by an actor. Expensive but probably our only option. She seems scared of reprisals and is very secretive. Her employers say she's Croatian. Not an illegal immigrant – she's here on a visa. Background still needs further checking. Pauline reports that Xsecs uses quite a few Eastern-European models.

ACTION: 1. Ray to query time of transmission: in view of subject matter this should go out later. We don't want to compromise on content.

2. Pauline to see if Xsecs has got established links with other agencies abroad.

3. Ian to approach Kristina's employers for more info: does she ever mention family, home, friends?

Frank Burnside

Archives suggest he's an undercover detective who takes things to extremes. Interesting, but much more newsworthy if he's 'crossed over'. Pauline witnessed him coming out of Xsecs yesterday as she was arriving. Burnside did not see her. She followed him and has footage of him entering a sex shop in Paddington. He came out six minutes later with a bag and caught a cab.

Evidence seems to confirm Dawson's story about Burnside: this is the same Praed Street sex shop which was virtually a private club for bent Met Police officers in the '70s. Looks like Burnside's gone back to his roots. He's acting alone and his behaviour is furtive. Pauline reports that when she returned to the agency Clare Miller seemed agitated and distracted. It's likely Burnside's blackmailing her as well as Dawson.
ACTION: Pauline to sound out Burnside's long-term associates, find out where he lives and build up a picture of his movements. Tony and Ian to follow him (with skeleton crew). Ray has kindly volunteered to check out sex shop.

Silks

Pauline unhappy about the situation and feels her cover has already been compromised too much. The team is sympathetic but Tony feels Pauline is close to a breakthrough with Dawson/Burnside and should continue. She has agreed to do a couple more nights.

TRANSCRIPT OF FILM, TAPE 331V/404. SILKS (DAWSON'S OFFICE).
09.03.00, 21.33
Dawson is sorting through some paperwork at his desk, totting up figures on a calculator. He enters them on a laptop, saves the

file to a floppy disk and ejects it. Whistling softly, he gets up and walks out of shot with the disk. Bizarrely, he jingles with each step. We hear the click of what sounds like a cabinet door being opened, then the sound of him tapping in a combination on the keypad of his safe. He returns a few seconds later, minus the disk, and feeds the hard copies into a shredder, watching as the machine spews out a spaghetti of paper. When it is done, he picks up his phone and dials a single number.

'Ange. About our little chat earlier. Send Emma in, there's a good girl.'

He reclines in his office chair, tilting it back and resting his boots on the desk. Tonight they are decorated with silver spurs, which explains the jingling noise. Dawson flexes his feet, admiring them, then swivels to retrieve a white stetson hanging on a peg behind him. He props it on his head, half-covering his face, and waits.

Two minutes later, there's a tentative knock on the door. Dawson ignores it. Another knock, louder this time. Dawson gives it five more seconds. 'Come!'

Pauline enters. She looks pale but musters a smile. 'You wanted to see me, Mr Dawson?'

'The lovely Emma.' Dawson tips up the brim of his hat with one finger, cowpoke-style. 'My own little Posh. Too posh for the likes of our punters, by the sound of it.'

Pauline swallows. 'Has someone... there was a gentleman yesterday... did he make a complaint?'

'Yeah, yeah, he came to me, mouthing off. Fat bastard. Wanted a bloody refund. As if.' He winks at her. Pauline looks confused.

'The thing is,' Dawson continues, still eyeing her from under his hat, 'you can't afford to be choosy in this job, love. You've gotta be up for it, d'you get me? It's what the punters expect.

You go turning them down, it knocks their confidence. They don't come back. That knocks my profits on the 'ead. Get my drift?'

'I understand. I mean, I thought it wasn't going to be a problem, at first, but I can see that – well, it is,' Pauline finishes lamely. 'It's just – my boyfriend – he found out where I work and he's so possessive, he stands outside watching the door. He'd kill me if I went with someone. Or he'd kill whoever I went with. Probably both.' She draws a shaky breath.

'Yeah, I heard all about his little performance yesterday. You'd better warn him: Steve got the old knuckle dusters out specially tonight. He's looking forward to meeting him again.' Dawson chuckles.

Pauline does not say anything. Suddenly, Dawson swings his boots off the desk and sits upright, leaning forward and looking at her intently. 'So. What am I going to do with you, then, Posh?

'I – '

'I got a bit of a dilemma, see? I've been trying to figure you out. You ain't what I'd call classic hostess material.' Dawson gets up and moves around the desk He walks behind Pauline, tracing the line of her bare shoulders with a finger. 'You're a natural with men, I'll give you that, sweetie. That's my problem.' He comes back round to face her and takes her chin in his hand, caressing her cheek. Pauline stares back into his eyes, hardly daring to breathe. Dawson puts his face close up to hers. 'You're too good with men.'

It looks as if he is going to kiss her but he does not. Instead, he lets go, steps back and perches on the front of his desk, arms folded. 'You've got the knack,' he continues softly, 'and it seems a crying shame to waste it.'

Pauline takes a step backwards and glances behind her. Dawson clearly thinks she's about to take flight. 'Just a minute, I ain't finished yet, Posh.'

'You're going to sack me. I might as well go now.'

'Tut-tut. Manners. You ain't been dismissed yet.' He rubs his hands together. 'No need to look so nervous, Posh. Unless you've got summat to hide. Have you?'

'No! Nothing.'

'Well, that's good. 'Cos I was beginning to wonder, you know? Why a nice girl like you wants to work in a place like this? Don't misunderstand me, we got a lot of nice girls here. Bright too – they ain't all toms. Not originally. But you're different.' He looks her up and down. 'It don't look like you need the money. You don't do drugs. You don't have kids – that I know of, anyhow. You gotta have some dark secret. It's the only explanation.'

Pauline stares at the floor. She takes a deep breath and then looks directly at Dawson, lifting her chin defiantly. 'You're right. I have.'

'You don't say.'

'Can I have a drink? I think I need one to tell you about this.'

'That big, is it?' Dawson leers at her. 'Be my guest.' He goes to a drinks cabinet and brings out a bottle of brandy, splashing it into a glass. 'Say when.'

EXTRACT FROM TAPED INTERVIEW WITH DS GARY HEDGES,
TAPE 82A/92, 27.06.00.
CHAMBERS: 'When did you realise the scale of what you were dealing with?'
HEDGES: 'I didn't. Not until the whole thing got blown wide open. He kept us in the dark about it.'
CHAMBERS: 'DCI Burnside didn't inform you about his connection with Peter Dawson?'
HEDGES: 'Nah.'
CHAMBERS: 'So where did you think he was when he disappeared?'

HEDGES: 'At home with his feet up. He was supposed to be off sick. That was the rumour, but there was all sorts of gossip flying around. Cal Wright overheard Burnside and Sutton having a barney but he couldn't tell what it was about.

CHAMBERS: 'But you weren't concerned?'

HEDGES: 'Sutton's a yes-man; Burnside ain't. They clashed sometimes – par for the course. I didn't mind the guvnor taking time off; I liked the extra responsibility. He knew we could handle things, me and Terri. I mean, DC Goldman. We were up to speed.'

CHAMBERS: 'Hardly. Burnside kept you clear of the agency and the club.'

HEDGES: 'He likes to lead the charge. He's always been one for that. It didn't occur to me it might be deliberate.'

CHAMBERS: 'Didn't you think the arson attack on his flat was odd? How did he explain that?'

HEDGES: 'He came in to work the next day looking a bit grey around the gills, coughing and that. I said, "Bit late in the day to take up smoking, innit?", 'cos he reeked, and he went, "I ain't; my trousers caught fire last night". I thought he was pulling my leg.'

CHAMBERS: 'Did he tell you what caused it?'

HEDGES: 'Just said some nutter had it in for him. The geezer stuck a petrol bomb through his letterbox. He didn't make a song and dance about it. It was pretty much business as usual, far as I recall.'

CHAMBERS: 'Someone tried to kill DCI Burnside and yet he acted as if nothing had happened? Weren't you at all suspicious?'

HEDGES: 'If my guvnor didn't make a big deal out of it, why should I? Shit happens – it's part of the job.'

CHAMBERS: 'That's what he wanted you to think, though, wasn't it?'

HEDGES [*reluctantly*]: 'Probably.'

CHAMBERS: 'How bad was the fire? Did Burnside report it?'
HEDGES: 'I don't think it was that bad, though it could have
been, if he hadn't managed to put it out. He said the hallway was
a mess and the living room got a bit scorched. I know he
reported it, 'cos I heard him on the phone. He rang SOCO and
told them to get over there. Sutton wanted him to be treated for
smoke inhalation, but Burnside said he was ok. They went
through into his office, which was when Cal was earwigging.
Burnside went out soon after without speaking to nobody.'
CHAMBERS: 'And it didn't occur to you that his life was in
danger? That the petrol bomb might not be a one-off?'
HEDGES [*stung*]: 'Yeah, well, hindsight's a wonderful thing,
ain't it?'

Diary, 9 March

I've never been so frightened in my life as I was tonight. I
thought Dawson was on to me. Angie had been treating me like
my cards were marked ever since I got in. She wasn't giving me
any punters, so I was left sitting at the bar feeling ostracised.
Then she came over with a big smirk on her face and said, 'Oh
dear, teacher's pet's in trouble.' I asked her what she meant and
she said Dawson wanted to see me and he wasn't happy. I went
cold all over.

I honestly couldn't read Dawson, which made it even more
scary. He was playing games with me, like it was a test or
something. At one point I didn't know if he was going to kiss me
or smash my face in. I even thought he might cart me off to the
Hotel Rosetta – or worse, the other place – and rape me. He was
touching me and being very intimidating. I don't know how I
stayed cool. (Well, I do: my legs had turned to jelly and I couldn't
have run away if I'd wanted to.)

Dawson said he knew I had a secret. I suppose I've always

known this moment would come, but I still wasn't prepared. My heart was pounding and my mouth went dry. I thought, you've got two options, girl. Either he knows 'cos he's found a camera or discovered he's being bugged, in which case he's winding you up before putting the boot in and you'll probably end up dead in a skip, or he's guessing there's something and calling your bluff. Then I heard my dad's voice in my head, saying, 'Paulie, you can talk yourself out of anything, you can', the way he used to, 'cos I always won him round when he was trying to tell me off. It was like a sign. So I looked Dawson in the eye and said, 'Yes, you're right.'

I was totally winging it. I made out I had this psychological problem with men that had taken over my life. I said it was a sex-fantasy thing: I was hooked on the power I had over men but terrified of the sex act itself because I'd been abused by my uncle when I was ten. Dawson seemed intrigued. I told him the experience had shattered my self-esteem and I was unable to have normal relationships. The only way I could relate to men was by continually reasserting myself over them, making them want me but not letting them have me. Working as a hostess let me play out that fantasy.

Dawson must have heard umpteen sob stories in his time, but for some reason he believed me. Perhaps because I was sobbing by then; big, shuddering sobs that seemed to come out of nowhere. He put his arm around me and gave me a squeeze and I cried mascara all over his white jacket and blurted out that I'd never told anyone that before in my life, ever. Amazingly, he was really sweet about it. He's usually so flash and heartless and treats the girls here like they're his for the taking (though he's never touched me until tonight). He told me not to worry, he wasn't going to force me to do anything I didn't want to do – quite the opposite. Then he dropped his bombshell. He said he wanted to promote me to greeter.

If Dawson had said he wanted to marry me, I couldn't have been more surprised. He said he was looking to update the club's image and I fitted the bill. I said, 'What about Angie, does she know?', 'cos I couldn't see the two of us working together, and he went, 'She's getting too old and too fat – huge bloody arse. And when she smiles the punters think she's gonna swallow them whole.' I couldn't help laughing, 'cos that just about sums her up. Just wish she'd been there to hear him say that. He called her in after I left. Knowing Dawson, I shouldn't think he was tactful.

The brilliant thing is, as greeter I'm not under any pressure to have sex with the punters. As far as Dawson's concerned, I'm a 'class act' and above all that. He said at some clubs they do, but he thinks it drags their reputation down. It's the best thing that could have happened for the investigation. I've got Dawson's confidence now and licence to move about anywhere. He actually said, 'Stick with me, babe, and you could really go places'! He seemed pretty excited. He also told me to 'lose the boyfriend'. Then he added, 'I think you'll find he ain't so keen after tonight. But don't take it personally, Posh. I'm doing you a favour.' When I left – he gave me the rest of the night off – I found Tony waiting for me in the car with a split lip, a black eye, a cut across one cheek and a bloody nose. I had to drive him to casualty. He's OK, but for some reason he wasn't interested in celebrating my promotion.

DICTAPHONE TRANSCRIPT, TAPE 39A/92
09.03.00, 20.22
BURNSIDE [*slurring*]: 'This is one for the record. Useful little gadgets, these. I never thought I'd get used to talking into a dictaphone when you handed these out, Sutton, but I'm sold on 'em now. Pity they ain't indestructible, like them black box voice

71

recorders. Then if I end up at the bottom of the Thames, you'd know all about it. We'll just have to hope that don't happen, eh? Not that you lot would care. Apparently, twenty-five years' service doesn't count for much.' [*Sound of Burnside pouring himself a drink and knocking it back.*]

'I don't like being taken off a case, Sutton. I don't like things being hushed up, either. You call a spade a sodding spade in my book; none of this poncing about hiding behind Yard-speak. If someone's setting me up, I've got a right to know. I'll find out anyway. I ain't gonna sit back while some bugger pulls my strings. Especially when that bugger's a turd called Peter Dawson. The fact he tried to chargrill my nuts speaks for something, you're right about that: he's scared his whole empire's gonna go down the toilet.

'This ain't about my personal safety. I don't need protecting from slags like that. I've wiped shit worse than Dawson off my shoe many a time. So what is it about, Sutton? How's he got to you? What are you, one of his VIP customers? I'm surprised I didn't see you down the club. Mrs Sutton ain't enough, eh? Though I always thought Beth looked a bit of a goer, myself. Still, it's not something you want your colleagues whispering about, is it? Wouldn't do your saintly image much good, not with Pepper going on...' [*He pauses and takes another drink. There's a long silence. Suddenly there's the sound of a glass being hurled and smashing on a hard surface.*]
BURNSIDE [*shouting*]: 'Shit. Shit. Shit...'

TRANSCRIPT OF TELEPHONE CALL, TAPE 363T/998.
FIREBRAND PRODUCTIONS.
10.03.00, 12.00
RECEPTIONIST: 'South London Press.'
CHAMBERS: '*Sun Hill Star*, please.'

RECEPTIONIST: 'Thank you.'

[Strains of the 'Blue Danube' waltz follow]

CHAMBERS *[to herself, sighing]*: 'Why do these places always have such crap music?'

FALLA: 'Newsdesk.'

CHAMBERS: 'Oh! Sorry. Hi. I'm trying to track down Steve Falla. Does he still work here?'

FALLA: 'Yes, for my sins.'

CHAMBERS: 'So you're – '

FALLA: 'Old reporters never die, they just get given the chess column. I jest, I jest. What can I do your for you?'

CHAMBERS: 'My name is Pauline Chambers. I'm researching a prominent police detective from your area for a TV documentary and I wondered whether you could help me. It's Frank Burnside. You've written a lot about him – I saw your byline in the archives.'

FALLA: 'Ah, how appropriate. Consigned to the mausoleum of microfiche.'

CHAMBERS: 'I didn't mean to imply… it's just you've obviously followed his career closely. I'd really value your contribution.'

FALLA: 'How kind of you, my dear. In that case I shall charge up the old grey matter. Let me see now, Frank Burnside. I haven't heard that name in quite a while. Why precisely are you doing him? Has our controversial Chief Inspector been making headlines again?'

CHAMBERS: 'Er, no, not exactly. It's a general piece. For a series we're doing.'

FALLA: 'Which is?'

CHAMBERS: 'It's called, um, "Rogue Males". About real-life maverick detectives, you know?'

FALLA *[chortling]*: '"Maverick". That's certainly one adjective for Burnside. I can think of several others that certain of his

73

colleagues used to bandy about quite freely.'

CHAMBERS: 'Such as? Do you mind if I record this, by the way? My shorthand's terrible and the producer will want me to get down all the details.'

FALLA: 'Not at all, be my guest. I expect your producer will want to hear what I sound like, for the programme.'

CHAMBERS: 'I'm sure he will.'

FALLA: 'Jolly good. So what do you want to know?'

CHAMBERS: 'Just preliminary stuff at this stage, then we can come back to you when the format's more developed. Perhaps take you out to lunch or something, get you to cast your expert eye over the profile.'

FALLA: 'Gladly.'

CHAMBERS: 'OK. Let's start with Burnside's career. He's had a pretty colourful past, judging by the cuttings.'

FALLA: 'I can only talk about Frank Burnside's tenure at Sun Hill. I believe he was in the Flying Squad and the Serious Crime Squad prior to that. Suffice to say his reputation preceded him. He didn't let niceties get in the way of his work, so inevitably there were fireworks. *Marvellous* copy, of course.'

CHAMBERS: 'Did you get to know him personally?'

FALLA: 'I made a few attempts to win his confidence but he made it perfectly plain what he thought of journalists. *Not* very complimentary, my dear, I should warn you.'

CHAMBERS: 'But from what you saw of him, did you think he was a good detective?'

FALLA: 'Good, yes. He was very effective. Fair, no. He used people terribly. And I couldn't put my hand on my heart and swear the man was honest, either. There was always, shall we say, a question mark over his propriety. Nothing was ever proven, I hasten to add. It was all circumstance and innuendo. And of course, he did pull off one or two tremendous coups...'

CHAMBERS: 'So in essence: hero or zero?'

FALLA: 'I beg your pardon?'

CHAMBERS: 'Do you think he's corrupt?'

FALLA: 'Oh, I see. Well, my own impression was that he batted for whichever side suited him, to coin a phrase.'

CHAMBERS: 'Do you know why he left Sun Hill?'

FALLA: 'He got promoted. He did an undercover stunt in Manchester and arrested a drugs dealer and several gangland leaders.'

CHAMBERS: 'Was this when he got involved with some mobster's wife?'

FALLA: 'Quite so. Burnside was always one for the ladies. Quite a charmer in his way, I'm told. I could never see it myself.'

CHAMBERS: 'He isn't married?'

FALLA: 'Good lord, no. Well, he wasn't, when I last heard. Seems highly unlikely. It's too late for a leopard like Burnside to change his spots. He always had a high turnover of women. Very big on blondes, I believe. Flashy types. It must have been mixing with all those prostitutes undercover.'

CHAMBERS: 'So he lives alone. Do you know where?'

FALLA: 'The last address I had for him was in Rotherhithe. I can look it up and e-mail it over to you, if you wish.'

CHAMBERS: 'That would be great. And what about his social life? Does he have any hobbies or interests? What about a local? Does he drink?'

FALLA: 'Burnside likes his scotch, but he's not a lush. The favoured Sun Hill watering hole has always been the Bay Horse, just up the road and round the corner from the station. I don't know if he drinks there any more, though. It depends whether he's moved.

'As to interests, I don't think he has any. The job's everything to him. I suspect he's absolutely terrified of being put out to grass

– he must be nearly fifty. Frank Burnside's the sort of policeman who drops dead a month after retiring because he's got nothing to live for. [*He pauses, then clears his throat*] Tragic, really. There should be more to life than work.'

TRANSCRIPT OF FILM, TAPE 42V/404. XSECS, 10.03.00, 11.50

Reception is empty. The phone rings. No one answers it and at last the caller gives up. Five minutes later it rings again. Still no one answers. Eventually, Clare Miller bursts into the room from her office wearing a face like thunder. She grabs the receiver. 'Xsecs. How can I – .'

She's too late. Slamming the receiver down, she barks, 'Joanne!', but gets no reply. Huffing, she checks her watch. At that moment, her receptionist enters, followed by Firebrand researcher Sam Gwilliam, who is dressed in ripped black jeans, DMs, leather jacket and a T-shirt held together with safety pins. They are laughing about something. Joanne, for once, is sparkly eyed and excited. Without preamble, Clare launches into her.

'Where have you been? Your break was over half an hour ago.'

Joanne's smile disappears instantly. 'Sorry.'

'Sorry *what*?'

'Sorry, Miss Miller.' She stares at the floor.

'Is that all you've got to say? The phone's been going mad, here. Why didn't you leave the machine on? While you're gadding about doing – ' she glances disparagingly at Sam ' – whatever it is you lot do, I might have missed an important call.'

Sam shoots a conspiratorial glance at Joanne. 'I'd better be off. See you six-ish.'

Joanne's eyes follow her out. Miller catches her look of

longing and says cattily, 'You've got no chance.'

'It's not like that. Sam's a – .' Joanne hesitates. Miller raises an interrogative eyebrow. Joanne blushes. 'She's into piercings and body art, like me. I was in that new coffee bar across the road and she came over and started talking.'

Miller smiles nastily. 'There you are. Give them a magnet and you can attract anyone.' She moves close and says threateningly, 'You sort your social life out in your own time, not mine. Do I make myself crystal clear?'

Joanne flinches. 'Yes, Miss Miller.' She slides out of range and goes to her desk. Clare Miller examines her watch again.

'Shouldn't the twins be back by now? When are they due over in Docklands?'

Joanne consults the desk diary. 'One o'clock. They're probably still having coffee. They came into the coffee bar while I was there.'

'And you didn't think to tell them to get a move on? Honestly!' Clare Miller sighs extravagantly.

'They were with another girl, gabbling away. I didn't like to go over. It looked pretty heavy.'

Miller freezes. 'Why do you say that?'

'This other girl was crying and stuff. Ana had her arm around her.'

'Was she a Croat too?'

Joanne looks surprised. 'I dunno. Probably. They weren't speaking English.'

'What did she look like?'

'Attractive. Dark hair. Olive skin. Couldn't see her tits. Want me to go snap her up anyway?'

'No. I'll go.' Miller, surprisingly, does not rise to the sarcasm. She fetches her coat. 'You've got work to do.'

TRANSCRIPT OF VOICEMAIL, TAPE 3T/998,
10.03.00, 12.05

GWILLIAM: 'Hi Tony, it's Sam ringing in with an update. I've made contact with Joanne Bennet. It went well and we're going to meet up tonight to discuss things in more detail. I've told her we're going for a video diary sort of approach, but that I need to build up a picture of her lifestyle before we do any filming. I've got a wire in my bag and I'll try and steer her round to Xsecs, but it might take more than one session. She's really nervous of her boss, and I can see why. Clare Miller's a right bitch – I'm in Starbucks at the moment writing up my notes, and she's just come in and given these two girls a really hard time. I assume they work for her. She was shouting, 'I know you've seen her, where is she?' They both looked terrified. Then she hauled them outside and marched them back to the agency. I'll mention it to Joanne when I see her; there might be something in it, you never know. Anyway, hope your face is feeling better now. Drink lots of soup! Catch you tomorrow. Ciao.'

DICTAPHONE TRANSCRIPT, TAPE 40A/92,
10.03.00, 16.45

BURNSIDE: 'OK Sutton, let's play it your way. From now on, consider these tapes *my* evidence. If I'm under investigation, don't expect me to just roll over. Smoke inhalation, my arse. I've had worse coughs after a night out in the boozer. I was up 'til two in the morning trying to figure it out. Why else would you want me off the scene for a few days? Like they say, just because you're paranoid, don't mean they ain't out to get you.

'It's gotta be something like that – or else Dawson's got protection. I'll buy that, too: he's too cocky to be operating alone. The question is, who's he taken out insurance with? And what do they do when he makes a claim – set fire to my shagpile? That's not a nice thing to do to a colleague, now is it? Option one don't look good for me; the other don't do much for you, Superintendent Sutton. And if you think I'm gonna rest up on sick leave while you or some bugger hangs my career out to dry, then you've seriously underestimated Frank Burnside.

'See, I've been on the blower today, making a few enquiries of my own. And I don't like what I'm hearing. There's still some people know what loyalty means, and they've been telling me questions are being asked about yours truly. Someone's playing Chinese whispers with my credentials and it don't take a genius to work out that's either the Pepper squad or CIB.

'Now CIB hate my guts, nothing new there. We have a formality we like to observe. They come along, accuse me of doing something I shouldn't, we have an argy-bargy and they back off when they can't prove it. I don't mind. It keeps life interesting. But Pepper I don't know about. Sounds to me like an exercise in political correctness; something to stop the government banging on about police accountability. If they are rooting out corruption, good luck to 'em. It's a hard task, I've done it before, with Countryman. But my guess is, they won't catch the real hard cases. Not enough of 'em to make the headlines. So they're going after coppers like me – coppers who've got their hands dirty doing the job – just so the top brass can shout about how they're cleaning up the force.

'It makes me sick to my stomach. You know, I might've played rough, I might've disobeyed orders, I might've done a whole lot of stuff that ain't in PACE, but there's a difference between bending the rules and ignoring 'em altogether. I know which side of the line I'm on. And after all the bodies I've nicked for you, Sutton, I'm surprised you don't.

'Remember that DCI on Tyneside, Dave Bonnet? The one running the show with Saul Anderson, head of the the local firm? He told me why he did it, why he crossed that line. He got passed over for promotion. All that effort and zilch. Too old. They kicked him in the teeth so he decided to go play with the other boys. "It's not about having a reason to take the money. It's about having a good enough reason not to." That's what he told me.

'Shot himself in the end, rather than face the music. Nearly shot me, too. The only reason he didn't was because a police marksman had him in his sights. And you know why he hated me so much? I'd let him down. He thought I was a used-car salesman with a sideline in importing high-grade sherbert. He thought I was like him, out for what I could get. A "partner in crime", those were his words. I think he even thought I was a pal. I'd busted him out of an illegal gambling club when the local woodentops raided it, I'd drunk his whisky, I'd kipped on his sofa.

'I turned out to be more like himself than he'd ever imagined – police officer, same rank – but unlike him I still had my integrity. That was what he couldn't stand. Not just that I was a copper, but that I wasn't bent. And even when I was staring down the barrel of his shooter, I never wished it had been any other way.

'I've been undercover a lot in my time, deep undercover. I've had to survive by my wits. I've had to prove myself to thugs and villains and psychos. I've been party to things you'll never know about. It's what I'm good at. I've had job offers worth far more than the Met'll ever pay me and there's been once or twice when I've given 'em some thought. I'm only human. But that's all I've ever done. Meanwhile there's bastards like Dave Bonnet in the force, controlling rackets, decapitating snouts and selling as much gear as they seize. So if you're helping the Pepper Squad with their enquiries, I think you'd better get your priorities straight.

[*Pause. Faint sound of traffic in the distance. In the silence, we hear the steady tick-tock of a clock. Burnside appears to be mulling something over.*]

'"If". Little word, big difference, ain't there? Because, if you ain't doing something like that, I've gotta consider the alternative. Like what's going on in my own back yard. Don't worry, pal, I'll find out. And you'd better be ready, because you won't see me coming ...'

TRANSCRIPT OF FILM, TAPE 77V/404. INTERIOR, IAN DI MICHELE'S CAR.
10.03.00, 14.09

There are two cameras recording footage: a concealed one, worn by Pauline, and a hand-held video camera that Ian occasionally uses to film better-quality sequences for the documentary. Pauline is also wired for sound.

The picture shows the road ahead as Ian's car bowls through Brixton. A black Escort XRi, throbbing to the beat of rap music, pulls out of a side street into his path. Ian slams on the brakes.

'Wanker!'

'I wouldn't say that any louder. Not if you want to keep your equipment intact. And I don't just mean the video,' Pauline says. 'You were going too fast, anyway.'

'It's impossible to go too fast in London. If you hit forty it feels like you're speeding.'

'Well, you are.'

'Hey! It's the only outlet my machismo gets.'

'What about Brian?'

'No comment.'

'Hah! Turn right here, then left at the next junction.'

Ian makes a dive across the oncoming traffic, to the blaring of horns. Pauline clutches the dash. 'Jesus! Isn't the fact I risk my neck every day working for Dawson enough for you?'

'Back-seat driver.' Ian slams the car into fifth, then immediately has to decelerate. They come to a halt behind a procession of double-decker buses. 'Anyway, you're Dawson's top chick; things should be a breeze now.'

'Yeah. Until he finds a camera in his bookcase. If Steve can do that to Tony…'

'Come on.' Ian pats her leg. 'It won't be for much longer. Anyway, Dawson won't hurt you. The bloke's obviously in love.'

'With me?' There is horror in Pauline's voice.

'He promotes you, creams your boyfriend and says the two of you are going to go places. Sounds like foreplay to me.'

'Oh my God.'

'Better crack this Burnside guy instead then. Talking of which –'

Pauline consults a London A–Z. 'Straight over the lights, then second left.'

'South Lambeth?'

'Yeah, a little road off the main drag. I'll tell you when.'

'Let's just hope he hasn't moved yet again.' Ian drums his fingers on the wheel as an elderly lady, bowed over, trundles in front of them with a shopping trolley. 'Come on, come on, deary.'

'Patience – '

'– is a virtue. Don't tell me; I don't possess any.'

'I was going to say it's good for your blood pressure. Now keep an eye out – it's somewhere along here on the right. This must be it. Yes. Turn!'

Ian swerves in front of a red Mondeo, provoking another barrage of honking. The camera's view is obliterated as Pauline covers her face with the A–Z.

'There was loads of room,' Ian says defiantly. 'What number are we looking for?'

'Eighty-six.'

The car slows to a crawl and hiccups over a speed bump. 'Must be on the other side, then. Yes, there. Bloody hell.' He pulls over and parks. 'Better get a shot of this.' [*The film fizzles and fades out, then comes on again. This time, we're seeing footage from the video camera.*]

The shot zooms in on a narrow, two-storey Victorian terraced house, unremarkable except for the blackened and blistered yellow paint on the front door. We hear Ian's voice. 'Well. That looks promising.'

'Umm. I wonder what happened.'

'That's your department, Sherlock.'

'We can't be positive it's his.'

'Well, let's stake it out, see if he shows. We can eat hotdogs or something, like in *Cagney and Lacey*.'

'*Cagney and Lacey*?' Pauline's voice comes out in a shriek. Ian swings the camera round, showing her doubled up in her seat laughing. 'Which one are you?' She sits up and wipes her eyes.

'The blonde one, of course.' His voice is deadpan. There's the sound of a door slamming. Ian swings the camera back to the house and catches Burnside outside, examining his paintwork.

'Shit.' The picture goes skywards, then dimly dark as the camera is put down with a clatter. Throughout the rest of the exchange, we focus on the Nike logo on Ian's trainer-clad foot. Pauline can be heard saying, 'What shall I do? He'll recognise me.'

'Crouch down on the floor.'

'Don't be stupid, there isn't room. Quick! He's crossing the road.'

There is the sound of seats creaking and a muffled protest from Ian. Heavy footsteps approach. Pauline hisses, 'For heaven's sake, kiss me like you mean it.'

'That's the problem.'

'Shut up.'

The footsteps draw level with the car. There's a smart tap on the windscreen.

'Oi.'

There is silence in the car.

He knocks again. 'Resident's parking only.'

'Bleuh.' Ian makes an indeterminate noise while Pauline enthusiastically snogs his face off.

'Way to go, mate.' Burnside slaps the roof of the car and walks off. Pauline and Ian separate, panting. Pauline speaks first. 'Are we tailing him?'

'Are you kidding? I think we can safely say we've broken our cover.' Ian slumps back in his seat. 'Not to mention my personal best.'

TRANSCRIPT OF TELEPHONE CALL, TAPE 382T/998, XSECS.
10.03.00, 14.35

MALE VOICE [*breezy*]: 'Hello.'

MILLER: 'It's Clare.'

MALE VOICE [*over crackly line; it's obviously a mobile*]: 'Is this gonna be the five-minute argument or the full half-hour?'

MILLER: 'What are you on about?'

MALE VOICE: 'I haven't found your little runaway yet, alright? I got someone on the inside looking but there's more than one of them places – '

MILLER [*cutting in*]: 'I know where she is.'

MALE VOICE: 'Yeah? How come?'

MILLER: 'She was here. She must have been hanging around outside. Ana and Irena met up with her.'

MALE VOICE: 'Hang on, I'm gonna pull over.' [*We hear the*

ticking of his indicator. The engine noise quietens and stops. He yanks on the handbrake then picks up the phone again.] 'So where is she now?'

MILLER: 'She's making her way to Kristina's – you remember, Davor's girl?'

MALE VOICE: 'Didn't something happen with her?'

MILLER [*crisp*]: 'You could say that.'

MALE VOICE: 'Dawson poached her. She threw a wobbly and threatened to tell Daddy. That was it, weren't it?'

MILLER: 'Yes. And guess who had to pay the little brat off and get her a job to keep her quiet. Davor sent her over to get catwalk experience. He'd have killed me.'

MALE VOICE: 'It was Pete's fault.'

MILLER [*snorting*]: 'You know Davor. He doesn't discriminate. Everything's black and white with him.'

MALE VOICE: 'What's the connection with these two girlies, then? They know each other?'

MILLER: [*hesitating slightly*]: 'So it appears. I didn't realise that, obviously. Apparently they were best friends back in Zagreb. Sanja followed Kristina over.'

MALE VOICE: 'Them twins tell you all this?'

MILLER: 'Eventually.'

MALE VOICE [*chuckling*]: 'Ouch!'

MILLER [*grim*]: 'Let's just say I haven't lost my touch.'

MALE VOICE: 'I remember it well. What did you use – the manacles and whip?'

MILLER: 'Oh, grow up.'

MALE VOICE: 'Ah, don't spoil my fun, Miss Miller. A bloke can still dream.' [*Lowering his voice*] 'What are you wearing?'

MILLER: 'For Christ's sake! I've got an important job for you and I don't want you blowing it.'

MALE VOICE [*talking dirty*]: 'That's lucky. I've got an

important job for you and I *do* want you blowing it.'

MILLER: 'Get your hands out of your trousers and concentrate. You'll get your reward if you do the job.'

MALE VOICE: 'Personally?'

MILLER [*sighing*]: 'Personally.'

MALE VOICE: 'Alright then. Go on, surprise me. I suppose you want me to pay this Kristina a visit.'

MILLER: 'I want you to do more than that.' [*Steely*] 'The question is, have you got what it takes?'

MALE VOICE: 'I'm surprised you need to ask me that, Miss Miller. I don't remember you having any complaints.'

MILLER [*ignoring innuendo*]: 'It's Sanja we're after, not Kristina. Got that? Kristina's living with a family in Hampstead, a big house up on East Heath Road. 'Caladon', that's what it's called. They would ask questions if she went missing. Sanja's a nobody, she's easy to get rid of. The police aren't going to waste time trying to find her. She's obviously got away from them once; they'll just forget about her.'

MALE VOICE: 'And what if these two have had a cosy little heart-to-heart about things? You're telling me Kristina's going to keep schtum if her best friend turns up out of the blue then just as suddenly disappears again?'

MILLER: 'She will if you get to Sanja first.'

MALE VOICE: 'Come on, Clare. Get real.'

MILLER: 'OK. It's a calculated risk. We'll just have to take it. Make sure Kristina doesn't see or hear anything. If Sanja's living on the streets, anything could happen to her.'

MALE VOICE: 'I'll play it by ear.'

MILLER: 'You do that.'

MALE VOICE: 'Brass tacks, Clare. What d'you want doing with her? I'm gonna need some backup here. I can't do it all on my tod.'

MILLER: 'I know, I know. You'll just have to pick your moment. Get her to the warehouse. I'll have a quiet word with Jonno. You can liaise with him.'

MALE VOICE: 'Does Pete know about this yet?'

MILLER: 'I had to tell him. The police have been asking questions. Don't worry, I glossed over the details.'

MALE VOICE: 'You've had the filth round? Why didn't you tell me?'

MILLER: 'Keep your cool. They haven't got any evidence. It's all a lot of hot air at the moment. And that's the way it will stay if we can shut that girl up. You just keep your end of the deal.'

MALE VOICE: 'That reward had better be good, Miss Miller. That reward had really better be good.'

Diary, 10 March

No work tonight, so I'm having a girl's night in, just me, a bag of popcorn, the cast of *Friends* and my fluffy rabbit slippers. I start the greeter's job on Monday, so I've got the weekend off too, though it creates a problem with changing the tapes over. I'll have to sneak in to Silks tomorrow morning and retrieve them. Still, the rest of the time's my own, which is a treat, plus I won't have Tony breathing down my neck (literally) because he's taken sick leave. Doesn't mean I'm going to let up on the investigation into Burnside, though. The opposite. I've had a brilliant idea.

It came to me just now. Ian and I had spent half the day dashing about in his car, trying to follow up the leads Steve Falla gave me. We found Burnside's place eventually – he'd moved, but the new owner had a forwarding address – though there was a bit of a hairy moment when I thought he was going to see me. I threw myself on Ian, which frightened the life out of him, or so he said. Actually, I think he enjoyed it. He definitely slipped me the tongue! (A 'conditioned response' he called it.)

We couldn't very well follow Burnside after that, 'cos he'd have recognised the car, so we decided to try and find his local instead and sound the regulars out. I stuck to halves, but by the time we'd checked out all the pubs in the vicinity, I was as pissed as a fart. A couple of the landlords recognised Burnside (I had a video grab of him from one of the covert tapes), but they both said he only came in on odd occasions, usually Saturday lunchtimes. If he drinks somewhere regularly, it's not in South Lambeth.

Ian suggested we try the Bay Horse, the pub where the Sun Hill crowd hang out, but I was tired and it was a bit of a hike so we decided to call it a day and go home. I crashed out when I got back and slept for nearly two hours, and woke up with a mouth like sandpaper. I was in the bathroom downing pints of water when I had this lightbulb moment: why not just front up to Burnside as me, not 'Emma', and chat him up?

It's risky, but time's running out and we need to get a result. Instead of pussyfooting around, waiting for Burnside to turn up at the club, I need to be proactive. I could come up with a story about why I was at Silks – say I'm an impoverished student or something – and spin him a line about why I overreacted when I saw him last time. I know there's a spark between us from the couple of exchanges we've had and, judging by what Falla said, Burnside's probably not attached. If I can get him interested in me, get him back to my flat, I can film him secretly and persuade him to open up. Then, when I've got his confidence, I can talk him into telling me all about his deviant practices and his set-up with that sleaze Dawson. Scoop!

Of course, all this depends on me actually managing to find him. Tomorrow's Saturday, so I've decided to try those two pubs at lunchtime and, if I don't bump into him there, I'll try the Bay Horse in the evening. It's feasible he'd meet up with his old mates for a bevy. I can't think what else to do, short of lurking in the street outside his house, which is way too obvious. I'm not going to tell Ian, Tony or anyone else on the team, then if I balls it up, they'll be none the wiser.

E-mail

From: Frank Burnside

Sent: 11 March

To: grhedges@hotmail.com

Subject: Request Update

Gazza

Sick leave overrated. Bored out of my tree here. I'll see my GP on Monday, get him to give me a once-over. That police surgeon doesn't know his arse from his elbow. I ain't working officially, but you know the score. Keep me posted by e-mail re. Dawson and the rest. Any news on Tomasic/Kristina? What about the shower girls?

Burnside

E-mail

From: Gary Hedges

Sent: 11 March

To: fburnside@cwcom.net

Subject: Re. Yr Message

Glad you're on the up. Me and Terri were going to wheel you round the canteen shouting 'penny for the guy', but we'll let you off. Any bloke who can set fire to his strides and still walk a straight line deserves a break.

No good news to report. NCIS couldn't get Tomasic to cough, but they're looking into his Zagreb operation. It's borderline — he almost certainly supplies toms to

the exhibition trade — but no one's admitting it. There's no evidence he's
recruiting for the smuggling ring, but then they've probably stopped shipments
while the heat's on. He gave an old address for his daughter and we've drawn a
blank with the au pair agencies here. Terri tried soft-soaping the shower girls but
she obviously wasn't their type. Sanja Gregovic has gone to ground, too, so we're
stymied all round at the moment. There must be more slags on the streets who
know Dawson's game. Want me and Cal to put the word out? Any other
suggestions?

Gazza

E-mail
From: Frank Burnside
To: grhedges@hotmail.com
Subject: Re. Yr Message — reply

Sent: 11 March

Fancy going to a conference in Croatia? See what Sutton says to that.

TRANSCRIPT OF FILM, TAPE 232V/404. INTERIOR, BAY HORSE PUB, SUN HILL.
11.03.00, 21.35

From the camera angle, Pauline is seated near the door. The film
is intercut with different shots from the concealed cameras in her
bag, watch and mobile.

A typical, Victorian-style London pub. It's a busy Saturday
night and the bar is already crowded with regulars including
several obviously off-duty police officers, who are celebrating a
colleague's birthday amid much ribaldry. Burnside is with them.
He is dressed casually in jeans and a black leather jacket and
appears relaxed, although his eyes betray a certain wariness. He
is standing on the edge of the group and does not join in with the

witticisms as the birthday boy – an amiable, well-covered Scot – unwraps his present. Instead, he signals to a taller, fair-haired man and draws him to one side. Their discussion is discreet but intense; it's clear Burnside doesn't want to draw the attention of the others. The other man appears to try and reassure him, but Burnside's expression is brooding and dark. He listens with narrowed eyes to what his friend has to say, then claps him on the back in a half-hearted gesture that suggests resignation as much as thanks.

The rest of the group drink up and shrug on coats, but Burnside remains seated by the bar. One of the women, a slim, attractive redhead, asks him to join them at a restaurant. Burnside's response is inaudible, but it's obvious he's declining the invitation. She throws him a lingering, slightly wistful look over her shoulder as she follows the others out. Burnside stares bleakly into his glass of whisky, drains it and orders a large one.

The picture is suddenly obscured and replaced by a closeup of an ample cleavage as a middle-aged woman in a revealing top looms over Pauline.

'Is anybody sitting here, love?'

'Er, no, help yourself.'

'Ta love. On your own, are you?'

The woman and her girlfriend commandeer the spare chairs at Pauline's table. Cleavage woman wears red lipstick and an assortment of gold chains and lockets that nestle in her bosom; her equally blowsy friend sports a beaded black tunic, dangly earrings and a tight blonde perm. Both stare at Pauline, who is in an open-necked white shirt and entirely unaccessorised, as if she is letting the side down.

'Um, well, sort of.' Pauline shoots a glance at Burnside.

The woman follows her gaze and winks at her. 'Join up with us then. We're on the pull too.' She and her friend shriek with laughter, making their jewellery jolt and jingle. 'Though that one's more in our range than yours, lovey,' she continues, nudging her friend and pointing out Burnside. 'You young girls have got to leave us mature ladies with something.'

Earring woman studies Burnside. 'Actually, he's not bad, Joan. What do you think? Is it your turn or mine? I'm losing track.' Burnside turns, catches her smirk, and flinches. Pauline is visibly panicked.

'Actually, I know him. I was just about to go and say hello.' She gets up hurriedly, scrabbling for her bag and phone.

Cleavage woman looks annoyed. 'Well, tell him there's two gorgeous, *experienced* ladies here who would love to be introduced. And we're drinking sweet white wine.'

'I'll mention it,' Pauline mutters, making a dash for the bar. Burnside is standing up to go as she reaches him. 'Hi,' Pauline says brightly. 'I thought I recognised you. It's Frank, isn't it?'

He does a double-take, then grins. 'Blimey. I didn't think you lot came out in daylight.' He glances at the street lights showing through the frosted glass windows. 'Still, you're probably safe.'

'I do have a life outside Silks, you know.'

Burnside stares at her, shaking his head.

Pauline seems momentarily unnerved. 'What?'

'You look completely different without all the slap.'

'Better or worse? You've forgotten my name, haven't you?'

'Emma.' He touches the side of his nose. 'And you look nicer without it. You don't need all that gunk. Unlike – ' He indicates his fan club. The two women raise empty glasses to him. Burnside scowls.

Pauline giggles. 'I thought I'd better come to your rescue. They were about to toss for you.'

'Toss for me? I'd swing for 'em first.'

'They want you to buy them a drink.'

'I can see that. Come on, let's move round the other side where we ain't got an audience.' He steers Pauline round the bar, one hand lightly on her elbow, and leads her to a quiet table in the snug. 'What can I get you? I'm not sure they run to champagne here.'

'Thank God for that. I've had enough to last me a lifetime. I'll have a Guinness, please.'

While Burnside is ordering the drinks, Pauline arranges her bag and mobile to get the best pictures. He returns with the drinks and sits down opposite her, perfectly framed by the shot. Pauline draws a deep breath.

'Actually, I have to come clean with you about something. My name isn't Emma.'

'You do surprise me.' He doesn't look it.

'It's Pauline.'

'Right.' Burnside takes a swig of his drink – he has switched to pints – and puts his glass down decisively. 'Anything else you haven't told me?'

'Like what?'

'Come on, what do you really do? Every other girl in that place is a "model". I never bought that story.'

'Are you saying I haven't got what it takes?' Pauline plays mock-offended.

'You've got in spades, but that ain't your real job.' He looks at her intently.

Pauline swallows. Her voice, when she answers, is husky. 'You're right. But it's not a job, as such. I'm a student. Hostessing's just a way of paying back my loan. I can cover it in about three months. Quite a few of the girls do it. Saves being saddled with debts for years on end.'

'Bit of free enterprise, eh?'

'You didn't seem to mind.'

'No. I didn't.' Burnside looks at her levelly. 'I enjoyed our little chats. Though I seem to remember I said something to upset you last time.'

'Oh. That.'

'All of a sudden, you went colder than Siberia.'

'I'm sorry. I was a bit – taken aback, that's all.'

'Not like an escort to be prudish.'

'I know. I got a rollicking from the boss about that.'

Burnside raises his eyebrows. 'And?'

'Strange as it may sound, he promoted me. I'm going to be greeting instead from now on.' Pauline examines her fingernails minutely.

This time, Burnside really does look surprised. 'Dawson promoted you?'

She glances up from under her lashes. 'Oh, do you know him?'

'Our paths have crossed before.' He is silent for a minute, then adds, 'I suppose he mentioned that? You being so thick with him.'

'He – he said something.'

'Don't tell me: he sang my praises and told you what a great geezer I am.'

Pauline eyes him speculatively. 'He said you were a bent copper and he was doing some business with you. Well, thinking about it.'

Burnside throws his head back and roars with laughter. Pauline looks unsure whether to join in or not. He slaps the table. 'You know something? You have really cheered me up. That toerag is so bloody predictable.'

'So, are you?' Pauline's voice is almost a whisper. Burnside is suddenly still. She tries being flirtatious. 'I came clean with you.'

'I didn't think we was at the "truth or dare" stage of our relationship, yet.' His face is stony. Pauline lowers her eyes. 'I meet all sorts at Silks. I'm not judging you – '

'Too right you're not. Because you know sod-all about it,' he says harshly. 'If you want to believe the word of a first-rate shyster against a senior police detective, go ahead. You ain't the only one. Your precious boss has been busy spreading the word.'

Another couple enter the snug and sit down within earshot. Burnside lowers his voice to a viscious hiss. 'Well, that's the pleasantries out the way. What d'you want to talk about now? Or have you had enough?'

'I'm sorry. It's none of my business.' Pauline looks upset. 'But you did sort of ask.' She sniffles into a tissue.

Burnside sighs heavily. He puts a hand on her arm. 'Yeah. Let's forget it, eh? I've had a pig of a day and that's a sore subject.'

'Just because I work for Dawson, it doesn't mean I like him. Or trust him.' Pauline juts her chin.

'Good. You'd be mad if you did.'

They drink in silence as a barmaid comes to collect glasses and wipe the table. Burnside leans back in his chair and regards Pauline, who is dabbing powder on her nose from a compact. 'Any particular reason?'

'He – he uses the girls.'

'Don't all the blokes there?'

'Not like that. I mean, at least they pay for it. He acts like – I can't describe it. Women are just toys to him. He takes them, he breaks them, then he just chucks them away.' She bites her lip, as if she's said too much.

'Pauline. Spit it out. What do you know?'

'Nothing. Nothing specific. I was just commenting – '

'No. You know something. And I need you to tell me.' Burnside is no longer laid back. 'That scumbag's got a sideline he don't go round advertising and I'm chasing my tail trying to find out what and where it is.'

'So is this an official interview?'

'It could be. I'd prefer to keep things friendly, though.' He glances at the other couple, who are looking curiously in their direction. 'Why don't I get you another drink? Same again?'

'Er, yes, alright. I'm just going to the loo.'

Pauline gets up, picking up her bag. Once in the deserted Ladies, she puts the bag down on the counter so that it films her own reflection in the mirror. What follows is effectively a piece to camera, narrated deliberately for a TV audience.

PAULINE'S VOICEOVER [*speaking in hushed tone*]: 'I've renewed contact with Frank Burnside informally in this South London pub, but he still doesn't know who I am. I'm hoping that, by taking advantage of the acquaintanceship we struck up in Silks, I can persuade him to divulge his real agenda. Peter Dawson claims Frank Burnside is a deeply corrupt police officer although, as we've just seen, Burnside has robustly rejected that accusation. He does, however, acknowledge that he and Dawson have a history, but seems reticent about elaborating on that.

'Now, the tables have been turned somewhat, and Burnside is asking me for help. It's a difficult position to call: on the one hand I can hardly refuse to co-operate; on the other, he may be trying to find out what I know for more devious reasons. By telling him what I know, I could be aiding and abetting him in, for example, blackmailing or undercutting Peter Dawson. Furthermore, if I was forced to hand over the evidence that myself and the team have so painstakingly gathered, he could bury it and we would be unable to expose either Burnside or Dawson and their criminal activities.'

There's the sound of raucous female banter from outside. She glances nervously at the door, then continues.

'I could slip away now – there's a side door in the corridor outside – but if I do, I lose any further opportunity to exploit the situation here. Plus, I'd be unable to return to Silks as Burnside would undoubtedly approach Dawson himself.

'If I take the risk and go back to Burnside, he's going to expect some answers. Possibly I could make some up, but I get the feeling he knows enough to tell when he's being lied to. He's a shrewd man and on the strength of our encounter this evening, I'm not sure I could stand up to being interrogated by him...'

Pauline rests her hands on the counter and hangs her head. She takes several shaky breaths, then looks up again, pushing the hair out of her eyes. Her face is drained of colour. When she finally speaks, her voice is no longer cool and professional but panicked and scared.

'Oh shit. I've really gone and done it this time.'

The door bursts open and two girls totter in, shrieking and laughing. One dives for a cubicle – 'I'm gonna wet me knickers if I don't go right this second!' – while the other joins Pauline at the mirror. Pursing her mouth, she applies lipstick, then stands back to admire the result. Glancing at Pauline she asks sympathetically, 'Boyfriend dumped you, pet?'

Pauline picks up the bag. We lose the picture but hear her answer: 'Other way round, actually. I just don't know how to break it to him.'

'Tell him he's history. That'll give him the message.'

'I think I'll leave him to work it out for himself.'

The door thuds shut.

TRANSCRIPT OF FILM, TAPE 45V/404. SILKS (PRIVATE SUITE).
10.03.00, 21.00
Dawson is entertaining three Japanese businessmen while a sour-faced Angie brings in a succession of hostesses for their perusal. So far, two have made their pick and have their arms round

giggling girls, but the third, an older man, is proving excessively fussy. After yet another hostess has been rejected, Dawson beckons Angie over and whispers in her ear. He turns to the increasingly awkward customer.

'We 'ave got one young lady I keep for really special guests. She's definitely… exotic. Quite a handful all ways round.' He pauses, grinning. 'I don't think you'll be disappointed.' The other two men speculate on this, with much laughter. The girls catch Dawson's wink and join in. The elderly Japanese remains unmoved.

Angie returns with a stunning, leggy, sloe-eyed brunette. Only a practised eye would register her too-perfect body as belonging to a transsexual, and the old man obviously does not make the connection.

'Ah-ha, yes!' His face lights up with something approaching wonderment. He pats the upholstered seat beside him. 'You come sit here. You very beautiful lady.'

The rest of the party is boisterously congratulating him on his choice when the door bursts open and a man enters. He is tall, with an upright, almost military bearing and is formally dressed in an obviously bespoke suit. He walks up to them and addresses Dawson, ignoring the others.

'You've been playing with fire, Peter. Haven't you?'

The Japanese look confused. Angie looks blank. The hostesses look fascinated. Dawson looks caught out. He stands up hastily. 'Not here, eh?' He inclines his head towards the group. 'Let's talk about it in my office.'

TRANSCRIPT OF FILM, TAPE 46V/404. SILKS
(DAWSON'S OFFICE).
10.03.00. 21.08
'I can't believe you did something so utterly foolhardy. And after I explicitly told you *not* to take the matter into your own hands.'

The tall man is already gunning for Dawson as he strides into his office ahead of him. This time, Dawson makes no attempt at pleasantries.

'Someone 'ad to do something. While you was sitting on your fanny in your ivory tower, I had Burnside crawling all over this place. And the agency. 'E's got Clare rattled and you know she don't scare easy.'

'So you put a petrol bomb through his front door to telegraph your concern. What did you think that would achieve?'

'I was 'oping it would shut the bugger up.'

'Then you should have arranged it better. He's alive and kicking arses all round the shop. I had to persuade the police surgeon to sign him off sick just to get him out of the way.'

Dawson looks as if the wind's been taken out of his sails. He digs his hands into his pockets and hunches his shoulders.

'I assume you got your so-called "specialist" to do the job? I hope so for your sake,' the tall man continues. He is at least six-foot-four and towers over Dawson. Next to the impressively fit, middle-aged man with his head of thick, dark, well-cut hair, the club owner cuts a ridiculous figure. 'Forensics have found a partial footprint outside Burnside's window. I wouldn't like to hear it had a Cuban heel.'

Dawson curses under his breath. He swings round the desk and slumps in his chair. ''E told me the gaff was well ablaze. Said 'e didn't hang around to check on Burnside, case some nosey parker clocked him.'

The other man looks grim. 'Well, while your ex-SAS chappie – and I can appreciate why they found him surplus to requirements – was botching attempted arson, I've had Frank Burnside ring-fenced from inside. The procedure is well underway. He won't be returning to duty. So you see, Peter, all you have succeeded in doing is complicating the situation unnecessarily.'

Dawson jumps to his feet, stung by his scathing tone. 'Now you just listen to me, Bigfoot, Burnside ain't gonna sit back and do nothing while you shuffle paperwork, even if he is at home. Even if you suspend him. *Especially* if you suspend him. That's like red rag to a bull. He'll have nothing to lose, mate. He'll go all out on this one.'

Dawson comes back round the desk and perches on the front edge, regaining his poise. 'What makes you so bloody sure your inquiry will shut him up?' He looks the other man in the eye, cocky now. 'Can't guarantee it, can yer? I tell you this: he won't stop shouting the odds until someone interferes with his vocal cords. And once he realises who's behind it – '

'He won't.'

Dawson sucks in his smooth cheeks. 'Burnside, he never forgets. That's something Mal's always said. "Frank never forgives and he never forgets." Your cards'll be marked, sunshine, and so will mine. Our entire operation is gonna go belly-up if Burnside catches on.'

'So what precisely are you suggesting?'

'Come on.'

'You can't just murder a police officer. Questions would be asked.'

Dawson raises an eyebrow.

'Besides, it's – well, is it absolutely necessary to go that far?'

'Bit late to be asking questions like that, innit?' Dawson goes over to the drinks cabinet and retrieves two crystal glasses and a decanter. 'You've had an easy time of it so far, Bigfoot, sitting back, taking the money, enjoying all the perks. No good getting squeamish now.'

He hands him a glass of cognac. 'I think it's time we did a little deal.' Dawson holds his glass in the air and admires the way it catches the light. 'If I sort Burnside, I don't want no more coppers sniffing round my club. And that includes Vice. Comprende? Unless you're thinking of taking him out yourself...'

His co-conspirator says nothing.

Dawson smiles. 'Leave it to me, then.'

The man squares his shoulders. 'You'd better make it good. I don't want this one rebounding. And don't use that bloody useless henchman of yours, either. Get someone who knows what they're doing.'

'Don't worry.' Dawson sniffs his brandy appreciatively. 'I'll do it myself. I can't think of anyone whose brains I'd rather blow out.' He salutes the man with his glass. 'To... Burnside. Let's hope the next twenty-four hours are 'appy ones. 'Cos tomorrow night – ' he consults his watch, '– will be 'is last.'

The tall man puts down his glass without tasting its contents and turns on his heel. He walks out of the room without a backward glance, back stiff as a ramrod. Dawson bellows with laughter and knocks his drink back in one.

TRANSCRIPT OF FILM, TAPE 233V/404. PAULINE'S FLAT, HAMMERSMITH. (PAULINE'S P.O.V.) 11.03.00, 22.30

Initially, there is sound but no picture. We hear laboured breathing. Someone is struggling to do something that involves ripping tape and buckling straps.

'Damn, damn!' It's Pauline's voice. More huffing and puffing and swearing, then a picture suddenly appears, a wobbly, out-of-focus shot of what looks like a bowl of fruit on a kitchen table. Pauline is wearing the camera and she's on the move, grabbing keys, phone, notebook, bag, diving about her flat so that the picture jogs up and down. The mike is recording not just her panicked breathing but her racing heart, putting a soundtrack on the scene: ba-dum, ba-dum, ba-dum.

She slams out of the flat, pounds down three flights of stairs and charges out into the night. The lens fogs in the cold air obscuring our view as Pauline jogs along the pavement and stops by her car. She jabs at the lock with stiff fingers, cursing again, and wrenches the door open. The engine starts, coughs and dies, inducing another stream of expletives. 'Don't flood. Please don't flood now,' she pleads. It starts second time. Revving loudly, Pauline pulls away from the kerb with a squeal of tyres and out into the Hammersmith traffic.

The next thirty minutes are a nightmare journey of blazing, bobbing lights, as Pauline screams along the Talgarth Road, zigzagging south-east to reach the Embankment. Flagrantly ignoring speed restrictions, black cabs and other drivers, she weaves in and out, overtaking slower vehicles and motoring down bus lanes, until she gets to Vauxhall Bridge. After crossing the bridge, she makes a mistake and turns down Wandsworth Road, thumping the wheel in frustration when she realises her error. Eventually she finds an opportunity to cut across and join South Lambeth Road. Heading back north, she passes a row of shops and the two pubs she had haunted looking for Burnside only that lunchtime. At the next corner she swerves deftly into the now-familiar side road and immediately slows down to a crawl. On her left, the curb is crammed with cars parked nose-to-tail, stretching all the way to the end of the street. On the opposite side of the road just past Burnside's house, parked up half on the pavement and straddling double yellow lines, is a black Ford Scorpio.

The big saloon's lights are off. At first, it's impossible to tell whether there is anyone in the car, then the dark silhouette of the driver becomes visible as he leans across to the passenger side, as if reaching for the glove compartment. As he straightens up again, we get a fleeting glimpse of his profile and long, straggly hair.

'Oh, shit!' Pauline throws the car into reverse, backing up almost to the junction until she can tuck in behind the first parked car. She switches off her lights, kills the engine and sinks down low into her seat. The hidden camera shot shows the driver's side window and the view from the wing mirror. Whispering – although there's no need – she delivers an urgent commentary.

PAULINE'S VOICEOVER: 'That's Peter Dawson in the car across the road. He's here to kill Frank Burnside. On the evidence of the secret tapes I've just seen, recorded last night at Silks, it's not Burnside who's corrupt but a fellow police officer, probably a very high-ranking one, judging by his influence. Whoever he is, he's in collusion with Dawson and desperate enough to go along with his scheme to murder Burnside.'

She risks a peep out of the window, craning her neck to get a glimpse of the Scorpio.

'It looks as I've got here in time to try and stop Dawson, although I'm not sure what I can do – '

Pauline breaks off as a car turns into the road, swinging out to avoid the rear end of her battered Polo. The driver – a black youth – glares at her as he goes past, and for a moment it looks as if he might stop, but he drives on. She heaves a sigh of relief. Lowering herself back down behind the wheel, she continues her narration.

'The longer I wait, the more danger I'm personally exposed to. I'm far too close to the corner here – that car nearly hit me – but my options are limited. I can't pull over and park facing the oncoming traffic like Dawson; it would draw too much attention. If I drive past him, he might recognise me. Besides, there's nowhere to stop. Here, I'm too far back to be identified, but also, possibly, too far back to intervene should anything happen. Also,

Dawson must have noticed me park and be wondering why I haven't got out. He might decide to come and investigate.

'There's one thing I can do, though – ' She turns and feels under the passenger seat, groping around in a deep litter of empty crisp packets, sweet papers, balled tissues and parking tickets, and finally produces a baseball cap, emblazoned with the legend 'Chicago Bulls'. Holding it up at chest height, so that it's caught on camera, she whispers, 'My ten-year-old godson left this behind a couple of months ago. I don't know if it'll fit, but it's the only disguise I've got. Though I might have some sunglasses somewhere.' She rummages in her bag. 'Yes!' Apparently she puts them on because her next comment, presumably not for transmission is, 'Great. I can't see a sodding thing now.'

Headlights illuminate the wing mirror. There's the distinctive ticking sound of a diesel engine, betraying a black cab. Pauline sits up. It barrels past close to her. Through the glass we see a fleeting glimpse of Burnside in the back. She raises a hand to signal to him, but he's already gone, and we're left with the image of Pauline's scared face reflected back at us. Breathing fast, she winds down the window, leaning out as far as she dares. The taxi's brake lights are on. It slows down and comes to a rattling halt opposite Burnside's house, a car's length or so behind the Scorpio on the other side of the road.

Burnside gets out and goes to pay the cabbie. The driver's door of the black car swings open. Quietly, Pauline opens her door too, just far enough to put a foot on the ground. Burnside jingles in his pockets for a tip. Dawson unfolds himself stealthily so that first his head, then his upper body become visible over the top of the car. He drapes his right arm casually along the roof, as if he is a neighbour stopping to chat. His left arm hangs by his side. Pauline gets out completely, standing up and keeping the open door in front of her as a shield. Dawson's eyes are fixed on Burnside. Burnside is bidding the cabbie goodnight. Dawson raises his left arm and hooks back his right shoulder. Something glints.

'Frank!' Pauline's shout is swallowed up by the chugging of the cab as it draws away. Dawson is levelling what looks like a sawn-off shotgun at Burnside's back. 'Frank! He's got a gun!' Burnside spins round at Pauline's scream, just as a shot rings out. He stumbles and catches at his side. Dawson strides round the rear of the car and stands, legs apart, a long mackintosh flapping round his ankles as if he's Clint Eastwood. He raises the gun again, taking careful aim. Burnside sees him and starts to make for the shelter of the parked cars.

Pauline runs into the road, waving her arms and shouting, 'This way! Come on! It's Pauline. Get in here!' It distracts Dawson long enough for Burnside to dodge between two vehicles and onto pavement. A car window shatters as Dawson shoots again. Cursing, he glances back at the cab, which has stopped further up the road, and seems to hesitate. Pauline scrambles back into her car. This time it starts first go. She flings open the passenger door. There's a dull metallic crack as a shot ricochets off the roof. Dawson is running up the street towards her. She switches the headlamps on full beam, hoping to blind him.

Burnside appears, gasping. Pauline revs the engine and slams the gearstick into reverse. He half-falls into the car and she takes off before he's even closed the door, almost tipping him out again. He makes another lunge and this time manages to shut it. There's blood soaking through his shirt and staining his jeans. Pauline is looking back over her shoulder, trying to reverse out into the main road, but there's obviously no gap. She doesn't see that Dawson has stopped and is standing in the middle of the road, pointing the gun straight at them.

'Get down!' Burnside roars. He yanks her towards him, so that she's almost face down in his lap. The picture goes black. There's the sound of the windscreen splintering into a million tiny fragments. We hear Pauline's terrified scream. Burnside takes charge. 'OK, go. Go!'

She gets up again and grabs the wheel. The lens is smeared with what appears to be Burnside's blood, rendering the rest of the footage into a surreal kaleidoscope. Through the fine tracery of cracked glass, Dawson's face appears in indistinct outline. Pauline stamps her foot flat on the floor and the Polo screeches out into South Lambeth Road into the path of an oncoming sportscar. There's a squeal of tyres from behind, but somehow the Mazda Mx5 manages to whisk round them.

'I can't see,' she yells desperately. They're sitting ducks: not for Dawson, who is running back towards his car now, but for the oncoming traffic. A van is bearing down on them fast, horn blaring.

'Just drive.' Burnside searches the mess on the floor and picks up a rubber torch.

'Oh, God,' Pauline whimpers, engaging first and pulling away like a learner.

'Cover your face!' Burnside orders. Shards of glass rain onto the bonnet as he knocks the window out. Suddenly, the view is clear, apart from the swirls of dried blood still on the camera lens. The volume of noise instantly trebles, so that every whoosh, roar, shout, honk, clank and hiss is picked up by the mike as if they're inside the car. Pauline accelerates out of trouble. 'Where's Dawson?' she yells above the racket of traffic.

Burnside twists in his seat, wincing as he does so, and glances behind. 'Making a quick getaway, I should think – in the opposite direction.'

'So where to now? Casualty?'

'I'll live,' Burnside growls feeling his oozing side, 'but your upholstery's going to be scarred for life.'

TRANSCRIPT OF SECRET FILM, TAPE 135V/404;
PAULINE'S FLAT, HAMMERSMITH.
11.3.00, 00.45

A clean, contemporary living room, all wooden floors, weeping figs and Ikea furniture. Strategically placed uplighters give the walls a warm glow, illuminating exhibition posters in clipframes and a collection of *objets d'art* in display boxes. The band Texas plays softly on an expensive minidisc and CD hi-fi system, which is set up on a home entertainment centre, a stacked arrangement of open cubes that also house the latest flat widescreen TV, a DVD player and a VCR.

Pauline, who has changed into trackpants and a red Gap fleece, is curled up on a sofa, her bare feet tucked under her. In front of her is a low table bearing a bottle of Bells whisky and two tumblers. She is pointing a remote control at the video, rewinding a tape, but from the hidden camera's perspective we're unable to see what it is. She looks up as Burnside pads into shot wearing a black dressing gown.

'I won't ask whose this is.' He plucks at the sleeve.

'My ex's. It was too nice to chuck. Unlike him.'

He smiles briefly. 'So where's my stuff? You binned that, too?'

'Being washed, with mine. A little blood goes a long way.' She stops the video. 'How do you feel now?'

'Like I've got what it takes to be a teabag.'

'What's that?'

'A little perforation.' He presses his side experimentally. 'Good job Dawson didn't have a sub-machine gun. I'd have been a rich, full-bodied blend quicker than you can say Typhoo.' He comes over and sits down beside her. 'And so would you. That was a stupid thing to do.'

'Thanks very much.' Pauline looks offended.

'You can't play Lois Lane around thugs like Dawson.' Burnside stares at her, his eyes glinting. 'What did you think, bloody Superman was going to swoop down and rescue you?'

'Actually, I thought it was the other way round,' snaps Pauline. 'I seem to remember rescuing you.' She leaps to her feet. 'Not that I've had any thanks for it.'

'Listen.' Burnside gets up too and takes her arm, pulling her round. 'I owe you my life. I can't thank you enough. But...' He looks into her eyes, as if trying to communicate something he can't bring himself to say.

'But what?' She's still defensive.

'Never mind.'

'You can tell me.'

'I said forget it!' His voice is harsh again. He sits down and pours two large whiskies. 'Come on, don't get the hump. Show me this video.' He shakes his head. 'I can't believe I didn't rumble you.'

Pauline rejoins Burnside on the sofa and swipes the remote off him. 'That's because I'm good.'

He raises his glass to her. 'I'll go along with that.'

'I'm honoured.'

'You should be. It takes a lot to impress me these days.'

Pauline flicks him a glance. Burnside isn't smiling. She zaps the tape on. 'This is where he comes in.'

We hear the unidentified man say, 'You've been playing with fire, Peter, haven't you?' Burnside frowns. He says nothing while Pauline plays the next tape, then asks her to rewind it and run it again. Eventually, she relinquishes the remote. He plays it three more times, jumping backwards and forwards, still not commenting. A sleepy black-and-white cat emerges from the kitchen and jumps onto Pauline's lap. She strokes it quietly, making the animal reverberate with purrs.

Burnside freezes the film and picks up his glass. He takes several gulps. Finally he says grimly, 'That – explains – a lot – of shit.'

'Are you alright? You look poleaxed.'

'Yeah, well it's not every day you witness a senior police officer conspiring to get you stitched up and assassinated.'

'Do you know who he is?'

'That's the clearest shot and the quality's still crap. I can't make the bastard out. His voice sounds vaguely familiar.' He rubs his eyes. 'Something's ringing a bell...'

'You're too tired to concentrate.'

'Probably. It's been a long, exciting day.'

Pauline yawns. 'I'm shattered.'

'Go to bed, then. No use sitting with me. I'll be chewing over this thing for hours.'

'Can't move. Cat's asleep.'

'Career girls and their cats... they're a substitute for everything these days, you know. Boyfriend, kids, sex life...'

'How d'you work that one out?' She sounds amused rather than affronted.

'Seen the way they advertise cat food lately? You give Tiddles a gourmet dinner, snuggle up with him on the sofa, then take him off to bed. What do blokes get? An M&S ready meal and "I'll call you". You tell me who gets the better deal.'

Pauline bursts out laughing. 'That says more about your sex life than mine.'

'Watch it.'

She pours them both another drink. 'So: have you got someone?'

'No. Not really.'

'What kind of an answer's that?'

'The only one you're going to get.'

Pauline sighs. 'Come on, give me something. What makes Frank Burnside tick? Here we are, thrown together, and I don't know anything about you.'

'I'm not sure I do, either.'

'That's a cop-out.'

'What d'you expect? I'm a cop.'

'You weren't always. What about your family? Have you got brothers, sisters? Are your parents still alive?'

'Mum died last year; my dad went five years earlier. Lung cancer. I've got one sister who I ain't seen in yonks and a younger brother I parted company with twenty years ago. That do you?'

'What happened? You sound bitter.'

Burnside pours himself more Scotch. 'Top up?'

'No, I'm fine. Tell me about your brother. Did you fall out over something?'

He is silent for a long while, staring into his glass. Pauline rubs his arm. 'Talking about it will make you feel better.'

'Talking about him makes me feel sick.'

'Why?'

Another long silence. Then: 'My brother's got a lot to answer for.' He takes another slug of whisky. 'Almost ruining my career, for starters.'

'Are you going to explain that?' she asks, when he doesn't volunteer any more information.

'Too long a story.' He peers at his watch. 'Isn't it past your bedtime? Even for a night-owl like you? Tiddles is looking tired.'

'Her name is Clarice.' Pauline tips the surprised cat off her lap and draws nearer to Burnside. 'And she goes out at night.'

Diary (extract), 11 March

Still can't make up my mind about Frank. I know I like him. I like him a lot. But I think he's stringing me along. After this evening I'm pretty sure he's not bent, but there's definitely more to him than meets the eye. Some of the stuff he says just doesn't gel with the other evidence, and he's very reluctant to talk openly, either about his work or his personal life.

That's why I'm still filming him. There's a deeper story behind all this; I can feel it. Call it journalistic instinct. I'm just not sure what it is. Frank knows I'm a reporter – I had to come clean about how I got the tapes – but he thinks I'm investigating Dawson. Which is true. I'm just keeping this going as a parallel investigation.

Actually, it's not even that. Now there's this internal corruption angle and they're gunning for Frank, the two stories have effectively merged. The whole thing's taken off in a direction we could never have predicted so I've no option but to run with it. I'm sure Tony will love it. After all, I'm using my initiative. I've got a fabulous car chase and shoot-out on tape. All the same, I might not tell him for a couple of days, just to see how the land lies.

Frank's forgiven me for bolting from the pub and we're going to pool resources. Not that I've got much choice. I can hardly refuse to co-operate with the police. There's lots I can tell him about Silks and Xsecs, not to mention all the evidence I've captured with the covert cameras. He's really excited about our eye-witnesses, too, particularly Kristina Tomasic. I'm going to take him to meet her tomorrow.

Anyway, it works both ways. We suspected there might be something going on with illegal immigrants, but we knew nothing about a smuggling ring or the agency's link with it. I can see the headlines now: 'Reporter–Detective Duo Reveal

Police Role in International Sex Smuggling Scandal'. It's going to be totally mega for Firebrand Productions, not to mention my career. I might even get an award.

As for the mysterious DCI Burnside himself, he did start to open up a bit this evening. Not much, just a crack. There's obviously a history with his brother. Frank seems to blame him for jeopodising his career or ruining his reputation somehow. I don't understand: all the cuttings I read have him down as this shit-hot detective nailing notorious villains and cracking crime rings. I'll just have to be more persuasive and worm it out of him.

I've decided the only way to find out the truth is to cross the line. It's hardly prostitution, is it, if you fancy the bloke and do it 'cos you want to? It's not like it'd be for money. And Frank's a man of the world. What was it Steve Falla said about him? 'He's got a high turnover of women.' So it's not like he doesn't know the rules.

I have to admit, it's proving harder than I thought. Considering his reputation, Frank's being a real gentleman. We sat up drinking til 2.30am, then I offered to let him share my bed, but he said he'd crash on the sofa. Talk about turning down an open invitation! I'm bit miffed, to be honest: how many fifty-year-old blokes get chances like that with gorgeous young twentysomethings? I'm putting it down to his injury – it's a flesh wound, but looks pretty sore. Still, seducing him has become a personal challenge now. I know it's highly unprofessional, but this isn't about work. It's about me.

FRANK BURNSIDE – HANDWRITTEN NOTE (DISCOVERED IN DRESSING-GOWN POCKET)

1. 'Bigfoot' = senior copper. Who?
2. Where have I seen him before? Serious Crime Squad? The

Yard? Vice? Flying Squad? Stafford Row? Barton Street?
Hendon? How far back does this go?

3. Is he working alone or in some kind of cell? Is Sutton part of
it? How high up does this go?

4. What has been done to 'ring-fence' me? Is 'Bigfoot' (or
someone else) feeding misinformation to Pepper/CIB?

5. Dawson: what next? Unlikely to give up now. House/car not
safe. Office?

6. Why am I being targeted? Am I missing the point? Is this
about something else?

7. Mal factor? What's he up to now? 'Bigfoot' & Dawson both
know him. Too significant to be coincidence.

8. NB: Pauline – motive?

TRANSCRIPT OF FILMED INTERVIEW WITH KRISTINA TOMASIC, TAPE 22V/404. PRIVATE HOUSE, EAST HEATH ROAD, HAMPSTEAD HEATH. 12.03.00, 14.30

A spacious, impressively designed conservatory overlooking a
well-tended garden. It is bristling with exotic potted plants,
including a lofty palm that reaches almost to the pointed ceiling,
and furnished in rattan draped with ethnic throws. The colour-
supplement effect is tempered by a scatter of garish plastic toys –
a trike, a doll's pram, a push-along truck – and an untidy pile of
muddy boots by the door. A radio, hidden somewhere in the
luxuriant foliage, is being drowned out by a red-faced baby,
which is flailing on its belly on the tiled floor. A teenage girl
shakes a rattle half-heartedly under its nose, which, if anything,
makes it cry louder. She looks up and starts as Burnside and
Pauline enter. A woman, out of shot, shouts, 'Kristina, visitors',
adding crisply, 'we're teaching Tobias to crawl. They get a much
better purchase on a hard surface.'

'Really?' Pauline says loudly. She smiles at the girl. Kristina blinks nervously. Conversation, due to the baby, is impossible. Burnside turns to the mother, who is hovering unhelpfully. 'I think what Tobias is saying is that he'd prefer to do his workout on a carpet. In another room.' She takes the hint with bad grace and scoops up the now-hysterical child. 'Don't be long. Kristina's here to work, not chat. Now don't forget,' she yells at the girl, 'you've got to get Katie ready for Scarlett's party at three.' She stomps off.

Burnside looks at Pauline. 'Poor bastard.'

'At least he'll have a privileged upbringing.'

'I meant the husband.'

Even the wan-faced Kristina smiles faintly.

The ice broken, Pauline gets down to business. 'Kristina, my name's Pauline. I work for a TV company, Firebrand Productions. You've talked to our researcher, Sam Gwilliam. She told me you were prepared to speak on camera about your modelling experiences.'

Kristina glances cautiously at Burnside. Pauline takes a deep breath. 'This is DCI Burnside. He's a friend of mine. You can trust him. He wants to hear your story as well.'

Kristina scrambles to her feet. 'What is DCI?'

Burnside looks her in the eye. 'I'm a police officer, Kristina. Now don't worry, I ain't here to make life difficult for you.' He nudges the toy truck out of his way with his foot. 'Looks like you've got enough on your plate as it is. I just want to ask you some questions.' He indicates an upholstered window seat. 'Shall we?'

Pauline nods to the girl. She sits down opposite them in a creaky rattan armchair, framing the shot. Kristina folds her hands in her lap and stares at her knees. Burnside clears his throat. 'I realise it must be difficult to talk about, but we need to know what happened to you so that we can stop the men who did it from hurting any more young girls.'

Kristina looks out through the rain-spattered glass of the conservatory. In the garden, the March breeze lashes a few brave daffodils. She says nothing. Pauline glances questioningly at Burnside. He nods.

'Kristina, you told Sam you wanted your identity kept secret. We'll honour that. But why? Who are you frightened of? Is it Clare Miller?'

The teenager looks up at the mention of Miller's name. 'She is a bad lady. Very bad lady.'

'I know. I worked for her, too. I still do – she doesn't know I'm a reporter.' Pauline grimaces. 'And you're right. She's a cow.'

Burnside rolls his eyes, but Pauline's struck a chord. Kristina nods enthusiastically. 'Miss Miller hit me and pull my hair.' She tugs her white-blonde plaits to demonstrate. 'She pull me across room like that.'

'By your hair?'

'Yes. She is wicked. She tell me to keep quiet about those men, what they did. She say it not bad, but…' Kristina's eyes fill with tears. She lowers her head, her shoulders jerking silently.

'Hey, it's OK. Take your time.' Pauline gets up and goes over, squeezing in on Kristina's other side. She puts an arm around her. The girl's wet face is in close-up. Burnside, in the background, obviously feels superfluous. He edges off the window seat and strolls round the conservatory, examining the palm's horny trunk with studied interest.

Kristina's sobs are heart-rending. Pauline comforts her. 'You poor thing, you're all alone and they've put you through hell.' She strokes her hair. 'I think you're so brave to have stood up to them. It must have taken so much courage.'

'I come here to model,' Kristina weeps. She looks up at

Pauline, tears dripping off her nose. 'Papa send me. He say London have many opportunities, much better than Zagreb. He say Miss Miller a friend of his, she will look after me, get me work.'

'What happened?' Pauline coaxes. 'Frank – DCI Burnside – told me he saw your details on the files at Xsecs.' She offers Kristina a tissue.

Kristina mops her cheeks. 'At first, it was good. I do some shoots, I do a fashion show, I make my book – you know?' Pauline nods. 'There was a magazine. I forgot, pardon me, forget – Mrs Watson, she always correcting me – what it is called, a teenage magazine.' She brightens for the first time. 'They really like me. But Miss Miller, she get time wrong and I go there too late. They pick another girl instead.' Her bottom lip trembles again. 'I think she do it on purpose. Ana, my friend, she say Miss Miller is jealous.' She takes a shuddering breath. 'After that, Miss Miller tell me she cannot get me work. She say I'm too – ' Kristina indicates her boyish figure and tiny breasts. She shoots a glance at Burnside, who is still apparently perusing foliage. He pretends not to notice. Leaning forward conspiratorially, she whispers, ' – you know, my bosoms are no good.'

'Did you tell your father the modelling had dried up?'

'Oh no. I am – ashamed. He so proud of me. He want me to be supermodel, like Kate Moss. He say I just like her.'

'You are. You're very pretty. And your figure's really in.'

Kristina sighs. 'This is what they tell me at magazine. That is why, when Mr Dawson come to Xsecs and offer me work, I go with him. He say I make many contacts, meet lots of photographers and directors and other models.'

'And did you?'

'Oh, yes.' Kristina starts to cry again. 'But it was making movies. And I had to…' She covers her face.

'Was it porn?' Pauline asks softly.

'Yes.'

'Did they force you to do things?'

'Yes.' Her face is wretched. 'Make sex with men, and women, and – ' She shakes her head.

'Did they hurt you?'

'Yes. Many times.'

'Did you tell them to stop?'

'Yes.'

'Did they?'

'No. Some of the men, they like it, if you cry. So I learn not to.'

Pauline squeezes her hand. She looks over at Burnside. He comes over and rejoins them on the seat.

'What was this place like, Kristina?'

She sniffs. 'Big, big house. Lots of stairs. Many rooms.'

'Do you know where it is?'

'I know it, if I see it. But I don't know where. In London, yes.'

'How did you get there?'

'Miss Miller, she take me at night, with some other girls. We go in van. We cannot see out.'

'What did it look like, from the outside?'

'It is white house, very tall. The door is blue.'

'Anything else? Did it have a garden? Railings? Can you remember a name or a number?'

Mrs Watson, Kristina's employer, pokes her head around the door. 'Kristina. Katie is waiting. I don't want her to be late.'

Burnside scowls at her. 'Kristina is helping with a police investigation. Which puts pass-the-parcel a very poor second.'

'I thought you said this was to do with the television?' Mrs Watson is outraged.

'It is, too,' Pauline says hurriedly.

'So why is this policeman here?'

Burnside stands up. 'Smuggling. Illegal immigration. Rape. Sexual abuse. Grievous bodily harm. The list's short because we've only just started. Do you pay National Insurance for Kristina, Mrs Watson? Does she receive the national minimum wage? Have you checked her visa expiry date? I assume you checked she's actually got a visa?'

'Well, I...' Mrs Watson backs out of the room. 'You must talk to my husband, he deals with all that.'

Kristina looks worried. Burnside sits back down. 'She won't do anything, love. She knows I'll hang 'em to dry. So, about this house?'

'It has black spikes on the wall. And bushes, high bushes. You cannot see from the road.' She frowns. 'I do not remember a number. There was a – what you say? – little sign by the gate.' She draws a rectangle with her hands.

'Sign? Like a plaque? A brass plate?' Burnside queries.

'Yes, a plate. But I cannot read the writing. My English...'

'Can you describe the area? What kind of road is it on?'

'I think it is a good area, like here.'

'Wealthy?'

She nods. 'There are many houses, all the same, tall and white. The road is not so busy, at night. It is funny shape – like this.' Kristina indicates a sweeping curve.

'A crescent?' Pauline suggests.

'Could be Notting Hill, somewhere off Ladbroke Grove,' Burnside says.

'Notting Hill, like the movie?' Kristina looks excited. 'I think maybe yes. I hear one of the men say something once.'

'OK, we're getting somewhere,' Burnside says, pleased. 'What were the other girls like?'

Kristina shakes her head. 'All different. But young, all young.

I see so many faces. It is hard to remember.'

'Were many of them refugees?'

Her face clouds suddenly. 'I don't know.'

Burnside and Pauline exchange glances. Burnside, sharp now, says, 'Kristina, we know who your father is and we know what he does. We're working with the National Crime Intelligence Service on this. There's no point in trying to protect him. We've already picked up a kid who fell off the back of one of his lorries.'

She looks mulish.

'Does the name Sanja Gregovic mean anything to you?'

Kristina is genuinely surprised. She opens her mouth to speak, then thinks better of it. Burnside's face darkens. Pauline lays a restraining hand on his arm and says, 'We think she came to Xsecs – or at least, the café across from the office. Sam saw a girl talking to Ana and her sister. Clare Miller got really heavy with them afterwards. From the description, it could be Sanja.'

Burnside looks as if this is news to him, too. 'If Miller's on her tail, Sanja's in trouble.' He curses under his breath.

Kristina chews her lip, still undecided about something.

'So if you know where she is,' Burnside continues, 'it's in your – and her – best interests to tell me.'

'No.' Kristina stands up abruptly. 'I must go to Mrs Watson. She will be angry I am so long.'

He takes a card out of his pocket. 'When you remember, ring me on my mobile. Or call Pauline.'

Pauline scribbles her home telephone number on the back of the card. She hands it to Kristina, smiling encouragingly. 'You've done really well. I know we can put a stop to this, with your help. You stood up against the bad men once, and you can do it again. Your father will be more proud of you for that. I promise you.' She gives her a brief hug. 'Call me, yes?'

Kristina does not meet her eye.

TRANSCRIPT OF TELEPHONE CALL, TAPE 527T/998,
MADE AT PAULINE'S FLAT.
12.03.00, 17.46

BURNSIDE: 'Trish?

TRISH: 'Yes?'

BURNSIDE: 'It's Frank.'

TRISH: 'Who?'

BURNSIDE: 'Frank your brother, that's who.'

TRISH: 'Jesus! You've got a bleeding nerve.'

BURNSIDE: 'Well that's nice. "Hello, how are you?" is more usual. Especially when you ain't seen someone for a year.'

TRISH: 'A year! More like five.'

BURNSIDE: 'You must have missed me at Mum's funeral, then. I was one of them blokes in black, carrying the coffin.'

TRISH: 'Don't you get sarky with me. That's the only time you've bothered to show your face since Dad died. What is it with you, Frank? You just turn out for funerals? Don't you do Christmas and birthdays?'

BURNSIDE: 'Look, sis, I'm sorry. It's – '

TRISH: 'Don't say "the job". Not unless they grant you a special licence to stop caring about people who are supposed to matter. Like your family. It's no wonder Shelley divorced you.'

BURNSIDE: 'Below the belt, Trish. You know what that tart did to me.'

TRISH [*ignoring him*]: 'I don't mind for meself. You can go to hell for all I care. But the kids don't get much, not now Mark's on disability. You could send them some cash for their birthdays. You must be raking it in. I bet you don't even know how old our three are.'

BURNSIDE [*sighing*]: 'I didn't ring for a fight. I'll send the kids a cheque – call it backpay for birthdays missed, alright?'

TRISH: 'So why did you ring, then? Must be something important for you to be buying favours.'

BURNSIDE: 'I can't win with you, can I?'

TRISH: 'Cut the crap, Frank. You baled out on us all years ago. If you'd helped with Mum and Dad, I might think better of you. But no. While you were busy playing cops and robbers, I had to nurse them and raise my three. On top of that, Mark had his accident. He can't do much, so it's been little old me trying to keep all the flamin' balls in the air. Don't blame me for being bitter. I've got good reason.'

BURNSIDE: 'I've got reasons too, Trish, but you ain't gonna listen, are you?'

TRISH: 'Yeah, right. Go on, then. I need a laugh.'

BURNSIDE: 'I was undercover for five years. It's like wiping out who you are. You can't contact friends, family. You don't have a life.'

TRISH [*unsympathetic*]: 'And which five years are we talking about here?'

BURNSIDE: ''93 to '98.'

TRISH: 'So the last two years you've been doing what?'

BURNSIDE: 'I don't have to justify myself to you. What about Mal? I notice you don't mention him. I thought he was the golden boy?'

TRISH: 'He does his bit. He paid for a private nurse for Mum, and he sends me money – you know, because of Mark. He's very generous.'

BURNSIDE: 'Didn't come to see his old mum off, though, did he?'

TRISH: 'Only because you were there. We talked about it – he said she wouldn't want her boys scrapping at her graveside. He paid his respects later. I went with him. You should've seen the flowers he bought.'

BURNSIDE: 'More to the point: is he keeping his nose clean?'

TRISH [*cold*]: 'I don't know why you talk like that about him. It was years ago. Yes, he went wrong, but he put it behind him and got on with his life. He's ever so successful now.'

BURNSIDE: 'Doing what?'

TRISH: 'Dunno exactly. He's got three or four companies. And he does loads for charity, too. He's a Rotarian.'

BURNSIDE: 'Yeah, and I'm a Rastafarian.'

TRISH [*suddenly weary*]: 'Why don't you just bury the hatchet, Frank? I mean it. I'm tired of all this rowing, it's doing my head in. We ain't got Mum and Dad, and we three… We could be a proper family, if we tried. Get together once in a while. If only for the kids' sake. They'd love to see their uncles.'

BURNSIDE [*hesitating*]: 'You really think Mal's changed?'

TRISH: 'I'm sure of it. Just give him the chance to show you.'

BURNSIDE: 'I don't even know where he lives.'

TRISH: 'I can give you his address. He's in Warwick. Hang on.' [*Pause. Sound of rifling through pages*] 'Here it is: 5, The Copse, Parklands. It's a new estate on the outskirts.'

BURNSIDE: 'Thanks.'

TRISH: 'So you'll go and see him?'

BURNSIDE: 'I might pay him a visit, yeah. Make it a surprise. Probably better that way. He won't have any… preconceptions.'

TRISH: 'I suppose.'

BURNSIDE: 'You'll keep quiet about it, then, eh? Let me and Mal work it out between us.'

TRISH: 'OK. If it means we can stop all this. And when are you coming to see me?'

BURNSIDE: 'I'll surprise you an' all.'

TRISH: 'Don't leave it too long, will you?'

BURNSIDE: 'I won't. Happy now?'

TRISH: 'Yeah. It's good to talk to you again, Frank. I've missed you, you know.'

BURNSIDE: 'Like a hole in the head.'

TRISH: 'No, really.' [*Laughs*] 'So why did you ring me then?'

BURNSIDE: 'I missed you, too, sis.'

TRANSCRIPT OF SECRET FILM, TAPE 136V/404.
PAULINE'S FLAT, HAMMERSMITH.
12.03.00, 21.12

Burnside and Pauline are sitting on the sofa, tucking into a takeaway pizza straight from the box. On the coffee table in front of them is a half-empty bottle of red wine. Another, empty bottle is on the floor. The curtains are drawn and the room is tastefully lit, as before.

Burnside stops chewing and gesticulates with a slice of pizza. 'What is this shit?'

'American Hot. What you wanted.'

'No, I mean the music. Bloody awful.'

'TLC.'

'Ain't that something you gargle with?'

'That's TCP.'

'Yeah. That's bloody awful, too.'

Pauline drains her wine and immediately tops both their glasses up. 'So what kind of music do you like?'

'Ah. There's only one. The King.'

'The King? Do you mean Elvis?' She's horrified.

Burnside grins and picks up an untouched garlic baguette, holding it like a mike. '"Love me tender, love me true..."'

'Stop!' She claps her hands over her ears.

'Well it slayed 'em in Newcastle. They couldn't get enough of my Elvis medley down the working men's club.'

'What were you doing? Moonlighting as an impersonator in a white suit and sequins?'

'Karaoke. Bit of R and R.'

She shakes her head. 'You surprise me. You really do. You're not – '

'What I seem? That's a bit rich, innit, coming from you.'

'Fair enough. But at least I'm consistent. You're a mass of contradictions.'

'And you've known me how long, exactly?' There's a touch of steel in his voice.

'OK, it's just a few days, but it feels like longer.'

'I'm sorry if I'm boring you.' He puts his pizza down, as if he's suddenly lost his appetite.

She sighs. 'You're not. Quite the opposite. You fascinate me. You intrigue me...' She's obviously fairly drunk. She moves closer to him and reaches out to touch his face. 'I've never met anyone like you. I feel like we connect.'

He takes her hand and squeezes it. 'I'm too old for you.'

'You feel it, too.'

Burnside stares into her earnest face for a long time, then defuses the moment. 'You're pissed, Pauline. Go to bed.'

'Come with me.'

'Don't be stupid.'

'I'm not. I mean it. I've learned a lot at the club. I could – '

'What are you, a slag?' He gets up angrily and walks out of shot. Pauline bursts into tears. We hear banging about in the kitchen, a tap running, kettle being filled. Pauline gets up and stumbles out of shot.

Two minutes elapse, then Burnside reappears with mugs of coffee. He puts them down on the table and flicks on the television. The news is on, an item about people made homeless by floods in Mozambique. Pauline returns, having patched up her

124

streaked mascara. 'I'm sorry. I know I'm a bit tipsy – '

'Try "totally wasted".'

'No! I know what I'm saying. It just came out really…
clumsily. I – I went the wrong way about things. To tell you the
truth, you make me a bit nervous.'

'Heaven help us when you're scared shitless. What do you do,
jump complete strangers?'

'Frank, give me a break. I'm trying to explain.'

Burnside passes her a mug of coffee. 'Drink that, then try it.'
He settles back to watch the rest of the news. The weather comes
on. 'Heavy rain, dangerous driving conditions.' He zaps the TV
off. 'Nice day for it.'

'What are you talking about?'

'I'm heading off tomorrow. Up to the Midlands. Got a bit of
business to see to.'

'Is it to do with the investigation?'

'Let's just say it might have a bearing on it.' His tone is grim.

'Come on, we're supposed to be helping each other. Quid pro
quo, that's what we agreed.' Pauline's composure is back. 'We're
a team, aren't we?'

'Hmm.'

'How is your side now?' She looks at him levelly.

'Alright! Just don't go shooting your mouth off until this is all
wrapped up. Agreed?'

'Agreed.'

'And I'm not in it. Agreed?'

'Agreed.' She shoots a fleeting glance at the camera.

'This is strictly to do with the Dawson case, the club and the
girls and whatever racket he's got going. Agreed?'

'We've been over this once. Yes!'

'Yeah, but you're a reporter. Scum of the earth and all that.
How do I know you're not lying?'

'How do I know if *you're* telling me the truth? Your reputation doesn't exactly inspire confidence. No one seems to know if you're a straight cop who likes to bend the rules or a bent cop who doesn't have any rules.'

Touché. They regard each other. Burnside narrows his eyes. 'And which horse are you backing?'

'Probably the former, though the other one seems to be favourite with the bookies.' She holds his gaze, chin uplifted.

Burnside snorts. 'So I'm supposed to believe you're a journalist with honour. Another rank outsider.' He stretches his arms in the air and folds them behind his head, stealing a sideways look at her. 'Long odds.'

'Bigger payout.'

'You cross me, I'll have you.'

'Is that your way of sealing a deal?'

'Nah. Normally I'm much more uncouth.'

They laugh and the tension is dissipated. Pauline rubs her bare arms – she's in a clingy cropped top and combat trousers – and Burnside pulls the throw off the back of the sofa and drapes it round her shoulders. 'Thanks.' She snuggles into it. 'So where are you going tomorrow?'

'See my brother.'

'Why? I thought you hated his guts.'

'I do.'

'So…?'

'He used to run around with Dawson.' He shoots her a sidewards look. 'Small world, ain't it?'

Pauline's jaw drops.

'Yeah. He wasn't anything then, just a lowlife with aspirations, but Mal thought he was a real Mr Big, know what I mean? He latched on to him, said Dawson was going places.'

'He was right.'

'So it seems.' Burnside shakes his head. 'I was gobsmacked when I saw him the other night. From housebreaking to hostess club. Now there's a fun one for Michael Aspel.'

'Was that when you and Mal fell out?'

'No, that was later.' Burnside's expression is unreadable. 'Don't get me wrong, I was no saint either when we was kids. I ran my own gang and Mal used to hang out with us. We were a right bunch of tearaways, but it was petty stuff, teenage troublemaking, mainly.'

'So what did Mal do?'

'Got himself nicked for burglary, along with Dawson. My old mum and dad were doing their nut. Mal was the youngest, the favourite son; I was the troublemaker. They never saw him for what he was. They begged me to do something. And being green and stupid, I did. Not for him, for them.'

'Were you a police officer then?'

'Yes. I was.'

'What did you – '

'Nothing. Nothing important. But somebody made it look like it was. And that's stuck with me ever since.'

'And Mal and Dawson? What happened to them?'

'They got off.'

'Oh.'

'Yeah.'

Pauline is thoughtful. 'Do you want to borrow my recording gear for your trip?'

Burnside looks thrown. 'Why?'

'Come on, Frank. I heard what Dawson said. He's still in contact with Mal, isn't he? You think the three of them could be in this together?' She climbs off the sofa and returns with her under-cover kit. 'This way, if he is, you'll have hard evidence. You might be able to nail this guy, whoever he is, if Mal decides to share.'

'Mal? Spill his guts in a brotherly heart-to-heart? I don't think so.'

'Talk him round. It's worth a try. You need all the insurance you can get.'

Burnside looks thoughtful. 'OK. Let's have a look at it.'

'Hey! I'm the expert here. Undo your shirt.'

Burnside gives her a wide-eyed look. 'Is this how you are with your punters?'

'Watch it.' She starts unbuttoning him. Burnside stares at her. He does not resist. Pauline slides opens his shirt, revealing his naked torso. A pulse quickens at the base of his throat. She slips the shirt off his shoulders and he takes his arms out, throwing the garment to the floor. She kneels next to him. 'Want me to show you how to strap it on?'

He nods dumbly.

'I'll have to tape the wires down. It's a bit painful ripping them off again. Especially for someone hairy like you.' She holds the mike in place, spreading the fingers of one hand across his broad chest while she trains wires over his shoulder with the other.

'Don't bother.' Burnside leans back against the sofa. He shuts his eyes.

'Why? You need to know how to do it properly.'

'I do.'

'Sure?' she whispers, bending over him.

'Yes.'

'It's the latest technology, you know. Very – sensitive.' Her hair brushes against his skin.

Burnside groans. 'Pauline. Stop. Torturing. Me.'

He opens his eyes and she's caught in their beam. They hold each other's gaze, as if negotiating something unspoken. A clock ticks loudly in the silence. He twists towards her and slowly, deliberately, reaches out, sliding his hands up her arms. Drawing her close, he bends his head to hers until their lips are almost touching. 'Are you sure about this?' he mutters hoarsely.

'Yes.'

The kiss is long and searching and hungry. It is Burnside who pulls away first. He holds her face in his hands, forcing her to meet his eyes, and says in a strange, harsh voice, 'What's your game, Pauline?'

'I'm not playing games, Frank.'

'Don't come the innocent with me. Anyone who can pull off the kind of stunts you've pulled off...'

'Frank. I may have pretended to be someone I'm not, but I've never faked my feelings for you. You can't manufacture sexual chemistry. It's either there or it's not. And it's there between us.' She takes his hands and places them on her exposed midriff. 'You're the one with all the equipment. If you don't trust me,' she breathes softly, 'search me.'

Diary, 12 March

I feel like a dizzy teenager. Frank kissed me. I really stuffed up the first time I tried it on, but even though he was angry with me, I could tell he wanted me. We had a chat and calmed down a bit, and then it just happened. Well, I suppose I did engineer it, but I still felt absurdly excited when he reciprocated. All the while he was snogging me there was this little voice inside my head going, 'Yes! He likes me! Yessss!'

It got pretty heated but when I suggested we go into my bedroom – I'm not into filming myself in the act (well, not when an entire production team's going to view it) – it sort of broke the moment. Frank said we were crazy to be getting involved and things never worked out in situations like this, and then he just clammed up. I asked him what the matter was, but he went all monosyllabic and moody.

To change the subject, I started talking about working at Silks tomorrow. Frank was amazed I was even thinking of going. I pointed out Dawson only saw me from a distance, and it was unlikely he recognised me in a baseball hat and dark glasses and a big quilted anorak – I had the collar turned up, hiding my chin. I mean, normally he sees me all dolled up and wearing corsets. Also, Dawson thinks my name's Emma and he would have heard me call out, 'It's Pauline'. By the time he did get up close, the windscreen was frosted with cracks and he couldn't see through it.

All the same, I'm not looking forward to going. The last time I saw my employer, he tried to shoot me, which makes the prospect of being face-to-face with him again very, very scary. But if I don't turn up for my first day in my new job, he's bound to suss something's not right. Besides, as I said to Frank, we need to know what Dawson's up to, now more than ever. And what if that other guy comes to the club again? It's vital I'm there to spy if we're going to nail them both.

Frank tried to talk me out of it. He said it wasn't worth the risk and he didn't want another death on his conscience. I asked him what he meant – we were pretty smashed on red wine and brandy by then – and he started telling me all about this woman called Kim he'd been in love with that he'd met on an undercover operation. I remembered the story in the cuttings and almost dropped myself in it by saying, 'Wasn't she some villain's wife?', but I stopped myself just in time. He said she got shot trying to protect him and he swore then he'd never put another person in that position.

I felt sort of privileged that he'd told me – apparently he's never talked to anyone about it before. It's obvious he really fell for her. He said at one point he even considered chucking in the job and leaving the country with her. I asked him if he'd ever been married and he said yes, and it was a disaster: his wife was a shopaholic who ran off with another bloke just after they'd bought this really expensive house, and it took him years to pay off all the debts she'd run up.

Turns out that was almost twenty years ago. I said, 'In all the time since, haven't you been tempted to settle down with anyone else, apart from Kim?' He admitted there had been another woman he'd really liked – a detective he'd worked with at Sun Hill called Liz – but not long after they got together she took a post in Newcastle and it had fizzled out because of the long hours they both worked and the distance. He looked sad about that and I felt quite jealous, even though I've absolutely no right to be.

After Frank had opened up so much, I began to feel really bad about using him like this. I thought, maybe I should just switch off the cameras and mikes here and stick to what we've agreed. Then I thought, well, he's a professional and I'm a professional, and we've both got jobs to do, and if we have some fun while doing them, where's the harm? It's true what I said to him earlier: I haven't lied about my feelings. There is this electricity between us. He's got this air of danger about him, like he could be really hard if he had to be. It's a real turn-on. That, and the way he looks at me with those piercing eyes. I'm not sure if they're green or grey – they almost seem to change colour, especially when he's angry. One thing's for sure, when he looks at me I feel caught, mesmerised. It makes my stomach flip over.

And I do go for older men, like I told him at Silks. Call it a father fixation or whatever, but that's me. Not that those relationships ever work out: the problem with older men is they're too controlling and stuck in their ways. I guess I just like feeling protected and cherished. Whatever the drawbacks, they do make you feel special. And when Frank held me in his arms,

131

I felt so secure and happy... But it won't last and it's no use being sentimental. I've got to stick to my plan and see this through.

DICTAPHONE TRANSCRIPT, TAPE 41A/92, 13.03.00, 12.14

BURNSIDE [*over traffic noise; he's obviously in a car*]: 'Well, boys, I'm still 'ere. Thought you'd got rid of me, didn't you? And you might have managed it, but for my little friend. You'll find out who, soon enough. Let's just say I know what I'm up against now. And from the evidence I've seen, someone's been a very naughty boy indeed. Probably more than one person.' [*The car slows down. We hear rapid bleeping; it sounds as if he's stopped at a pedestrian crossing.*]

'This could just be the tip of the iceberg, which is why I ain't trusting nobody. I'll solve this myself and until I've got it wrapped up I ain't standing in line for some toerag to take a pop at me. Dawson's botched it twice, so I assume you've got a professional on my case.' [*He revs the engine and moves off again*] 'He'll have to find me first. I ain't stupid enough to go back to my house, or to the office for that matter, no matter how many bleedin' messages you leave on my mobile, Sutton. I'm touched you consider my health sufficiently recovered to return to work so soon, considering last Friday you wanted to sign me off sick, but I'm sticking with the doc's advice. He took my blood pressure, then said I was stressed. Gave me this lecture on stress being one of the biggest killers of middle-aged men. Of course, he didn't know I had a posse after me, but I think I'll lay low for a bit, like he said. Can't do any harm, can it?' [*Burnside's accelerating now; clearly on a faster road*]

'So here I am, taking it easy. Thought I'd hire a motor, get out of town, blow the old cobwebs away. I'm going to see someone I ain't visited in a long while, 'cos I reckon he holds the key to this. I know what Dawson's racket is – I've got a witness on tape describing it all – and I've got a fair idea who his importer is. But this is about something else, innit? You finish me off; some other detective'll have Dawson and Miller. I've been missing the point. This is personal. This is about something I know; something that could drop a lot of people in deep shit. I ain't exactly sure what it is yet, but I'm getting the broader picture. What puzzles me is, who this mystery copper is. See, I know his voice, but I can't put a name to it. I will, though. It's niggling away. I'll get there.'

TRANSCRIPT OF TELEPHONE CALL, TAPE 390T/998;
FIREBRAND PRODUCTION OFFICE, SOHO.
13.03.00, 14.10
DILLON: 'Tony Dillon.'
BURNSIDE: 'This is Frank Burnside.'
DILLON [*hestitating*]: 'How did you…?'
BURNSIDE: 'Don't worry, pal, your reporter will give you the gory details. I assume the lovely Pauline does work for you?'
DILLON [*still sounding stunned*]: 'Er, yes. She does.'
BURNSIDE: 'Just checking. You can't be too careful, these days. So many flies on so many walls. It's hard to know which ones to swat.'
DILLON [*recovering*]: 'Pauline's a highly reputable journalist who is working on a major undercover investigation for us. I'm sorry I can't be more specific – '
BURNSIDE: 'I'm way ahead of you, mate. Things have moved on a bit since you lost your front teeth. I think you'd better give her a call.'
DILLON: 'How did you know – ' [*checks*] 'Yes, I will. Is she alright? She's not in any trouble, is she?'
BURNSIDE: 'Who with?' [*Laughing, realising*] 'Nah. She's doing

a grand job. I owe her one. She saved my life.'

DILLON: 'She did?'

BURNSIDE: 'Yeah. And she almost got herself killed in the process. That's why I want you to rein her in.'

DILLON: 'Sorry, I don't follow...'

BURNSIDE: 'Look. Pauline's a gutsy girl. She's got initiative and brains and she's very... forward. But she don't know where to stop. She thinks she's gonna solve the Dawson case single-handed, but she ain't. She's gonna wind up dead.'

DILLON: 'Is that some kind of threat?'

BURNSIDE [*snorting derisively*]: 'Not by me. But Dawson won't think twice if he twigs she was the one foiled his assassination attempt.'

DILLON: 'So what are you saying? Call her off the story, at this point?'

BURNSIDE: 'Unless you want to carry the can when her body's discovered in a back alley. Which wouldn't be good publicity for your little peep-show, would it?'

DILLON [*offended*]: 'This isn't some sordid excuse for voyeurism. We're offering a window on the criminal underworld.'

BURNSIDE: 'Except that most of your footage is of punters in a hostess club drooling over young girls' knockers.'

DILLON: 'Do you include yourself in that?'

BURNSIDE [*sharp*]: 'I was there undercover as part of a major police investigation involving Crime Operational Command Unit, NCIS, the Vice Squad and Immigration. Don't push your luck, Dillon. The only reason I ain't clamping down on your documentary right now is because Pauline's co-operating with me.'

DILLON: 'And I'm supposed to believe she wasn't coerced into this by a heavy-handed copper?'

BURNSIDE: 'Ask her yourself. I ain't got the time to sit here arguing the toss with some poxy documentary director who thinks he's Quentin bloody Tarantino. And as for being heavy-handed, you'd better look in the mirror.'

DILLON: 'What do you mean by that?'

BURNSIDE: 'I think you know what I'm talking about, lover-boy.' [*He pauses. Dillon has no answer to this.*] 'So, you'll stop Pauline going to Silks tonight?'

DILLON [*grimly*]: 'Don't worry, I'll be speaking to her right away.'

BURNSIDE: 'Good. Tell her "no hard feelings". She's done fantastic – but it's up to me from now on.'

DILLON: 'That's it?'

BURNSIDE: 'It's in her own best interests, believe me.' [*He clicks the mobile off*]

DILLON [*shouting*]: 'Sam! Get me Pauline on the phone! Now!'

TRANSCRIPT OF FILM, TAPE 400V/404. THE COPSE, PARKLANDS, WARWICK.
13.03.00, 15.20

Burnside is wearing the recording gear, camera and mike. When the tape commences, he is in the car, parked up on the road outside Mal's house. He gets out and stretches, weary after the long drive, giving us a swift pan of the exclusive new housing estate. It's a twee country dream: half-a-dozen large, individually designed 'executive' homes clustered around a landscaped circle of green and a pond. The houses, sheltered by a windbreak of mature pines, represent a mishmash of architectural styles – fake Tudor, fake Georgian, cutesy eaves, olde-worlde beams, even a turret. The close is set well back from the main drive and is eerily quiet; only the cawing of rooks in the tall trees and the drone of a light aircraft disturb the peace.

Burnside takes it all in and shudders. 'Give me Brixton any day.' He locks the car and goes in through the side gate of an imposing, manorial-style property. A black BMW is parked outside a double garage, its open boot crammed with plastic bags full of groceries. The front door is also open. A blonde comes out of the house in leather trousers and stiletto-heeled boots. Burnside, his feet crunching on gravel, walks towards her. 'Can I help you with those?'

She swings round, alarmed. 'You stay away from me!' She starts to runs towards the house, yelling, 'We've got dogs!' Burnside jogs after her, the camera bobbing. Suddenly her foot skids on the gravel, buckling under her, and she falls. Shouting and scrabbling, she kicks out at Burnside as he reaches her. 'Piss off! Don't you touch me! Get away!'

He steps back out of range of her pointed heels. 'I ain't going to hurt you. I was going to help you up. I was going to help you carry those bags.'

'Who are you?' She sits up, her hair comically wild, dirt on her chin.

'My name is Burnside.'

'It can't be.'

'I assure you it is. Come on.' He goes to assist her, but she flails an arm at him.

'I can manage.' She gets up, examining the gravel embedded in her grazed palms. 'Ow.'

'Better do something about that. Got any Dettol?

She scowls. 'Who are you to give advice?'

'At a guess, I'd say I'm your brother-in-law. Though you look a bit different to Mal's last missus.'

She eyes him shrewdly. 'I'm his third. Debbie. You must be Frank.'

'That's right,' he says. 'Is Mal here? Or is he – working?'

'He's at the depot. He should be home by six. You should've rung.'

'No worries. I can shoot over to the depot, catch him there. Where is it?'

Debbie looks cautious. 'Mal doesn't like being disturbed at work. I'll call and tell him you're here.' She fishes a mobile out of her bag, plugging in a natty earpiece, and punches a memory button. 'Hi darling, it's me.' [*Pause*] 'I thought you'd like to know we've got a visitor. It's your brother.' [*Pause*] 'Yeah.' [*Pause*] 'I don't know. Come to see you.' [*A longer pause. She listens, looking up at Burnside under sooty lashes.*] 'Well I was surprised, too. But he seems... friendly.' [*She winks at him.*] 'OK, so you'll be back at the usual time? Fine, I'll give him a cuppa. See you then. Love ya. Bye.' She flicks the phone off and gives Burnside a hundred-watt smile. 'Mal's delighted. He says he's dying to see you again.'

'Me too,' Burnside says genially. 'So, now you know I ain't a blagger, you go and see to that hand and I'll bring in the shopping.'

'OK,' she agrees, dusting herself down. 'But no funny business, understood?' The grin says she's flirting.

Burnside laughs. 'And we've only just met. Don't worry, you're safe with me, love. Hasn't Mal told you what his big brother does?'

'Yeah,' she replies drily, looking back over her shoulder, 'I know all about you.'

TRANSCRIPT OF FILM, TAPE 401V/404. THE COPSE, PARKLANDS, WARWICK.
13.03.00, 18.30
Mal has still not arrived home. Debbie and Frank are in the living room, a long, spacious room furnished with chintz sofas

and heavy, reproduction furniture. A dried-flower arrangement occupies the open fireplace and a collection of china dogs takes pride of place in an illuminated display cabinet. Frank, nursing a large whisky, sits in an armchair opposite Debbie, who has a gin and tonic in her hand. She has changed into a tight grey skirt and a clingy pink short-sleeved sweater, and wears a string of pearls. Their lustre suggests they are real. She checks her watch. 'I can't think what's keeping him.'

'Maybe he had some unfinished business to attend to.' Frank takes a drink. 'Those the dogs you were on about?' He indicates cabinet. 'Shouldn't think they'd scare many burglars.'

She giggles. 'We've got a gadget you can set. If someone triggers it, they get the sound of two snarling Rottweilers.' She leans forward confidentially. 'I can't stand the hairs, myself. Couldn't have a real one.' There's the noise of a car drawing into the drive. Debbie leaps up. 'Here's Mal. At last.' She hurries to greet him. Frank stands up and moves over to the display cabinet, another shelf of which is devoted to a collection of shields, engaved bowls and trophies. It's impossible to make out the inscriptions, although a framed photograph given pride of place is obviously of Mal receiving an award from a minor Royal.

A voice behind him says, 'Long time no see, bro.' Frank turns around. Mal is standing in the doorway, still in his overcoat, his left hand resting lightly on the doorframe, his right hand deep in his pocket. Apparently he is concealing something, for the pocket protrudes bulkily. There is more than a passing resemblance between the two men, although while his older brother's hair is receding, Mal is completely bald on top. He is taller than Frank and looks fit, as if he works out.

'Take your coat off, sweetheart,' Debbie says, from behind him. Frank says nothing. Mal, unsmiling, keeps his eyes on

Frank's face, prolonging the suggestion of menace. Slowly and deliberately he removes his hand from his pocket and places a mobile phone on a side table next to him. He shrugs his coat off, leaving Debbie to catch it, and walks into the room.

'Frank.' He claps his hands together in a show of bonhomie that strikes an false note after the charade in the doorway. 'To what do we owe the pleasure after all this time?'

'I've been thinking about the past,' Frank replies evenly. 'Thought it was time we... drew a line under it.'

'I couldn't agree more.' Mal extends a hand. Clearly, he sees disbelief on Frank's face, for he laughs. 'Yeah, Frank, it's that simple. I been waiting for you to come see me for – how many years? I could hardly visit you, could I? Not after the send-off I got. So it's been up to you to produce the old olive branch. I'm chuffed, mate.' He grabs Franks hand and wrings it, then turns to Debbie. 'Go and get something special out the wine cupboard. We got Bolly, ain't we?'

'It won't be cold.'

'So what?' He slaps her rump as she departs and she squeals kittenishly. When she's out of earshot, he turns to Frank and hisses, 'Lovely girl, Debs, but not too much upstairs. Still, looks the part, don't she?'

'She's an attractive woman.'

'Yeah, used to be a model. Bit past it now, but she knows how to keep me happy.'

Frank gesticulates at the room. 'You've done well for yourself. Debbie showed me round. It's quite a spread.'

Mal throws himself down in an armchair. 'Can't complain.' He looks up at Frank. 'Go on, then, ask me. I know you're dying to.'

'What?'

'How I come by this pile.' He grins.

'Alright.' Frank strolls over to the fireplace and stands with his back to it, surveying the room. Last time I saw you, you didn't have enough cash to open your own bank account and you were breaking into places like this. Nicking stuff make you aspirational or something? What did you do – take swatches from the curtains on your way out the window?'

Mal roars with laughter. 'Still cracking 'em like a good 'un, Frank.'

Debbie comes in on the end of this with a bottle of Bollinger and three flutes. 'It's lovely to hear you both getting on,' she announces breathily. She makes a show of bending over with the tray. Mal whistles. Debbie smiles indulgently and hands him the bottle. 'Pop the cork for me.'

'Any time.' He winks at her. She pouts at him.

Frank clears his throat. 'You didn't answer my question, Mal.'

The cork flies off with a loud retort, just missing a crystal chandelier. Mal pours three foaming glasses. 'Patience, Frank.' He hands him a glass. 'A toast. To... reunions. May they always be such happy ones.'

'Cheers,' Debbie says enthusiastically, clinking glasses all round. Mal raises his glass in a half-salute. Frank does the same. They drink.

'And now, my pumpkin, I want to talk to Frank alone.' Mal puts his arm around Debbie, giving her a peck. 'So why don't you go and cook us something in that designer kitchen of yours?'

'But – '

'And none of that microwaved rubbish.' He propels her with a little push. 'Delia Smith would give her eye teeth for that set-up. Go and give me some bloody value out of it.'

She departs reluctantly. Mal sinks back into his chair. He drains his glass, refreshes it, and turns to Frank, teasing him. 'So you want answers, do you? What's little brother been up to in

140

the past twenty years? That sort of thing?'

'Don't mess with me, Mal. Trish says you've changed, and that's the only reason I'm here, to see for meself. According to her, you've become a pillar of the community, besides going up in the world. It sounded too good to be true so I thought I'd better check it out.'

Mal spreads his arms wide. 'It is true. All of it. I'm a reformed character. Have been since you put me right. I've gotta lot to thank you for, Frank.'

'Funny. That's what Dawson said – or words to that effect.'

'Dawson? Pete Dawson? You seen him recently?' Mal does astonishment quite convincingly. 'What's he up to these days, the old lag?'

'I thought you might be able to tell me that.'

'We lost touch, Frank. A long time ago. He was a bad influence, you said so yourself. That day at court, remember? We was standing outside after the case got thrown out and you came storming over and gave me an ear-bashing in front of everyone.'

'And you listened to me? That must be a first.'

'I did a lot of growing up over the next few years, Frank. A lot. It was a struggle, I admit it, but I was determined to get out of… all that.' He gets up and brings the bottle over, topping up Frank's glass. 'I got a job with this removals company, humping bloody pianos about 'til I nearly broke me back. Then I got a job as a driver. Then I got in with the boss, got in on the management side, giving quotes and all that. And it went from there. Five years on, I had me own business. Got a house, got a wife, got a decent motor. Four years later, I had another business – taxi cabs – a better house, a better wife, a better motor. You keep trading up, see? That's the key. Then I branched out into limo hire, minibuses, that sort of thing. Now I've got me own showroom just down the road, another one in Brum and one

planned for Coventry. Betcha never thought you'd see the day!'
He slaps Frank on the back, fortuitously missing his hidden
wires. The picture disappears as a connector is jolted out of
place, but sound remains.

'Very impressive.'

'So what about you, bro? Things going well? How's life in the
force?'

Frank pauses. 'Never a dull moment,' he replies.

Diary, 13 March

I was hauled into the office by Tony this morning. He was
absolutely steaming because Frank rang him on his mobile and
told him to pull me off the investigation. Tony recorded the
entire conversation – he stuck a pick-up mike on the phone as
soon as the receptionist told him who was on the line – so I was
able to hear it myself. Obviously he didn't know what had
happened over the weekend, so he was furious about not being
kept informed. I explained that events had moved too fast to tell
anyone, which was almost true. Once I'd brought him up to
speed, he calmed down a bit. With the financial constraints we've
got – all the covert recording gear took us way over budget – the
powers that be are screaming for a result, and now things have
progressed so dramatically we've got a better story than any of
us ever imagined. Ray was very impressed and congratulated me
on my initiative, so Tony had to start being nice to me again,
although he looked really pissed off when he realised Frank had
spent the weekend at my flat. Not that I gave him any of the
intimate details! Needless to say, he didn't appreciate being
warned off by Frank, either, though no one else got the reference
and I didn't enlighten them.

As for me, I was angry that Frank had rung to check me out,
but I suppose I should have expected it. He's a detective; he's

hardly going to just take my word after the way I've deceived him. He might've known the shit would hit the fan at my end, but I suppose that's part of his plan, too. It's obvious he regards journalists as the scum of the earth, so he's not exactly the sort to co-operate with a TV programme unless he's desperate (which he was). Now that he's got my evidence and a witness, he seems to think he can dump me and finish the job by himself, the bastard.

I'm trying to be objective about it. It's tit for tat, that's what I keep telling myself: I've used him; he's used me. We're both professionals trying to get a job done, so it's fair dos. But in my heart I'm going, 'Yes, but he kissed me. We connected. I like him. I don't want to be play these games.' And I think he genuinely cares about me, otherwise he wouldn't try and stop me going to Silks. Equally, of course, it might be that he thinks I'll get in the way or dent his credibility – or, even more humiliating, solve the case before he does. Now that would be something, wouldn't it?

We haven't decided what to do about tonight. Tony and Ray were having a meeting about it when I left, and I'm sitting here waiting for one of them to ring me. Everyone's agreed it's risky, but if we do as I suggested and have backup outside and inside the club, I can't come to much harm. Personally, I want to do it. I wasn't sure before, but since Frank went and stuck his oar in, it's like it's a challenge. I'm going to prove to him that Pauline Chambers is not a girl to be messed with.

I wish he'd ring me.

TRANSCRIPT OF FILM, TAPE 82V/404, SILKS. 13.03.00, 22.30

The club is starting to fill up. There is no sign of Dawson. Pauline, in her new post as greeter, is introducing a group of drunken businessmen to several hostesses. The men, who are sitting at a large circular table, are big and boisterous and one of the girls hangs back nervously. She taps Pauline's arm. 'Excuse me.'

Pauline, who is trying to attract a waiter to take their order, turns round. 'Yes?'

'I'm Teresa. I'm new here and...' She glances at the rowdy group. One of the men beckons to her. 'Come on, love, don't be shy. We don't bite. Not yet, anyway.' The others guffaw loudly. Directly behind them, the camera picks up grizzled producer Ray Dunthorne enjoying a tête-à-tête with a lissom Nigerian called Patti.

Pauline sees the tension in the young new girl's face and whispers, 'Smile.' Teresa forces a half-hearted smile to her lips. 'Don't worry,' Pauline hisses, 'the first time's the worst. Soon it'll come automatically. A lot of this will just wash over you.'

Teresa nods, biting her lip. Pauline takes in the gawky stance, the self-conscious hands. 'How old are you?'

'Eighteen.'

'Seriously? I won't say anything.'

'Well... sixteen. Nearly.'

Pauline cocks her head. 'Serious pocket money, eh?'

Teresa stares at her feet. 'It's not for me. It's for my boyfriend.' She looks up at Pauline, her eyes brimming with unshed tears. Pauline steers her away from the group. 'I'll be back with you in a minute, gentlemen. If you could just excuse us...' She takes Teresa over to quiet corner and sits her down at an unoccupied table. 'Do you really want to do this?'

Silent tears drip down the girl's cheeks. Pauline's voice is harsh. 'This "boyfriend" – is he on drugs? Or is he your pimp?'

She sniffs. 'It was coke. But now he's on heroin. He's out of his head most of the time. He said...' She starts crying again. Pauline hands her a paper napkin. The girl dries her eyes. 'Thanks.'

'I suppose it was either you doing this or he'd be forced to turn to crime,' Pauline guesses.

'How did you know?'

'It's a common story.'

'Is it?' She looks surprised.

Pauline gets up. 'Yes. And it never ends happily. My advice is to ditch him before you get sucked in too. And get the hell out of here before you wind up a tart like all the rest.'

'But you're the head hostess. Surely you're not supposed – ?'

'Off the record,' Pauline says, 'I don't encourage minors. It's bad for the club's image.' She puts an arm round her shoulders. 'Why don't you leave now? I'll cover for you.'

Teresa falters. 'I can't. I can't do it to Alan. I love him.'

'Jesus!' Pauline snaps, losing patience. 'Then clean up your bloody face and get back to that table. I've got work to do.'

The girl's face crumples. 'But how do you... I mean, we're supposed to keep them drinking, aren't we? How do you do it, without getting drunk? I'm not... well, I'm not really used to booze.'

Pauline spots Dawson winding his way towards her through the tables. He is wearing an unusually sober suit and dark glasses. 'See those big ferns all round the place? You water those. Frequently. They love champagne, it makes them grow like wild fire. Now go.'

Dawson watches the young girl stumble away. 'Trouble?'

'All sorted now.'

'Then get back to the desk. They're queuing up out there. I've had to take some through myself.'

'Sorry.' She makes to go, but he catches hold of her bare arm and holds it in a vice-like grip. 'I can trust you, can't I, Posh?' He pauses. It's impossible to read his expression behind the shades.

Pauline winces as his fingers bite into her flesh. 'Of course.'

'Good. 'Cos I wouldn't like you to let me down. Not after all the... confidence I've shown in you.' Dawson draws closer, so

145

close that his voice booms into the mike. 'That would be a big mistake.' He releases her arm, stroking his nail up her skin. Pauline shivers. 'What's the matter, darlin'? Someone step on your grave?' Dawson chuckles. He runs his finger over the hollows in her shoulder, tracing the delicate collarbone, and encircles the back of her neck between forefinger and thumb, rubbing gently.

'Thing is, Posh,' he whispers. 'I'd hate to have to discipline you. But if I thought you was being disloyal' – he glances after Teresa – 'or failing in your duties, I might have to lick you into shape. Know what I mean?' He hooks her face towards him. Pauline swallows. Dawson grins suddenly. 'You and me, babe, we'll get along alright. I can tell. Once we've worked out our… priorities.' He strokes her lips with his thumb. 'I reckon I'm the man you've been waiting for.'

From across the room there's a loud crash as Ray deliberately knocks an ice bucket off its stand. Dawson, distracted, turns round. 'Another one bites the dust,' he says softly, pursing her mouth as if she's a naughty child. He holds her like that for a second, as if trying to read behind her eyes, then lets go. 'I'll see you later, doll,' he says, making it sound as much a threat as a promise. 'I'd better sort that punter out.'

The tape stops at this point. It has been spliced and edited together with another sequence, because the next frame code shows the later time of 23.22. Pauline has obviously managed to secrete a camera into the reception area, because the viewpoint is above the greeter's desk, looking down. We see Pauline enjoying a discreet coffee during a lull in proceedings. She bends over, massaging an aching calf, and doesn't notice Angie come in. Angie looks comical. She has swapped her ankle-length evening gowns for an unflattering pair of white trousers and a halter top, which

146

merely accentuates her flabby arms and crepey neck. Her hair, which was formally drawn back severely, is loose and rather wild, and her favoured Paloma Piccasso-style make-up appears to have been abandoned for pink lipgloss and glitter eyeshadow. As soon as she begins to speak it becomes clear that she is very, very drunk.

'Hey! Service!' Angie slaps her hand down on the desk.

Pauline bobs up, startled. 'Oh! Hi Angie. What are you doing here?'

'Never mind "what am I doing here". What are you doing here, you skinny little bint?' Angie spits, leaning across the desk.

'Angie, I'm sorry, I didn't ask for this. Dawson just sprung it on me.'

'Yeah, like he sprung the sack on me – after eight bloody years in the job. You must be well pleased with yourself.'

Pauline spreads her hands helplessly. 'Honestly, I – '

'Honestly!' Angie cackles with laughter. 'Honesty isn't exactly your strong suite, is it, Emma? If your name *is* Emma, of course. Which I doubt.'

'What do you mean?'

Angie fishes in her shoulder bag. 'When I finished my shift yesterday, I helped myself to a drink or several behind the bar – I thought, "why not, he owes me enough" – and I spotted this attached to a dusty old bottle of curacao.' She produces a micro-video camera with a flourish, as if pulling a rabbit out of a hat. 'I assume it's yours?'

'Why would you think that?' Pauline flannels.

'Come on. You're new, you're uppity, you won't sleep with the punters. It's a mystery to everyone why you're working here. But if you're spying, well – suddenly it all makes sense.'

At that moment one of the regulars – an elderly and very rich eccentric – enters. Pauline, looking daggers at Angie, escorts him into the club and takes him to his usual booth. He is swiftly dealt

147

with and she returns to reception, where Angie is playing with the tiny camera, dropping it from one palm to another. 'What's it worth, *Emma?*' She throws it up in the air and catches it. 'What's it worth, not to tell Dawson?'

'For God's sake, put it away.' Pauline tries to snatch it out of Angie's hands, but the older woman is too quick for her.

'I would say it's priceless,' Angie slurs, snapping her bag shut. 'Judging by your reaction.' She leans close to Pauline. 'Which puts me in a very strong position. You see, I don't want money. I want revenge.'

She goes as if to walk past Pauline. Pauline, glancing back over her shoulder into the club, puts her arm out. For several seconds they tussle, panting, then Pauline appears to give up the fight. 'OK,' she bluffs, breathing fast. 'Tell Dawson. It doesn't matter. I've got backup inside and outside the club. He's completely surrounded. We're just waiting for the right moment to arrest him. You go to him with this and we'll have you, too. Tipping him off makes you an accessory. You'll be looking at ten, maybe fifteen years.' She folds her arms.

Angie blinks. 'You're a policewoman?'

'Keep your voice down!'

'I – I never realised. I thought you were an undercover reporter, or something.'

'Well you thought wrong. I'm DI Chambers and you are imperilling an international criminal investigation. Hand over that evidence.'

She does so, stunned.

'Good. Now get out of here before Dawson sees you and starts asking questions. We don't want him alerted.'

Angie backs away. 'What will happen to me?' she whimpers, suddenly pathetic.

Pauline observes her coldly. 'Someone will be round to talk to you. We don't consider you a major player, so if you cooperate fully, the CPS might be persuaded not to prosecute. Unless I discover evidence to the contrary.' She waits until Angie is out of the door and then collapses into her chair, inadvertently kicking over her coffee and making a black puddle on the carpet. 'Oh, shit,' she curses, betraying what sounds like a sob. She buries her head in her hands, her shoulders shaking silently.

DICTAPHONE TRANSCRIPT, TAPE 42A/92, 14.03.00, 09.00

BURNSIDE [*on the road again*]: 'Thought you might appreciate an update, boys. Just in case I don't live to see you in court. For the record, copies of these tapes are going to someone I can trust, so if you nab me, they'll do the rest. One way or another, I'll have you. I'm getting warmer. I've got the pieces of the puzzle. All I need now is the big picture, to see how it all fits together. And that's coming along nicely, thanks to my brother and his missus.' [*He pauses, presumably to do a manoeuvre. It sounds as if he's opened the window, as the traffic is much noisier. Burnside mutters 'Come on', under his breath. He releases the clutch and accelerates onto a fast road. There's the roar and rush of heavy vehicles. It appears he's on a motorway. He changes up through the gears and buzzes the window shut again.*]

BURNSIDE: 'Where was I? Oh, yeah, Mal...' [*He is interrupted by his mobile going off. He lets it ring and listens to the voicemail. It's DS Gary Hedges from Crime OCU. The two tapes have subsequently been spliced together so that we can hear the message.*]

HEDGES: 'Guv, are you there? It's Gazza. Listen Frank, I'm worried about you.' [*Pause*] 'There's a hell of a stink going on back at the factory; Sutton's tearing his hair out – what there is left of it, anyway – 'cos no one seems to know where you are. I told him you'd sent me an e-mail, said you was coming in on Monday, so when you didn't show, I went round your house. Thought you might've taken a turn for the worse or summat. That was when one of the neighbours told me there'd been a shoot-out outside your place on Saturday night. She thought you'd been hit. Another old boy said he thought you got away in a car. Nobody's seen hide nor hair of you since. I checked it out when I got back, 'cos I ain't heard nothing on the grapevine. A taxi driver reported it but the gunman was off the scene by the time they got an ARV and an ambulance round. I don't know why Sutton ain't mentioned it. He's more obsessed with having the Pepper squad on his tail. Some commander from the Yard wants your nuts in the grinder and he's giving Sutton hell. Anyway, if you get this, give us a ring. Anything I can do and all that, goes without saying. See you around, Guv. Cheers.' [*The phone clicks off.*]

BURNSIDE [*drumming his fingers on the steering wheel*]: 'Thanks, Gazza, I owe you. Sounds like you're one of the good guys. Question is, how many of the others can I trust? This thing gets deeper by the minute. Nice to know I could've bled to death in the street before anyone got there. I wonder who organised that? Our mystery copper really wants shot of me… Sounds like he's keeping his options open by mainlining the Pepper squad as well: what I'd call a "whack me or sack me" approach. So, who is he? That's what I need to work out, and fast. At this rate, I ain't got many lives left.

'Mal said something yesterday that made me think: "Remember that day in court?". Funny he should bring that up, 'cos it's been on my mind, too. If this is about something beyond the current investigation, something I've been involved with – and it's gotta be, else certain people wouldn't be so keen on shutting me up – then it's the only lead I've got. It was a poxy case, didn't even go to trial, but it's the one time after I joined the force that I had contact with both Mal and Peter Dawson. I didn't exactly come out of it smelling of roses, neither.' [*Burnside pauses. There's the 'tick-tock' of his indicator as he overtakes. He's powering up the outside lane.*]

'There was Mal and Dawson up in front of the bench for theft. Prosecution had a cast-iron case, but the Met. Police solicitor was so bleeding useless the judge threw it out. That's why the pair of 'em got off. It had nothing to do with yours truly sticking his oar in and trying to persuade the OIC to drop the charges against my brother, despite what went round afterwards.' [*Wet splats of rain on the windscreen. Burnside puts on his wipers. He raises his voice over the drumming of rain on the car roof.*] "Bent Burnside", that's what they used to call me behind my back. I didn't care, 'cos I knew the truth, but it stuck. That kind of label can be hard to get rid of, specially when you operate the way I do. Those post-graduate pen-pushers on Pepper are probably lapping it up... Jesus, sodding roadworks.' [*The car engine slows. The wipers bash away louder. It's pelting down outside. Burnside sighs and continues.*]

'I can't work out what relevance this might have – yet – but it's worth going back to the original case file. Something might show up; perhaps a name I can pin on this other bloke. What did Mal call him? "Bigfoot". I haven't had a clear look at his face, but I know his voice. He's a player; he's gotta be involved somewhere down the line. It's obvious he knows who Mal is. Either they go way back, or he's in on some sort of deal with him now.

'I know Mal's up to something. I don't buy that "reformed character" stunt for a minute. He always was a shifty beggar, telling porkies and landing other kids in trouble. Mal never did nothing out of the good of his heart; there always had to be something in it for him. According to his bird, he's raising money for charity, being decorated by royalty and turned into Warwick's answer to Daddy Warbucks. It don't add up.

'One thing's for sure, he doesn't put it about at home. She ain't too happy in the marital nest, if this morning's anything to go by.' [*Laughs drily*] 'I was surprised they even put me up. I wasn't expecting breakfast in bed – not that kind, anyway.' [*He laughs again.*] 'Apparently, Mal's all talk and no trousers and Mrs Burnside the third is feeling a bit neglected. She reckons he gets his kicks with toms, which wouldn't surprise me, especially if he is up to something with Dawson. Question is, what? If Tomasic's supplying the smuggling operation, which we ain't got proof of, how would Mal fit in? You don't bus illegal immigrants into the country like they was on a charabanc, and you don't hide 'em in stretch limos, neither.' [*It sounds as if Burnside's unwrapping something – a mint perhaps. He sucks on it thoughtfully.*]

'So, what are the facts? Trish said Mal's got three or four different companies, but all he's told me is, he's in the motor trade. When I pressed him on it, he changed the subject. Correction, Debbie started blethering on about his commendations, like I give a toss. Yesterday, she told me he was "at the depot", not "at the showroom" or "at the garage". When I offered to drive over there, she said he didn't like casual visitors. Hardly the attitude of your average car dealer. This morning, he shoots off at the crack of dawn without saying goodbye to his long-lost brother. Then, when I ask his wife where he's gone, she offers me the choice of full English or continental. And she didn't mean coffee and croissants...' [*Another pause.*] 'Damn!' [*He thumps the steering wheel in frustration, hitting the horn by mistake. It blares loudly.*] 'The bitch was covering for him! How could I have been so bleedin' stupid? He's sodding well got away!'

EXTRACT FROM TAPED INTERVIEW WITH DEBBIE BURNSIDE,

TAPE 88A/92, 22.06.00

CHAMBERS: 'What did you think when your husband's older brother just turned up out of the blue? They hadn't spoken for about twenty years, had they?'

DEBBIE: 'I thought he was going to mug me, at first.'

CHAMBERS: 'Why?'

DEBBIE: 'He looked a bit… dodgy. A bit, you know, rough around the edges. Mal's made me very security-aware, being on my own all day in that big place. He's always said not to trust anybody who turns up without an appointment. Especially strange blokes. Of course, I didn't know who Frank was, then.'

CHAMBERS: 'Did he introduce himself?'

DEBBIE: 'Yeah. I thought he was joking, until I saw the resemblance between them. I knew Mal hated his guts, had done since they was kids. I couldn't believe his nerve.'

CHAMBERS: 'What did you say?'

DEBBIE: 'I was nice as pie to him. Had to be. I rang Mal; he told me to keep him sweet.'

CHAMBERS [*acid*]: 'And how far did he mean you to interpret those instructions?'

DEBBIE: 'Mal knows I can be very… imaginative. He wouldn't mind what I did, so long as it did the trick. Which it did.' [*She laughs*]

CHAMBERS: 'When was this?'

DEBBIE: 'Next morning. He was asking all these questions so I…distracted him.'

CHAMBERS: 'How?'

DEBBIE: 'Simple. Lifted up the duvet and asked, "Mind if I join you?".'

CHAMBERS: 'And he didn't resist?'

DEBBIE: 'Not really. Not like he meant it.'

CHAMBERS [*sounding thrown*]: 'Did Frank say if he had a – a girlfriend, or anyone? Did he seem guilty about what he was doing?'

DEBBIE: 'He didn't mention anyone. Why? Was there?'

CHAMBERS: 'I – don't know. You tell me.'

DEBBIE: 'Well, how should I know? Frank seemed to enjoy the service. He was a bit pent-up. Know what I mean?'

CHAMBERS: 'Are you saying he seemed sexually frustrated?'

DEBBIE: 'I'm saying he was more than ready for it.'

CHAMBERS: 'Didn't he question your motives – his brother's wife seducing him?'

DEBBIE: 'No. He seemed to get a real kick out of it. I think he thought he was getting back at Mal, know what I mean? Course, the laugh was on him, but he didn't realise it.'

CHAMBERS: 'Are you a prostitute?'

DEBBIE: 'Hey, girlie! I'm a respectable married woman.'

CHAMBERS: 'Just because you've got a ring on your finger doesn't mean you're not a slag. One that's well past her prime by the look of it.'

DEBBIE: 'Are you allowed to talk to me like this on a television interview?'

CHAMBERS: 'Don't flatter yourself. Do you really think I'm going to broadcast anything a tart like you has to say?'

DEBBIE: 'What did you ask me here for, then?'

CHAMBERS: 'I just wanted to know, OK?'

DEBBIE: 'Oh, I get it. You went with him, too, didn't you?'

CHAMBERS: 'No!'

DEBBIE: 'And you've got the nerve to call me a slag. What is it: want to compare notes?'

CHAMBERS [*screaming*]: 'Get out!'

E-mail

To: gary.hedges@crimeocu.gov.uk   Sent: 14 March
From: fburnside@cwcom.net
Subject: Info needed

Tried to get you on the blower but no reply. Voicemail too risky. Your instincts were right. Person or persons are out to get me, hence the propaganda: We're talking major league, Gazza, so keep schtum. You're the only one I trust. Don't let me down.

I need you to look up an old two-hander from late 1979: Peter Dawson and Malcolm Burnside, charged with burglary at Rochester Row nick, subsequently acquitted at Horseferry Road magistrates court, summer 1980. I want anything you can get on it, right away. Ring me on my mobile.

Also need you to do a search on Malcolm Burnside. (DOB: 19.09.55. Home address: 5 The Copse, Parklands, Warwick.) He claims to be in motor trade; has dealerships in Warwick & Birmingham. Try Companies House as well as PNC. Could be missing link in Playmates. And yes, he is my brother.

EXTRACT FROM TAPED INTERVIEW WITH DS GARY HEDGES,
TAPE 83A/92, 27.06.00

CHAMBERS: 'Let's move on to when DCI Burnside made contact with you after he'd apparently "gone to ground". What was your initial reaction?'
HEDGES: 'I was relieved he was still with us. Thought he might've been lying dead in a ditch after hearing about that shoot-out.'
CHAMBERS: 'Which no one had mentioned at work?'
HEDGES: 'Not until I started asking questions, no.'
CHAMBERS: 'Did that strike you as odd?'
HEDGES: 'A bit. What with Sutton running round like a headless chicken, I thought something must be going down.'

CHAMBERS: 'Did you mention that to any of your colleagues?'

HEDGES: 'Yeah, DC Terri Goldman.'

CHAMBERS: 'What was her response?'

HEDGES: 'She said we should stay out of it.'

CHAMBERS: 'But you didn't.'

HEDGES: 'I couldn't, could I? Not after he sent me that e-mail.'

CHAMBERS: 'What made you think you could trust Burnside? By the sound of it, no one else did.'

HEDGES: 'Copper's instinct. There's times you've just got to make a judgment call.'

CHAMBERS: 'That was brave of you.'

HEDGES [*laughing*]. 'Dunno about that. Sounded like he was being fitted up from inside. That was when I started looking over my shoulder, too.'

CHAMBERS: 'Had Burnside ever mentioned having a brother with a criminal record?'

HEDGES: 'Nah, he never talks about his personal life. It didn't surprise me, though. He looks like he's come from that kinda background, know what I mean? Rough and ready. I reckon he could've gone either way. If he hadn't become a copper...'

CHAMBERS: '... he might have become a villain? Interesting theory.'

HEDGES: 'It's a fine line, darlin'. As we've seen.'

CHAMBERS: 'So did you find the case files he asked you to get?'

HEDGES: 'No. They was gone. I had a talk to the clerk at the dead files store; she said they'd probably been destroyed. All she had was what was on the index: name of the prosecuting solicitor, which was Keith Gaughan, and the OIC. I forget his name.'

CHAMBERS: 'OIC?'

HEDGES: 'Officer in charge.'

CHAMBERS: 'Oh, right. Did you follow them up?'

HEDGES: 'Yeah, thought the guvnor would want me to. Turned out to be quite revealing: the OIC – it was Hugh somebody or other – retired on medical grounds six months later. Reading between the lines, I think he had a nervous breakdown. He committed suicide in 1982. Gaughan left the Met. and went into private practice soon after the case was dropped. He was still working then; had a partnership in Bromley.'

CHAMBERS: 'What about Mal Burnside? Did you find anything on him?'

HEDGES: 'No records after the burglary case in 1980. It looked as if he'd kept his nose clean. He had a couple of garages – second-hand dealerships, nothing flash. He also had a registered haulage company, which Frank hadn't mentioned.'

CHAMBERS: 'How did you get this information to DCI Burnside?'

HEDGES: 'Rang him, didn't I? He told me to get over to Whiteley's shopping centre. Found him drinking coffee in the internet café, cool as a cucumber, surrounded by backpackers. I told him what I knew and he said he thought his brother must've got something like that. He reckoned Mal's the one who brings the girls over for Dawson in his lorries. Said he thought he'd done a runner by now. That's when I broke the news from NCIS that Tomasic had disappeared too.'

CHAMBERS: 'So what course of action did you both decide on? Presumably it was just the two of you in on this?'

HEDGES: 'I wanted to bring Terri in, but Frank said he couldn't afford to trust no one else. It was like he was on some kind of mission. I didn't ask him about it; I thought, it'll all come out in the wash. He said he was going over to Bromley to find Gaughan. He told me to fetch Tomasic's daughter from Hampstead and drive her round Notting Hill, see if she could identify Dawson's porn palace. Then I was to take her to a safe house.'

CHAMBERS: 'What about the missing girl, Sanja?'

HEDGES: 'Burnside said Kristina was probably protecting her. Told me to give her the old patter, persuade her to talk.'

CHAMBERS: 'And did you?'

HEDGES: 'Well I would've, if I'd been able to find her. When I got there, her employer was tearing her hair out. Said she should've been home with the kiddies two hours ago.'

TRANSCRIPT OF FILM, TAPE 53V/404. KEITH
GAUGHAN'S OFFICE, BROMLEY.
14.03.00, 12.50

An exterior establishing shot of Gaughan's office, which has its premises in a dismal, single-storey concrete shopping mall left over from the 1960s. The area is going to seed, made unfashionable by the huge, glittering retail extravaganza known as The Glades which now dominates the town centre. Burnside, who is wearing the secret camera, pauses outside, so that the nameplate bearing the legend 'Gaughan, Quentin, Marks' is recorded. He enters and finds himself in a narrow corridor. The solicitors' office is through a door off to the left. Burnside goes through and speaks to a grey-haired woman in a navy cardigan, who is obviously the receptionist.

'Is Keith Gaughan here?'

'He's at lunch at the moment. Are you early for an appointment?' She pecks at a computer keyboard, peering short-sightedly at the monitor.

'I don't need one.' Burnside shows her his warrant card. 'Where's he gone?'

'The, er... across the road, I believe.' She pinkens slightly.

Burnside peers out of the window. 'The Cross Keys?'

She gives him an embarrassed smile. 'He should be back by two. Can I take a message?'

'Don't bother.' Burnside turns to go, then turns back again. 'What's he wearing?'

'A sports jacket and – and a bottle green tie. Yes, bottle green,' she repeats, half to herself. She rolls a ballpoint between her palms, pondering this description. 'And I *think* he had a mustard-coloured scarf on...'

Burnside is already out of the door.

TRANSCRIPT OF FILM, TAPE 54V/404. CROSS KEYS PUB, BROMLEY.
14.03.00, 12.55

A smoky town-centre pub. It's full of regulars, mainly men. Three decorators in paint-spattered clothes are arguing over the racing pages of the *Sun* at the bar. A wizened old boy in a flat cap chips in from his seat in the corner. A few suits from nearby offices occupy tables. Sitting by himself, drinking what looks like a large gin and tonic, is a bald man in his late fifties fitting Gaughan's description. He is reading *The Times*. Burnside goes over to him. 'Mind if I join you?' His tone is sarcastic.

Gaughan glances at the empty table next to him. 'There's plenty of space over there.' His voice sounds petulant; clearly this disruption of his lunchtime routine isn't welcome.

'So there is.' Burnside sits down opposite him. 'But it's you I want to talk to.' Gaughan gives him a severe look over half-moon spectacles. 'Do I know you?'

'I doubt it. But you know my brother.'

'I meet a great many people in my profession.' Gaughan shakes the paper out. He scans the obituaries with a keen eye.

'His name's Burnside. That ring any bells for you, Mr Gaughan?'

Gaughan lowers the paper warily. He looks at Burnside again. This time he spots the resemblance. His air of superiority dissolves. 'Oh dear, I – ' He reaches for his glass and takes a large gulp. His hand trembles, slopping some of it on the paper.

'I see it does.' Burnside sits back, folding his arms.

Gaughan glances around nervously. 'How is, er – ?'

'Malcolm.'

'Yes, that's it, Malcolm.'

'He's an extremely successful businessman, worth a fortune.' Burnside pauses. 'Don't you want to know how Peter Dawson's doing, too?'

'Dawson. He was the… older man, wasn't he?'

'Or you could call him the ringleader. It was his show.'

Gaughan attempts a feeble smile. 'A clever customer, as I recall.'

'Too clever for you.'

Gaughan fishes a handkerchief out of his top pocket and mops his shiny pate. 'You know how it goes. One can't win every case, much as one would like to.'

'Yeah, well only a total incompetent could have got that case chucked out,' Burnside snarls. 'Are you?'

'I take great offence at that remark,' Gaughan blusters. 'I have a highly successful partnership and an excellent professional record.'

'So what went wrong then? Dawson should've gone down for what he did. So, by rights, should my brother. But they didn't, did they? They walked free. What was it – a bad hair day?' Burnside leans across the table towards him. 'Or were you offered an incentive to lose it?'

'I – I resent your implication.' Gaughan downs the rest of his drink in one. The glass clatters as he puts it on the table.

'I ain't implying nothing. I'm stating the facts as I see 'em.' Burnside is getting into his stride now. 'I always thought you were just crap at your job and that's why I copped the flack for you ballsing up the case. But now I'm beginning to see things differently. Briefs up for a bit of match-fixing... it happens.'

Gaughan blinks rapidly. 'Who are you? What do you want with me?'

'I'm DCI Frank Burnside. I'm the fall guy,' Burnside replies, calculatingly. 'Someone bunged you a backhander, didn't they? Must have been a bloody good one for you to leave the MPS. Who was it, eh? Dawson? Couldn't have been Mal, he was stony broke. Or was it one of the others?'

'I absolutely deny it.' Despite his vehemence, Gaughan is queasy pale.

'Of course you do. And I ain't got any proof. Let's just call it a shot in the dark. And I've had one of them recently.' Burnside knits his fingers, pinning Gaughan's paper down with his forearms. 'But let's just say, for argument's sake, that I'm right. What makes a twenty-year-old burglary so important? What was it they nicked? I've been racking my brains, but I can't remember. It's got to be something impressive. Artworks? Jewellery? Forged notes? What? See the way I'm thinking, Mr Gaughan?' Gaughan purses his lips. He does not answer. Burnside continues. 'The case file's vanished into thin air. At least one senior police officer's conspiring to kill me. Dawson's made two attempts on my life. And my brother's gone walkabout. That's just for starters. I keep coming back to this because it's all I've got to go on. So if you know something...'

Gaughan gets up from the table, almost knocking over his chair in his haste. 'I'm afraid I really can't help you.' He winds his scarf around his neck. 'It was all a very very long time ago and my memory isn't what it was. I barely remember the case.'

Burnside stands up too. He skirts the table, blocking Gaughan's exit. 'I think you remember it plain as day. You're shitting yourself now, ain't you, wondering what's going on? Who's gonna be next

161

in line for the chop, that's what you're thinking. 'Cos it'll all come out, with or without your help. I'm that close now.' He holds his forefinger and thumb a centimetre apart. 'So why don't you save yourself the hassle? Get it off your chest. I might even be able to get you protection – if you think you're gonna need it.' He takes a card out of his wallet and stuffs it into Gaughan's top pocket. 'Don't think about it too long, will you?'

Gaughan winds the scarf tighter. 'Is this an official police investigation?' he asks querulously. Burnside does not answer. Gaughan steps round him, shoulders hunched. 'I thought not.'

TRANSCRIPT OF TELEPHONE CALL, TAPE 621T/998, 14.03.00, 13.25

BURNSIDE [*abrupt, on mobile*]: 'Hello.'

CHAMBERS: 'Frank? It's Pauline.'

BURNSIDE: 'Oh.'

CHAMBERS: 'Is that all you've got to say for yourself after doing the dirty on me?'

BURNSIDE: 'Look. I'm sorry for raining on your parade, Pauline, but I had no option. I couldn't have you putting yourself at risk.'

CHAMBERS: 'And you thought calling my boss would stop me? You don't know TV people very well, do you Frank? We don't let little things like that stand in the way of a good story.'

BURNSIDE: 'Well it's your life.'

CHAMBERS: 'Yes, it is.' [*Silence.*]

BURNSIDE: 'So you went there?'

CHAMBERS: 'Yes.'

BURNSIDE: 'What did he do?'

CHAMBERS: 'Wouldn't you like to know?'

BURNSIDE: 'Don't muck me around, Pauline. This is no time for games.'

CHAMBERS: 'Games? Me? That's a good one, coming from a man who's got his hand up my T-shirt one minute and dumping me the next. One who didn't even have the decency to tell me to my face.'

BURNSIDE [*sighing*]: 'Pauline, it wasn't... personal. You don't realise what's going on here. You're way out of your depth.'

CHAMBERS: 'Oh, I know what's going on. We were supposed to be a team. Now you've got what you want from me – and a bit extra besides – you're going to wrap it up and claim all the glory.'

BURNSIDE: 'I don't believe I'm hearing this. Is that all you can think about? Who's going to get the credit? You're even more selfish than I thought.'

CHAMBERS [*backtracking*]: 'No! It's not – it's just that I thought we had something, Frank. We were doing well, working together, weren't we? Then, all of a sudden you hung me out to dry.' [*Her voice starts to crack*] 'How did you think I'd feel?'

BURNSIDE: 'Pauline? Are you crying?'

CHAMBERS [*sobbing*]: 'No.'

BURNSIDE: 'What happened at the club?'

CHAMBERS: 'Dawson...' [*She cries even harder.*]

BURNSIDE: 'Did he hurt you?' [*Pauline does not answer.*] 'Pauline, are you alright?'

CHAMBERS [*through tears*]: 'No, not really.'

BURNSIDE: 'Stay there. I'm coming round.'

Capital Radio, 14.03.00, 14.00
'Capital news, it's two o'clock. I'm Jane Sanderson.

    'A four-year-old girl is thought to have been snatched from Hampstead Heath this morning together with her teenage childminder and another girl.

    'An eye witness spotted two men forcing sixteen-year-old au pair Kristina Tomasic and a dark-haired girl into a van. Little

Katie Watson, who was in the charge of the Croatian au pair, was later discovered to be missing. Police think she may already have been inside the white Ford Transit, although they haven't ruled out the possibility that she could be lost on the Heath. Her six-month-old brother, Tobias, was found abandoned in a pushchair nearby. He was unharmed. The identity of the third girl is not known.

'Teams of specially trained searchers are already scouring the Heath looking for signs of the missing girl. Meanwhile, Katie's parents, Marie and Gerald Watson, are preparing to make a televised appeal on the BBC's *Six O'clock News*. As yet, police have been unable to trace Kristina Tomasic's family.

'A motive for the abduction is not clear.'

TRANSCRIPT OF TELEPHONE CALL, TAPE 622T/998, 14.03.00, 14.12

BURNSIDE: 'Hello?'

HEDGES: 'It's me, Guv. Bad news.'

BURNSIDE: 'You're late, ain'tcha? I just heard about it on the car radio. Or is there something else I won't like?'

HEDGES: 'Sorry, Guv. Got a bit... tied up. Lotta red tape going on.'

BURNSIDE: 'What are you on about? Where are you?'

HEDGES [*hesitating*]: 'At the office.'

BURNSIDE: 'I told you not to go back there! Are you deaf or daft or what?'

HEDGES: 'I didn't have no choice, boss.'

BURNSIDE: 'Jesus! What happened? Can you talk?'

HEDGES: 'Not for long. Sutton's watching me like a hawk. I'm on me mobile, on the roof. Don't think anyone saw me go up.'

BURNSIDE: 'Go on.'

HEDGES: 'I got to the Watsons' house, to get Kristina, and Mrs W was going mental 'cos they hadn't come back. She'd already called the local nick by then. To be honest, I didn't know whether to duck out and let 'em get on with it, or pull rank and take over. Either way was gonna look odd, seeing as I'd just turned up out the blue. Then she started rabbiting on about you being there the other day and asking questions. She seemed to think it was all connected. I felt I had to stay and cover our end, find out what was going down. The two coppers from Hampstead arrived while I was still on the doorstep, so I didn't get a chance to bugger off anyway.'

BURNSIDE: 'And once they knew Crime OCU was involved...'

HEDGES: 'I told 'em I'd handle it, but some CID sergeant fancied himself, didn't he? Called our lot for information on the case. Next thing, Sutton's on the radio and telling me to get my arse back here.'

BURNSIDE: 'He ask about me?'

HEDGES [*embarrassed*]: 'Yes, Guv.'

BURNSIDE: 'What did you tell him?'

HEDGES: 'It wasn't Sutton, Guv. He said things had gone way beyond him. There was this bloke from Pepper waiting to interview me. Commander Webster.'

BURNSIDE: 'And?'

HEDGES: 'I couldn't not co-operate...'

BURNSIDE: 'Yeah, yeah, I know. I don't blame you, Gazza.'

HEDGES: 'He said you was suspended as of now.'

BURNSIDE: 'That don't make much difference. My whole life's on hold 'til this is over.'

HEDGES: 'I gotta go, Guv. Someone's coming.' [*The line goes dead.*]

Diary, 14 March

I'm still feeling numb after what happened last night. First of all Angie staggered in dead drunk, shooting her mouth off about having found a secret camera. (I knew someone would find one soon; my luck's been holding out for far too long.) I thought she was going to drop me right in it with Dawson, but I managed to shut her up by pretending I was an undercover police officer. It's an offence, but that was all I could think of at the time and I was totally desperate.

I was on tenterhooks anyway because Dawson was being so creepy and menacing towards me. It wasn't like he'd guessed what I was doing there; more as if he was playing some sort of perverted mind game. I remembered what Ian had said about Dawson having feelings for me, and it made my skin crawl. I tried to get away as soon as we closed, but Dawson said he wanted me to have a drink with him in the private suite – some excuse about celebrating my first day in the new job. I went to the loo and got rid of the kit but when I tried to call the others on my mobile, the battery had run out. Of course, that was the one contingency we hadn't planned for.

It was awful. Dawson put this porn video on and said he thought I might 'relate' to it. I didn't know what to expect. My heart was thumping like crazy. He said, 'Don't look so worried, Posh; Daddy's here.' Then he poured me champagne and sat with his arm around my shoulders. I nearly got up and ran out there and then, but I thought he would catch me. I haven't got much of a turn of speed in three-inch spike heels. I didn't know whether the secret camera in the private suite was working, but the thought that, if Dawson raped me, it would all be on film wasn't any comfort. It was like I would be participating in one of his sick home movies – except that this time I would be the one who had set up the camera.

At first I couldn't make out what was going on in the video. The lighting was terrible. What was weird was that Dawson apologised for this, like he was some kind of art-house film director. He said, 'Normally, my productions are much classier, but I thought you'd appreciate a bit of what we in the business call cinema verity.' (Yes, that's how he pronounced it.) Then, suddenly, the lighting went from being really dark to really bright, and there was this man sitting on a sofa and a girl lying face-down across his lap. She was dressed in school uniform and had her knickers around her ankles and he was spanking her. You couldn't see their faces, because he was leaning over her, whispering stuff like, 'Who's Daddy's naughty girl?' She was crying and going, 'Me, me', so he spanked her again, harder. Then he said he'd stop if she did 'something special' to please him. No prizes for guessing what that was. That was when I saw her face, 'cos the camera zoomed right in. It was Kristina.

I couldn't help gasping. I could see Dawson out of the corner of my eye. He still had his shades on but I could tell he was watching me, waiting for my reaction. I realised then what this was all about. He'd got off on that story I'd made up about being abused as a child and this was his way of trying to regress me to that same state of vulnerability. It was obvious what scenario he was going to want to act out once the film was over. The man climaxed, which was shown in such lurid detail it made me want to gag. When the camera panned up and I saw his face, I couldn't hold it in any longer. The man looked just like my father.

The fact that I vomited all over Dawson's suit was probably what saved me. Whatever reaction he was expecting, it wasn't that one. He had to take off his glasses to see where to mop it up, and that was when I noticed he had two livid shiners. I thought he must have been beaten up, but there were no marks anywhere else on his face. He caught me looking, mumbled 'eyebags' and slammed the shades back on as if he was really embarrassed. I started apologising like crazy and backing out, saying I had to get home because I felt ill. He didn't try and stop me; he was too busy wiping off the puke. Thank God for Dawson's vanity.

I was awake half the night going over it in my mind. When I did eventually sleep, the nightmares were worse than anything I'd allowed myself to remember. It was all such a muddle: stuff about Kristina and the investigation – at least I'd seen concrete proof, at last – mixed up with a montage of images from my childhood and early adolescence. Thinking about it now, the man wasn't even that much like my dad. It was more his age, and the fact that he had silver hair and looked quite distinguished. What disturbed me was the image Dawson had so crudely planted. It fed on my subconsicous, eating away at my dreams like a maggot. Dad and I were always so close. It was like him and me against the world, after Mum died. I suppose being a diplomat's daughter made me pretty self-confident: I remember accompanying him socially to parties and events, thinking I was so grown up and clever. It was almost as if we were a couple, but I never saw anything wrong in it. He used to say how proud he was to be with a pretty girl like me, and hold my hand and stuff, and people who didn't know used to think I was his girlfriend and nudge each other. We used to get a real kick out of it, seeing who we could fool, giggling about the looks on their faces. It was only play-acting. That's what I thought. But my dreams were nagging me. How had my father seen it? And why hadn't he gone out with other women? He used to say, 'Paulie, you're quite enough for me.' Were we unnaturally close?

When I woke up I felt little and scared and desperate for someone to confide in. That was why I phoned Frank. That, and I just needed someone to yell at. He's on his way over now. I wasn't going to film him any more, not after what happened between us on Sunday night, but since he's chosen to cut me out of his investigation I've changed my mind. After all, I might not see him again and I've got to wrap this documentary up somehow. I need to know what, if anything, he's discovered. I'm not going back to work at Silks again, no way. I'll call Tony later and tell him.

TRANSCRIPT OF FILM, TAPE 138V/404. PAULINE'S FLAT, HAMMERSMITH.
14.03.00, 15.06

The sofa's in shot, as before. At the moment, it's occupied by Clarice, Pauline's cat. We hear footsteps squeaking as Pauline crosses the wooden floor and opens the door, presumably to Burnside's knock.

'How are you now?' It's the first thing he says and his voice betrays concern.

'A bit better now. Got it out of my system. Here, let me take that.'

Burnside walks into view, minus his leather jacket. He is holding a plastic carrier bag. He looks around.

'Cup of tea?' Pauline shouts.

'In a minute. I want to talk to you, first. Come in here.' He scoops the cat off a cushion. It lands on the floor with an offended yowl.

'Ah, baby.' Pauline squats down to stroke the animal.

'Hey.' Burnside sits down, patting the space beside him. 'Sit.'

'I'm not a pet dog. And I don't take orders – especially from you.' She remains standing, blocking the shot of Burnside, then realises this and moves to the far end of the sofa, perching on the arm.

'Come on. I've brought an olive branch.' He holds out the bag. Pauline can't quite reach it. She slides off the arm and grudgingly shifts a little closer. She peers inside and fishes out a whopping box of Thornton's.

'Anyone would think you were feeling guilty.' She looks up at him. 'Are you?'

'No. Just don't like hearing girls cry.' He takes her hand. 'What did Dawson do to you?'

Pauline shakes her head. 'Made me watch a porn video, starring Kristina Tomasic.'

'Then what?'

'He was about to get me to re-enact her role when I threw up on his second-best Paul Smith. We kind of lost the moment.'

'Nice one.' Burnside squeezes her hand. 'Nothing else happen?'

'He didn't connect me with your miraculous escape in South Lambeth, if that's what you mean.'

'So what got you so upset on the phone?'

'Christ, Frank! If you'd had to watch some poor teenager being forced to commit – '

'OK, OK.' Burnside holds up his hands. 'I'm an insensitive bastard. You ain't the first to tell me that.'

Pauline tears the cellophane off the chocolate box. 'Anyway,' she says nonchalantly, 'what have you been up to?'

'This and that.'

'Frank!'

He eyes her suspiciously. 'You still working on the case?'

'Let's say I'm tying up the loose ends. Come on, share.' She moves closer. 'Who else have you got in your corner?'

She's hit a nerve. Burnside glowers. 'As of now, absolutely no one. According to my sergeant I've been suspended and someone from Pepper's after my scalp. Which reminds me.' He taps his lips with his fingers. 'Webster, Webster... I know that name.' He pauses. Pauline proffers the chocolates. Burnside absentmindedly picks one out and continues, 'There was a David Webster at

Stafford Row. He was a sergeant then. Tall fella, droopy 'tache, sideburns, West-Country accent. Looked like a bleedin' hippy and sounded like Worzel Gummidge. It can't be him. Can it?'

He looks at Pauline as if expecting an answer. She shrugs. Burnside's expression darkens. 'He used to roll his "r"s. Very distinctive.'

'So?'

'That tape you got of Dawson and Bigfoot. Can you find it?'

'Yes.'

'Put it on.'

Pauline looks as if she's going to object to being ordered about again, then thinks better of it. She unlocks a strongbox and produces a cassette. 'Should be on this one. Hang on, let me check... yes.' She slots it into the VCR and fast-forwards the cassette, checking the time code against an index, which she keeps out of Burnside's sight. 'Here we go.'

Burnside stares at the screen intently, straining to catch every nuance as the tall man spars with Dawson:

'So you put a petrol bomb through his front door to telegraph your concern. What did you think that would achieve?'

'I was 'oping it would shut the bugger up.'

'Then you should have arranged it better. He's alive and kicking arses all around the shop. I had to persuade the police surgeon to sign him off sick just to get him out of the way.'

'There!' Burnside shouts. 'Stop and rewind it to, "Then you should have arranged it better". Listen to the way he rolls his "r"s. And on "arses" and "surgeon".'

Pauline complies. 'I'd say he's got a very educated voice. But there is a faint burr.'

'Play a bit more,' Burnside instructs, sitting forward.

'I assume you got your so-called specialist to do the job?
I hope so, for your sake. Forensics have found a partial
footprint outside Burnside's window. I wouldn't like to hear
it had a Cuban heel.'

'Did you hear it there? On "forensics" and "partial"?'

'Not to mention "Burnside",' Pauline adds dryly. 'That's
where it's strongest of all.'

'You know what this means?'

'Tell me.'

'If this is Webster – the same Webster that's running Pepper –
the entire operation's bent from the top down.'

'And Pepper's supposed to be rooting out corruption in the
Met?'

'Burying it, more like, from the sound of it. No wonder...'

'Are you sure it's him? Webster's a common name and the
accent's not that obvious. I didn't pick up on it first time round.'

'It's been twenty years. Long enough to tone his act down,
especially if he fast-tracked through the ranks, which he must
have. You don't get promoted to commander looking like
bleedin' McCloud and sounding like a yokel.'

'Mc-who?'

'You're too young.'

Pauline frowns. 'Why's it called Operation Pepper, anyway?'

Burnside gets to his feet. 'Sergeant Pepper. Think of the first
line.' Pauline is still frowning. 'Jesus. The bloody Beatles. Are you
trying to make me feel old?' He strides out of shot. 'I need to
take a leak.'

'It's about lonely hearts. The band sings it at Silks,' she shouts
after him.

Burnside laughs mirthlessly. A door bangs.

While he's out, Pauline checks the recording time left on the camera. We see her face up close, so close that it's not a face, more a landscape of distorted features. She steps back and we regain the perspective. Pauline regards the minute lens, hands on hips, as if it were an interlocutor accusing her of something, then she shrugs and returns to the sofa.

A few minutes later Burnside's back, jubilant. 'I've got it.' He sits down next to Pauline. His eyes are glowing. 'I've just remembered. Outside the magistrates' court, after Dawson and Mal were acquitted. They were with a couple of other blokes, talking about something. I didn't take much notice at the time; I was too intent on bawling Mal out. He reminded me about it yesterday. My mind's been coming back to it on and off ever since. One of them had a 'tache and collar-length hair. It was David Webster, I'm sure of it.' He clicks his fingers. 'Piece of piss.'

'You've lost me.'

Burnside looks as if he hasn't heard her. 'It doesn't get me that much further, though.'

'Why not?'

'I know who. I know where. But I still don't know why.'

TRANSCRIPT OF FILM, TAPE 139V/404. PAULINE'S FLAT, HAMMERSMITH.
14.03.00, 17.30

Burnside and Pauline are playing back the footage he shot at Mal's. They are sitting together, comfortable but not intimate. Pauline is scribbling notes in a reporter's pad. They do not talk while they watch the tape. Eventually, Burnside points the remote at the TV and freezes the video.

'Would you buy a used car off of that man?'

Pauline puts down her pen and picks up a mug of tea from the low table in front of them. 'Nope. Not after that little stunt of his at the start.'

'Which one?'

'What we girls would call, "is that a gun in your pocket or are you just pleased to see me?".'

Burnside snorts. 'Mal always overdid it trying to impress the ladies.'

'*She* seems impressed with him,' Pauline jeers. 'What a bimbo! Talk about trophy wife.'

Burnside looks faintly discomfited. 'She tried to tell me they weren't getting on, but I think she's in this with him.'

'Really? I can't believe there are all these women involved in exploiting other women. Clare Miller, Debbie Burnside… I mean, the men you can understand…' Pauline sips her tea thoughtfully. 'So, let me get all this straight: you think Davor Tomasic recruits the girls in Zagreb through his agency and ships them to London hidden in Mal's lorries?'

'It's a possibility.'

'And he's got some sort of arrangement with Xsecs?'

'At a guess I'd say Miller keeps a few for appearances, like those twins and Kristina, and feeds the rest through to Dawson. He gets his mileage out of 'em, flogs 'em to the ponces and it's all downhill from there.'

'But the other eye-witnesses…' Pauline jumps up and returns with a foolscap folder. She pulls out pictures and hands them to Burnside. 'Suzanne Kelly, Catherine O'Leary. Pretty young English girls. They've both got potential as proper models. Why would Miller and Dawson risk using kids like them? They were bound to speak out.'

Burnside shrugs. 'They probably aren't representative. Remember what Kristina said? The minute it looked like she was getting a break – something that didn't involve showing tits or arse – Miller sabotaged it. Maybe she did the same with the other two. If Dawson came sniffing around like he did with Kristina and made them some sort of cushty offer, they'd 've leapt at the chance, same as she did.'

'That doesn't make sense.' Pauline frowns. 'Surely Miller would want her models to be successful.'

'Reverse psychology.' Burnside taps the side of his head. 'Believe it or not, Clare Miller used to be a model. Not the *Vogue* kind, I grant you. Fetish mags. Whips, rubber, manacles, masks. I shouldn't think that was her first choice when she started out, either.'

'You think she's just jealous? That's a bit twisted, isn't it?'

'The female mind...' Burnside arches an eyebrow at Pauline. 'Is infinitely twisted. As I've learned to my cost.'

'Hah!' She is about to hit him with a rolled up newspaper when a high-pitched ringing signals a mobile going off. Both Pauline and Burnside start patting pockets and reaching for bags. It turns out to be Burnside's. He waves at Pauline to be quiet. 'Hello? Superintendent Sutton... No, I've been on sick leave, as requested... Suspended? Why? No...no... you've got it all wrong, sir... Someone's giving you misinformation... Yeah, well that's where it's coming from... It ain't ridiculous, sir, and I'll prove it to you... It makes the world of difference. Look sir, I'm being set up. Now I don't know how much you know... Frankly, I don't know who I can trust. I've had two attempts on my life, how do you explain that?... That's rubbish... Keith Gaughan?... Dead?... When?...Of course it ain't....Yeah, I saw him lunchtime. We talked. That was all... No! Forget it. No. I ain't coming in... Well you'll have to find me first.' He punches the 'off' button and hurls the phone across the room, sending Pauline's cat skittering for the door. 'Bastards!'

'Come on.' Pauline holds his arm. 'Calm down.'

Burnside's eyes are steely. 'They're closing in. I'm so near, and yet I keep coming up against a bloody brick wall.'

'Who's dead? And what's it got to do with you?' she asks anxiously.

'Keith Gaughan. Used to be a Met. Police solicitor. I went to see him today. His secretary found him shot dead in his office half an hour ago.' Burnside bows his head. 'Gaughan was the only name Hedges could dig up connected with Mal and Dawson's burglary trial. The only one still alive, anyway – the OIC topped himself – that's why I went to see him.' He looks up at Pauline again, his face weary. 'I didn't have anything on him, not as such; it was just a fishing trip. But when I mentioned the name Burnside, he started sweating and I figured I might be on to something. That's when it occurred to me someone might've bought him off originally.'

'Bought him off? You mean, paid him to lose the case?'

'Happens more than you'd think.'

'What did he say?'

'Denied it, didn't he? But it got him rattled. He must've spoken to someone about it afterwards and they decided to buy his silence permanently. I'd feel sorry for the bugger if Bromley Police hadn't found my card on him. I'm the chief suspect.'

'Oh, God.'

'Yeah.' Burnside gets up and walks out of shot.

Pauline gets up too and (presumably) joins him. We hear her say, 'They don't know about me, though, do they? So they won't know where to look for you.'

'I can't stay holed up here. The only chance I've got now is to nail Dawson and persuade him to talk.'

'How will you do that? Dawson won't confess. Not if this Commander Webster's calling the shots.'

'I'll think of something. Let's get part one out the way, first.'

'Who? You and me?' Pauline sounds excited.

'Forget it. Anyway, I thought you never wanted to see that

176

rhinestone cowboy again.'

'I do if it means seeing him in handcuffs.'

'Clare Miller's rubbed off on you, I see.'

'Frank! I'm serious. How else are you going to get inside Silks? Security have been briefed not to let you near the place and they won't bother being polite. You should have seen the mess Steve made of Tony's face.'

'I wish I had.'

Pauline ignores this and continues. 'Whereas I can walk in as normal, no questions asked, and let you in through the back when the coast's clear. Da-dah!' She returns to the sofa and flings herself backwards onto it, arms outstretched.

'Ain't Dawson gonna be surprised to see you back at work?'

'I'll front him out, don't worry.'

Burnside walks back into the frame and sits down again beside her. 'You're doing it again, Pauline.'

'What?' She shoots him a comical sidewards look.

'Your Lois Lane impersonation. What if Dawson tries it on again? I can't burst in through locked doors to rescue you.'

'Frank Burnside in tights. Now there's a thought.' She runs a hand lightly over his thigh, giggling.

'You're behaving like a kid.' He takes her roughly by the shoulders and forces her to look at him. 'A man died this afternoon because I went to see him. Kristina Tomasic's been kidnapped, plus two other girls. That lunatic Dawson tried to kill the pair of us. And you still think this is some wild gig that'll bag you the scoop of the century. For Christ's sake, Pauline, get real!'

'Ow, you're hurting me.'

She tries to wriggle free but Burnside's grip is vice-like. He shakes her, his eyes blazing. 'It's not a game!' He's shouting in her face. 'You could get killed.'

'So could you. Let. Me. Go!' Burnside releases her. Pauline rubs her shoulders. 'And trying to intimidate me won't help. If Dawson doesn't get you, Webster will. He's not just going to suspend you, is he? You'll be – rubbed out – that's what they say, isn't it? Before you get the chance to drop him in it. Then they'll all get away with it.'

Burnside glowers.

'Admit it. You need me.'

He stands up. 'I've got Hedges.'

'His hands are tied, you told me.'

'He'd turn out as backup, I know he would.'

'With the rest of the cavalry close behind.'

'It's a risk I've got to take.'

'OK.' Pauline stands too, facing him. 'You still haven't told me how you're going to get into Silks.'

Burnside is silent.

'Admit it, you need me.' She moves closer to him.

Burnside's mouth twitches.

'Say the words: "I need you, Pauline".'

Burnside tries not to, but he can't stop the smile.

'You can do it. "I".'

'I.' The smile reaches his eyes.

'"Need".'

'Need.' He takes her by the shoulders. Gently, this time.

'"You".'

'You.' He draws her to him, wrapping his arms around her.

'"Pauline".'

'Pauline.' He breathes the name into her hair.

She tilts her face up to gaze at him. 'See. Wasn't difficult, was it?'

'You twisted the meaning.' He brushes her lips with his, slowly, deliberately; a soft, teasing lip-kiss. His mouth moves over her eyes, her nose, her chin, her neck, her ears, her throat. Pauline tips back her head, her eyes closed, swaying against him, letting him graze on her exposed skin. He puts a hand in her hair, pulling her back up, and plants his mouth on hers. They kiss with sudden savagery, teeth clashing, tongues lashing. When they finally pull apart, both are panting. 'Like I said.' Burnside unbuttons her blouse and slides down Pauline's bra strap. He bends his lips to her breast. 'Infinitely twisted.'

E-mail

From: Frank Burnside   Sent: 14 March
To: gary.hedges@crimeocu.gov.uk
Subject: Playmates climax

Gather you're on overtime. My fault no doubt. Sorry you copped the flack. Assuming Sutton's requisitioned your mobile. Meet me at Silks, 21.30. May need backup. Delete this.

Burnside.

E-mail

From: Gary Hedges   Sent: 14 March
To: fburnside@cwcom.net
Subject: Playmates climax – reply

Will do.

PS: HGV registered to M. Burnside Haulage has shown up on security video from Maidstone Services. Time code fits with assault on Sanja Gregovic. Surprise, surprise. I double-checked tapes this afternoon after what you said. Terri reviewed them last week, she must have missed it.

'...The parents of missing four-year-old Katie Watson have issued an emotional appeal for her safe return. The little girl, who is asthmatic and needs to use an inhaler, disappeared this morning on Hampstead Heath. Katie was out walking with the family's au pair and another girl when two men jumped out of bushes and dragged them into a van parked nearby. Police were initially unsure as to whether the four-year-old had actually been abducted or simply left behind, like her baby brother. Rescue teams have been combing the area for six hours now and, having found no sign of Katie, the feeling is that she must have been snatched with the two teenagers.

'Fifteen-year-old Croatian Kristina Tomasic had been with the Watsons only two months and spoke limited English. Nobody knows who her companion was, or whether it was Kristina or Katie who was the object of the kidnapping. Gerald Watson is the owner of Pulp!, a company that has revolutionised plastic mouldings, and it's thought that his personal fortune, valued at around 2.2 million pounds, could be the reason behind his daughter's disappearance. Police are said to be following up several leads, though as yet no ransom has been demanded. The van was later discovered in Greenwich...'

Piece to camera by Pauline Chambers,
14.03.00, 20.00
Pauline is sitting at her dressing table. She is wearing her 'Posh Spice' corset, flashy diamante earrings and a broad velvet choker, which she adjusts to cover a lovebite. The set-up is being recorded by an ordinary camcorder, positioned on the bed behind her. Reflected in the dressing-table mirror is the cramped, untidy room. The duvet is rumpled and several pillows lay scattered on the floor. Pauline, dropping her jaw, applies black mascara to her

thick eyelashes. Her hand trembles slightly. She stops and, looking in the mirror, addresses the camera.

PAULINE'S VOICEOVER: 'As you can see, I'm getting ready to go out. This is going to be my last undercover assignment at Silks and, probably, my most dangerous. My encounter with Peter Dawson last night, unpleasant though it was, revealed proof of his home-grown porn industry and confirmed our eyewitness's statement. I am returning to the club tonight because, this time, we are going to arrest him. Using the element of surprise, DCI Burnside and myself intend to overpower him before he can put up a fight. It's our best chance of success, but the plan's not without risk. Dawson has access to guns and, as we've experienced, knows how to use them.'

Pauline picks up a brush and applies powder, dusting her nose, forehead and chin meticulously. She seems calm and composed. Gesticulating with a lipstick, she continues. 'What makes this all the more perilous is that we can't rely on police backup. In fact, we may have less to fear from Peter Dawson than the police themselves. Corruption in the Metropolitan Police is at the heart of this story, something our team could never have predicted when we set out to expose Dawson's underage sex scandal.

'Even more incredibly, at least one "bent" senior policeman is part of an operation designed to root out corruption within the force. This individual has been using his influence to frame the investigating officer, DCI Burnside, a ruse I initially fell for. It was some time before I realised that Burnside was not, in fact, the villain of the piece, but a hero.' Pauline applies the red lipstick, pursing her mouth into an 'O' and then blotting her lips with a tissue. She applies another coat and bares her teeth in a bizarre snarl to check for smears.

'Being a professional, Frank Burnside himself wouldn't describe himself in that way; as far as he's concerned, he's just doing his job. He's a reserved man who, I am quite sure, wouldn't submit to being filmed voluntarily. While I respect and admire his modest stance, I feel his story deserves to be told, hence the continued use of secret cameras. It's deceitful, I know – Frank Burnside and I have become close friends during the course of this investigation – but, in the end, he may come to thank me for it.'

Pauline fluffs her short spiky hair with her fingers and rubs hair gel into it, accentuating the 'Posh' look. Looking straight into the mirror, she continues her narration. 'After all, we have no other witnesses. It's our word against the might of the Met. We need the cameras to prove that to you. Burnside's protagonist has a contract out on his life. He's also got him suspended from duty and very probably framed him for the murder of a solicitor, Keith Gaughan. At this very minute, on this man's instructions, Burnside's fellow officers from Crime Operational Command Unit are trying to find him to bring him in. As Burnside himself said to me earlier, "They're closing in".'

She swivels round to face the camera, her face now an unnatural, over-made-up mask. She wears the minute frown of a TV presenter being serious. It's as if, by talking in journalese, she is distancing herself from what she's about to undertake.

'That is why tonight's operation is of the utmost secrecy. Only myself and DCI Burnside will be taking part, with backup from his most trusted sergeant. Even by alerting him, we may have put ourselves at risk. We know his movements are being monitored but we can't afford to tackle this entirely by ourselves. Unknown to Burnside, I will have my own crew standing by outside the club as well. *Whatever* happens this evening, they will record the outcome.' She shivers suddenly; a chink in the armour. Standing up, she announces, 'I suspect it's going to be an eventful night.' With that, she switches the camcorder off.

TRANSCRIPT OF FILM, TAPE 234V/404. SILKS (PAULINE'S P.O.V.). 14.03.00, 21.30

The camera is bobbing along a narrow corridor in semi-darkness, like a creepy steadicam shot in a slasher movie. There is a soundtrack of clacking heels and rapid breathing. In the background, faint music, overlaid with the just-discernible sound of angry male voices. The camera-wearer, Pauline, stumbles and swears, causing the picture to dip and swoop. Limping slightly, she hurries on, around a corner and down an echoing flight of stone steps, stopping at a blue fire door with a bar across it. Above the doorway, a neon 'Exit' sign flickers feebly. Another sign on the back of the door reads 'Warning! This door is alarmed'. She twists round, checking behind, then pushes down hard on the bar. The door bursts open with a noisy clang, revealing Burnside standing in the dark.

He checks his watch. 'On the dot.' His breath comes out in a white cloud. He rubs his gloved hands together.

'Quick, come in. You've got ten seconds.' Pauline yanks him inside. The door slams shut. She tenses. No alarm sounds.

Burnside puts an arm around her shoulders. 'You OK?'

'Yeah. Just,' she replies in a low voice. 'Something's going on, though. Dawson's in his office having a mega row with someone. I couldn't make out who it was. Watch the steps.' At the top she freezes and holds up her hand. 'Wait!' There's the squeak of footsteps coming towards them. Pauline looks at Burnside, her eyes wide with fear. There's a door on their left. Burnside tests it. It opens. They creep inside, Burnside pulling the door quietly to behind them. The space is pitch black. In the darkness, their breathing sounds extra-loud. The footsteps draw closer. Pauline swallows. The footsteps are outside the door. The two of them hold their breath. The footsteps carry on, jogging down the stone steps. We hear the exit door clang, then slam shut. Pauline and Burnside exhale.

'How often is that exit used?' he mutters.

'Don't know. The bar staff sneak out for a fag break. They've got some sort of system with the key. You can't wedge the door open or all hell breaks loose.'

'Better stay here 'til they've gone back, then.' He fumbles for the light switch. Suddenly the cramped space is flooded with light. The camera is pointing at a mop head. 'Looks like we're in the caretaker's cupboard.' Burnside grins at Pauline. 'I was hoping for the girls' changing rooms.'

'Behave.' She nudges him. 'And switch that light off. It might show up from outside.'

'Murder in the dark.' Burnside obviously gropes her, for Pauline yelps.

'Jesus! Don't say that. And don't do that, either.'

'Spoilsport.'

The back door clicks open two minutes later, signalling the return of the smoker. They fall silent. Once again, the footsteps pass by without pausing. When they are well clear, Burnside and Pauline slip out into the corridor. They walk swiftly, not speaking. The music – an inevitable Beatles medley – grows louder. Beyond the (almost) soundproofed door into the club's main area, the resident combo is singing 'Can't Buy Me Love'. Burnside, who has taken the lead, mouths 'Dawson's office?' Pauline points to a short flight of steps off to the left, this time leading upwards. They mount the steps and are taken round to the right, where they come to two doors. Behind the first one comes the sound of raised voices.

'... so what were you planning on doing? Throwing a teddy bears' picnic down the depot?' It's Dawson's voice.

'I wasn't *planning* on bringing the kid. But we 'ad no choice. She was making too much bleedin' racket and she was holding on like a limpet. We couldn't hang about so we shoved her in too.'

Burnside glances at Pauline, frowning in concentration.

'And now you've got every copper both sides of the river out looking for 'er,' Dawson seethes. 'Bigfoot can't help, it's gone way beyond him. Whose bright idea was this? Yours or Clare's? No, don't tell me. You ain't got the gumption; it must've been madam. Stupid bleedin' cow. What she want to snatch Kristina for? She wouldn't say nothing, she's got Davor's interests to protect.'

'It was just supposed to be that girl Sanja. But they was all together – '

'So you thought you'd get three for the price of one. Nice one.'

Burnside leans close to Pauline and breathes, 'It's Mal.'

'Well, I ain't the only one keeping the filth busy. How long before they find your paw prints on Gaughan, eh?' Mal's voice sounds a triumphant note.

'They won't. I took precautions.' Dawson cackles at his little joke. 'And your brother made it so easy for me. Bigfoot was killing himself when I told him.'

'Yeah, well, Frank's too warm for my liking.' Mal retorts. 'He was sniffing round mine yesterday. And if he's talked to Gaughan...'

'Gaughan didn't say nothin'. I made sure of that before I popped him.'

'Yeah, but when Frank's got the scent, he don't give up. You hit him, he comes back at you, harder. Bigfoot says he's gonna spring him, but will he do it in time? See what I'm driving at?' Mal pauses, then adds: 'I mean, we're expendable, you and me. If Frank talks, Bigfoot'll deny everything. And guess who'll carry the can.'

Burnside throws open the door.

TRANSCRIPT OF FILM, TAPE 235V/404. SILKS
(DAWSON'S OFFICE).
14.03.00, 21.36
(Footage has been taken from the fixed-position camera in Dawson's office.)

'Good point, Mal.' Burnside strides into the room. 'I think we've all learned something here. Never trust a copper.' Dawson and Mal, caught unawares, look gobsmacked. When Pauline sidles in after Burnside, Dawson's jaw practically hits the floor. 'Don't bleedin' well stand there, girl; call the police,' he expostulates. 'Number's on the till behind the bar. Tell 'em it's me. And tell 'em I've got Frank Burnside in me office.' He smiles nastily. 'They'll love that.'

'Too late, pal. They're already on their way.' Burnside's smile is equally dangerous. 'I went through a different channel. Just to make sure. Like I said, you can't be too careful.' He glances at a clock on the wall. 'Should be here about now.' Without taking his eyes off Dawson and Mal he says to Pauline, 'You're a greeter, ain't you? Go and make them welcome ' She acts fazed and casts a look at Dawson. Dawson leans back in his chair, playing it cool, still in his shades. 'He's bluffing, Posh. Burnside's a wanted man. They'll 'ave him.'

Burnside propels her with a sharp push. 'I said "go".' Pauline leaves. 'Not you Mal,' Burnside says to his brother, who is half out of his seat. 'You ain't going nowhere. This ends here.'

Mal gets up and takes a step towards him. 'And you're gonna stop me, are you?'

'I beat the crap out of you last time and if necessary I'll do it again.'

'Yeah, well that was twenty years ago. Look at the state of yer now.' Mal is in Burnside's face. He is taller than him, and looks fitter. They eyeball each other. Burnside lifts his chin. He does not budge.

There is a metallic click. It's a gun being cocked. We cannot see it – Dawson is out of shot – but the sound is unmistakable. Burnside and Mal swivel round. Dawson, off camera, drawls, 'Boys, boys. This ain't the playground, it's the West End. The wild West End.' He savours the phrase, rolling his tongue round it as if he's been waiting to use it for a long time. 'We sort things out different, here.' The glint of a Beretta semi-automatic pistol catches the light as it noses into the frame. Dawson is standing with his back to the hidden camera, presumably almost right beneath it because his stiffly extended right arm is all we can see of him. He waves the muzzle at Mal. 'Stand aside, partner.'

Burnside looks at his brother. 'I've got you down for smuggling and kidnapping but not murder.' He flicks his eyes at Dawson. 'Makes a big difference. That nutter's looking at least one count of murder and two of attempted murder, not to mention all the other stuff. You give me the low-down on that and I'll make sure your co-operation is taken into account.'

Mal hesitates. Dawson waves the gun again. 'Mal. Get out the way.'

'Who do you think he's going shoot next after he's blown me away?' Burnside says, ignoring Dawson. 'You've been his stooge for too long, Mal. Can't you think for yourself any more?' He moves closer and mutters, 'You won't make it out. My backup's going to be here any minute. Dawson knows that. He'll shoot me, then shoot you, make it look like we had a fight. You were right about being expendable. You're even more expendable than he is.'

'I'm warning you.' The pistol is steady in Dawson's hand.

Mal steps back. 'We was just discussing Frank's last will and testament. He said he'd leave me all his worldly goods – if he had any.' His laugh is hollow, scornful. Apparently he joins Dawson, for he moves out of the picture. Dawson chuckles. 'I 'ope you kissed goodbye while you was at it.'

Burnside is left standing alone under the stark fluorescent striplight. His forehead glistens with sweat. 'Are you going to stand by and let that freakin' cowboy murder your own brother, Mal? Ain't our past worth anything? Growing up together, pulling birds together, being in the gang together, fighting side by side?' Mal is silent. Burnside swallows. 'Remember that time, when we was up against Burrows' mob? When John Harding had a knife at your throat? I looked out for you, didn't I? He gave me this – remember?' Burnside yanks up his sleeve, revealing a scar on his forearm. 'I always looked out for you.'

Still Mal says nothing. Burnside lowers his arm. Dawson tenses his arm. Burnside stares straight ahead.

Dawson's finger is on the trigger. 'Hasta la vista, baby.'

Mal's hand clamps down on the pistol. The shot misses.

Unbalanced by the kickback and Mal's intervention, Dawson is easily overcome. 'Hey! What d'you do that for?'

Mal is walking backwards now, away from Dawson, holding the gun on him. 'Because.'

'I don't understand,' Dawson whines. 'Give me the gun. Don't listen to him.'

'Maybe I should've listened to him.' Mal is standing midway between the pair of them now. The hand holding the pistol shakes uncontrollably. 'If I had, I wouldn't be in this mess now, would I?'

Burnside visibly relaxes. 'You've done the right thing, Mal. I can help you. But you've got to give me that first.'

Mal turns round to face him slowly, still pointing the piece.

'Put it down, Mal. Then we can work something out.'

Mal takes a step closer. We can't see his face, only Burnside's. One step more and the gun is against Burnside's chest. 'Did you think,' Mal begins, 'that I would miss an opportunity like this?' He jabs him with it. *Brother.*'

Burnside pales under his tan. 'What are you playing at?'

'I'm not playing at anything.' Mal's voice is cracking, hysterical. 'I just didn't want Pete here to have all the fun. I've been dreaming of this moment for a long, long time.' He's losing it. The gun is practically dancing a tattoo on Burnside's ribs.

'Oh, Jesus.'

'That's right. You start praying.' Mal presses the muzzle into him.

'What did I do?'

'What didn't you do.'

'Tell me, then.'

'I have had to live in your bleedin' shadow all my life. Do you know what it feels like, to come second? Not just second, but a piss-poor second. To be little brother to big Frank, head of the firm?' He pokes him again. 'You ain't got the faintest idea, have you? While you was swaggering about, being cock of the walk, I was being bullied and picked on. When you weren't there, of course.'

Frank regards the wavering gun with popping eyes, his hands raised in submission. Mal, relishing his power, is spraying sentences in his face. 'Oh, yeah, it may have been "Burnside's manor", but there was only one Burnside, wasn't there? Only one that counted. No one wanted me in the gang.' He prods him in the chest again. 'And it was the same with birds, remember? They all went for that mean and moody act of yours. When we went out on the pull, you got the babe, I got the dog. It was like I was bleeding invisible when you was around.' He is ranting now. 'I didn't want you fighting my battles. I wanted people to respect me for being me. That's why I joined up with him.' He jerks his head in Dawson's direction. 'It was the best way I knew to break free of you.'

'You're remembering it all wrong,' Frank growls. 'You were the favourite. Couldn't put a foot wrong at home. You were the golden boy.'

'I ain't talking about what those two old coots thought. On the street, that's where it mattered.'

Frank's eyebrows shoot skywards. 'I don't believe I'm hearing this. I had to fight to earn that reputation and I had to fight to keep it, every single day.' Suddenly, he is on the attack, apparently ignoring the gun. 'I was the one copped all the flack. I don't recall you being glassed, or beaten up or hauled down the nick to be cautioned. I don't recall Dad taking his belt to you. He used to drag me back home and I'd see your face looking out the window, all butter-wouldn't-melt. You loved it. You had it bloody easy, you did.'

Mal's face is suffused, livid. He sticks the Beretta under Frank's chin. 'I ain't gonna stand here arguing the toss with you, brother.' He jabs him with the muzzle. 'I don't need to.'

From across the room, Dawson shouts, 'Just blow his bleedin' brains out, Mal, for Christ's sake!'

Distracted by the interruption, Mal's eyes leave Frank's face for a split second. It's all Frank needs. He sidesteps to the right, grabbing the barrel of the piece, pushing its nose upwards. The two men wrestle for control. It's an oddly silent fight, no shouts or yells, just huffing and panting and straining. Dawson keeps well out of range. Mal still has his finger on the trigger. He and Frank sway together, mirroring each other, their arms locked on

190

the gun: it's almost balletic. Suddenly, Mal manages to push Frank off balance. He staggers, falling backwards over a coffee table, taking Mal down with him. There's a sharp crack – someone's head – and a cry. We can't see who's hurt; it's difficult to make out what is happening. They scrap behind the low table, grunting. A chair leg splinters and snaps like balsa wood. Magazines and an ashtray go flying. Someone is making a choking noise.

The choking noise gets louder, becomes gurgling.

Dawson tiptoes into the picture, craning his neck.

The gun goes off, the bullet shattering an Art Deco lampshade. Pieces of red glass rain down on the white carpet like drops of blood. The gurgling ceases. There's a sharp intake of breath, followed by a sudden, violent thrust, a bone-crunching punch, an awful moan. One hand holds the semi-automatic aloft.

'Burnside!' The voice is a hiss of pure hate.

The arm is yanked down. The gun goes off again, the retort echoing round the room. This time, the carpet is spattered with real blood.

TRANSCRIPT OF FILM, TAPE 236V/404. SILKS (PAULINE'S P.O.V.).
14.03.00, 21.46
Pauline is tottering through the main area of the club, weaving her way past waiters, hostesses, punters. We get a succession of rapid close-ups in the dim light: someone's striped tie, a girl's upholstered cleavage, a tray of dead glasses, the dandruff-speckled collar of a man's jacket. The club is packed and noisy, raucous laughter ringing out from a garrulous stag party, champagne corks popping amid cheers and applause. Through the fug, a tall man is just visible, his height putting him head and

shoulders above the crowd. He strides away from the camera, heading purposefully towards a door near the bar marked 'Private'. Pauline is following him, at a distance. There is no sign of DS Gary Hedges.

She lingers outside the door for a count of ten, then goes through. On the other side of the not-quite-soundproofed door, the volume level drops to a dull roar. She pauses. Heavy footsteps tread the corridor ahead. Pauline takes off her high heels and pads noiselessly after them. We retrace the route she and Burnside took earlier, up a short flight of stairs and round a corner. The door to Dawson's office is open. Apparently, the tall man has gone inside. She inches closer, hugging the wall. A voice with a faint, but unmistakable Bristol burr can be heard saying, 'Good try, Peter, but I really don't think that you, of all people, are in any position to bargain.'

Dawson snorts. 'What? You're so bent you make old Burnside here look like a bleedin' saint. And that's saying something.'

Someone groans heavily. Pauline catches her breath.

'Thanks for nothing, pal.' It's Frank's voice. 'If that's your idea of sweet-talking, you're digging yourself in deeper every minute.' Pauline exhales again. Staying out of sight, she peers through the half-open door. The camera shows blood and glass everywhere. There's a body on the floor, wedged behind a coffee table. It's Mal. He appears to be curled up in a foetal position, clutching his leg. He groans again. 'For God's sake, somebody help me. I'm dying here.'

'You'll live for another ten minutes while we sort this out,' Frank snaps harshly. He chucks him a white linen teatowel, presumably from a wine bucket. 'Wrap this round it and stick your leg up on the table, keep it elevated.'

Pauline pushes the door gently. Instantly, there's the ratcheting noise of a gun being cocked. The door swings open. Burnside is pointing a revolver right at her. She screams.

'Jesus, Pauline. I nearly shot you.' He swings back to cover Dawson and Webster – for it is he – who are standing against the far wall with their hands on their heads. 'Where's Hedges?'

'"Pauline"?' Dawson's query is simultaneous.

She opens her mouth to speak, but Webster interrupts. 'DS Hedges is currently tied up at the office with some extremely pressing paperwork – namely, the warrant for your arrest.' He smiles the unruffled smile of a player holding all the cards. Glancing at the clock he continues, 'I expect him here shortly, but don't think he's going to come riding to your rescue. Quite the opposite.' He turns to Dawson and mutters, just loud enough for everyone to hear, 'Then we can put a stop to this tedious business and all go home.'

Clearly Dawson doesn't share Webster's confidence, for he ignores him and says to Burnside, 'Look, Frank. I ain't exactly sure what you know – and I certainly ain't sure who that scheming little bitch is,' he glares at Pauline, 'but I've got enough to nail this geezer for a lifetime. Considering what matey boy's got lined up for you, that's gotta be worth doin' a deal. Whaddya say?'

Webster sighs, feigning boredom. 'You're bluffing, Peter. I'm sure even Mr Burnside – I'm afraid you've been stripped of your rank and number *in absentia*,' he nods at Frank, 'has the intelligence to realise that.'

'You wanker,' Dawson snarls. 'You think you're so bleedin' clever, don't you? So far above me, Mr high-and-mighty policeman. Well, I ain't stupid. I got my insurance. You're stuffed, mate.' He turns back to Frank and waves a hand at a Hi-Fi system in the corner. 'Switch on the tuner and press "play". There's a tape already in there.'

TRANSCRIPT OF AUDIO CASSETTE, TAPE 90A/92.
CONCEALED TAPE MADE BY KEITH GAUGHAN, LOCATION,
DATE AND TIME OF RECORDING UNKNOWN.
(FOUR VOICES ON THE TAPE HAVE BEEN IDENTIFIED:
THOSE OF DAVID WEBSTER, KEITH GAUGHAN, MALCOLM
BURNSIDE AND PETER DAWSON. A FIFTH MALE VOICE
APPARENTLY BELONGS TO SOMEONE CALLED WILKINS.)

WEBSTER [*muffled but audible*]: 'What in Christ's name were you thinking of, man? We agreed: no guns. That was a condition, remember? Do you think for one minute we'd have cut you the slack otherwise?'

DAWSON: 'No.'

[*Sound of a door creaking open. Apparently it's Gaughan joining the meeting, for the voices become louder and clearer.*]

DAWSON: ''ey! What's 'e doing 'ere?'

WEBSTER: 'Come to check he's made the right career move. Haven't you, Mr Gaughan?'

GAUGHAN: 'Um, well, yes, you could, er, put it like that.'

DAWSON [*to Webster*]: 'I suppose you told 'im we'd be 'ere.'

WEBSTER: 'What a short memory you've got, Peter. You and Mal wouldn't be here at all now if it wasn't for this – gentleman. I think he has a right to see where his next paycheck's coming from. Especially since it's unlikely to be the MPS. Is it, Keith?'

GAUGHAN: 'Er, no.'

DAWSON: 'Being booted out, are yer?'

GAUGHAN: 'No. Absolutely not. DS Webster and I both think it would be a propitious time for me to set up in private practice.'

DAWSON [*laughing*]: 'He's being booted out.'

WEBSTER [*sharp*]: 'Let's concentrate on your own future, shall we, Peter? Your's and your sidekick's here. Because after Saturday's little fiasco, it may not be quite as rosy as you think.'

DAWSON: 'Yeah, well, we'll have to lay low for a bit. But we was gonna anyway.'

WEBSTER: 'You murdered a police officer. PC Underwood had only been in the job eight months. His wife's expecting their first child. Poor bastard's fatherless already. The Press is going mad. We're being railroaded by public sympathy. Upstairs is expecting a result.'

DAWSON: 'Look, we was wearing masks. No one could've recognised us. Bell didn't see nothing, he was inside the hotel. The courier scarpered. And the driver was hiding on the floor of his cab. I don't see what you're so frigging worried about.'

MAL: 'It ain't like Cook's firm's gonna be makin' a song and dance about how they lost two million quid's worth of stolen diamonds.'

WEBSTER: 'Not publicly. But Neil Cook will leave no stone unturned to find them. I wouldn't be so damn cocky if I were you.'

DAWSON: 'We got you lot to protect us, ain't we?'

WEBSTER: 'I don't recall Wilkins or myself agreeing to that. Do you?'

'WILKINS': 'No.'

WEBSTER: 'So there's only one thing for it.'

DAWSON: 'What's that?'

WEBSTER: 'You two get out of London – preferably out of the country – tonight. Before this blows up in everyone's faces. There's no rush on the gems. Start flashing them about now and you'll have the Amsterdam lot on your tail.'

DAWSON: 'You sayin' our snout will grass us up?'

WEBSTER: 'Cook and Bell are going to interrogate every single person who knew about this. And they won't mess about.'

MAL [*shuddering*]: 'Nah. I heard what they did to that other geezer. And that was for shunting Neil's motor.'

WEBSTER: 'It's not only Cook's lot. The courier might start talking. The hotel doorman might have a partial description. The taxi driver might have heard you speak. More eyewitnesses could come forward. It's just not safe.'

DAWSON: 'I always fancied going somewhere 'ot.'

MAL: 'I was gonna go up North anyway, stay out of Frank's hair.'

WEBSTER: 'Which brings me to the problem of Burnside.'

MAL: 'Yeah?'

WEBSTER: 'Not you, man. Your brother. He saw us all together.'

'WILKINS': 'Most of us.'

DAWSON: 'Come on, guys, stay cool. All Burnside knows is, his brother's been a naughty boy, he's slapped his wrists and banished him to Brum. 'e was so mad Mal was up on a charge that 'e didn't even notice who he was talkin' to. I bet yer.'

WEBSTER [*conferring*]: 'Peter could be right.'

'WILKINS': 'Nonetheless…'

WEBSTER: 'Put out a smokescreen?'

'WILKINS': 'Exactly.'

MAL: 'What do you mean?'

DAWSON: 'He means, let Frankie boy take the rap for us getting off last Tuesday.'

MAL: 'How?'

DAWSON: 'Yeah, how?'

WEBSTER [*clearing his throat*]: 'I don't know whether you were aware, Malcolm, but when Frank heard you'd been charged with burglary, he personally intervened on your behalf. I gather he told the officer in charge it was a first offence and there were mitigating circumstances and asked him to drop the charges.'

MAL: 'I didn't know that.'

WEBSTER: 'No. Well, it didn't cut any ice with Hugh Parry so he obviously gave up on the idea. Which is not to say that we

need to...' [*He mutters something inaudible to the other man.*
They confer in low voices and seem to reach a conclusion.]
WEBSTER: 'Good. That's settled. Plus it draws the attention
away from Mr Gaughan's hapless muddling of his witnesses,
which I'm sure he'll be glad about. Best to start up your own
practice with a clean sheet, eh, Keith?'
GAUGHAN [*muttering, embarrassed*]: 'Quite so, quite so.'
 WEBSTER: 'And as for you two, you'd better start packing.'
[*Scraping noise of chairs being pushed back*] 'Drop me a line
with your whereabouts, Peter. I'll let you know when things have
calmed down here.'
DAWSON: 'I can't just drop everything and disappear. I got stuff
to sort out. Not to mention my bird. She'll go mental.'
WEBSTER: 'Oh, and no postcards.'

TRANSCRIPT OF FILM, TAPE 237V/404. SILKS
(DAWSON'S OFFICE).
14.03.00, 22.00
Commander David Webster, ignoring Burnside's barked
instruction to the contrary, sinks onto a chair. He holds his head
in his hands. Only then is it possible to see that his thick, dark
hair is in fact thinning at the crown. Mal, on the floor, has
stopped groaning and started shivering. He is deathly pale.
Pauline looks at him with concern.

'This is stupid. He's lost a lot of blood. You've got to call an
ambulance.'

Burnside indicates Dawson's phone. 'Do it from there.' He
stares down at his brother impassively for several seconds, then
turns to Dawson. 'Chuck us your coat.'

With obvious reluctance, Dawson hands over an expensive
trench from a coat hook behind him. Burnside squats down and
drapes it over Mal. He feels his forehead, checks his pulse.

Dawson edges towards the door. Pauline, busy on the phone, doesn't notice. Webster is too absorbed to notice either. Burnside is examining Mal's leg. Dawson, his back to the door, depresses the handle gently, flicks a glance in the direction of Burnside's bowed head, swings round and bolts.

'Frank!' Too late Pauline spots the open door.

Burnside scrabbles to his feet. He's still holding the gun. 'Give me the tape!' he yells to Pauline. She ejects it and throws it to him. Burnside pockets it and starts out of the door. Pauline follows him out. 'What shall I do?' she hisses.

'Just keep Webster there.'

'How?'

'Lock them in if you have to.'

TRANSCRIPT OF FILM, TAPE 238V/404. SILKS (BAR). 14.03.00, 22.01

(The tape has been put together using footage from the remaining secret camera behind the bar and in-house security videos.)

Back in the bar, things are hotting up. The resident band, upgrading their repertoire from the Beatles, is playing a BeeGees medley and the tiny dance floor is thronged with couples making out to 'How Deep is Your Love?' The smoochers are broken up by Dawson, who practically falls through the connecting door and launches himself into the crowd like a guided missile. Scattering couples in his wake, he cannons into a waiter, sending the young man sprawling. A bottle of champagne smashes, to general hilarity from the pie-eyed punters.

Dawson stumbles but manages to stop himself falling by catching hold of a chair. Looking over his shoulder he hurries on, stepping on toes, barging into backs, knocking against people. The volume of complaints increases as, several seconds later, a ruddy-faced Burnside explodes out of the same door and charges after Dawson bellowing, 'Out of the way!' A drunk attempts to stand his ground, swaying in front of him with a stupid leer. Burnside decks him with a punch. Dawson is weaving in and out of tables, heading for the main entrance. It looks as if he might make it. Burnside tries a different tactic. He pulls out a gun. 'Police! Stop that man.'

Pandemonium ensues. Punters assume it's a raid and leap to their feet. Hostesses scream. Chairs are overturned. The staff go into emergency drill, dropping whatever they're doing and bundling for the rear exit, ignoring the predicament of their employer. Dawson is swamped. He lashes out, but only succeeds in felling a potted palm, which impedes his progress even further. He is wrestling with a panicked hostess, who is trying to get past in the opposite direction, when Burnside catches up with him and holds the gun to the back of his head. 'Don't tempt me, Dawson,' he breathes, panting. 'It's a while since I last held a firearm. I'd hate it to go off in my hand.'

Suddenly, the tide of people fighting to get to the main entrance is stemmed by the appearance of half a dozen uniformed officers. Hedges is with them. He scans the chaotic scene, looking for Burnside. Neither Burnside nor Dawson is visible. One of the officers shouts. 'Everybody sit down and stay calm. Go back to your seats.' People see the uniforms and become subdued, shuffling to their former tables. A few attempt to argue the toss and are informed that, if they leave now, it will be in a police van. This has the desired effect. Only when order has been restored do we see Burnside standing over a kneeling Dawson, with the gun trained on him. He looks up at Hedges. 'You took your bleedin' time, didn't you?'

Before Hedges can answer, Webster strolls into the room. He glances at his watch and says coolly, 'Far from it. DS Hedges is right on time. Good work, men.' He nods to the other officers, who have formed a cordon across the main entrance. 'Carry on, Hedges. You can arrest him now.'

'I assume you mean this scumbag.' Burnside prods Dawson with a foot. 'I'd cuff him before he does another runner.'

Hedges looks at Burnside, then at Webster, then at Burnside. 'Guv, I – '

'And after you've nicked him, nick this bastard.' Burnside indicates Commander David Webster. He sees his deputy's confused face. 'I ain't joking, Gazza. This is the bloke behind it all, the geezer who tried to have me topped. He's the one that's been setting me up. He's the one that's bent.'

The room falls silent. Hedges swallows. 'Guv. I've come – I'm under orders – to take you back.'

'Well, get on with it, detective sergeant,' Webster interrupts brusquely. Hedges hesitates. 'For heaven's sake, man, don't listen to Burnside. He's desperate, he'll say anything.' Still Hedges hesitates. Webster's laid-back façade begins to slip. 'DCI Burnside is on suspension pending a full enquiry by Operation Pepper. I cannot go into the nature of his offences, but I assure you they are being taken extremely seriously. Superintendent Sutton will confirm all of this.' His face darkens. 'Now do your duty, or I'll have you suspended as well.'

Hedges can barely bring himself to meet Burnside's eyes. When he does, their accusing glare stops him in his tracks. Webster sighs impatiently and signals to a uniformed officer, who steps forward obediently. 'You. What's your name?'

'Sergeant Pitson, sir.'

'Right, Pitson. It seems Hedges here doesn't have the stomach to arrest his own guvnor. Disarm Burnside and cuff him.'

Pitson lays a hand on Burnside's arm. Burnside shakes him off angrily. 'I ain't finished here yet.' He turns to Hedges. 'What did you think? All that stuff I told you was a load of porkies? Ask her.' He nods at Pauline, who has followed Webster from Dawson's office and joined the circle. 'Ask him.' He jerks his thumb at Dawson, who is being restrained by two other officers. 'Ask my brother. He's through there.' Burnside points to the connecting door. 'Or better still, listen to this.' He produces the tape from his pocket. 'You'll find this explains everything.' His stare challenges Webster to trump this. Webster has one last try.

'That – tape – is a fake. A hoax. It has obviously been made with the intention of incriminating me by Peter Dawson, and once a voice analysis expert has listened to it, they will confirm that. As for taking the word of a common prostitute' – he flicks a scornful glance at Pauline – 'or criminals like Dawson and his associate, I'm sure I don't need to spell out *their* reliability. The fact that he's Burnside's brother speaks volumes.'

Stalemate. Nobody moves. Pauline looks at Burnside, eyebrows raised. Burnside nods. She steps forward and says, 'Commander Webster. The first thing you need to know is, I'm not a "common prostitute". I'm an undercover reporter.' Dawson's puffy face – he has lost his dark glasses – contorts into a snarl. Webster looks taken aback. 'The second thing you need to know is that I have been secretly filming in this club for several weeks. I've got a *lot* of interesting stuff on tape.' She pauses for impact. Dawson is having to be forcibly restrained. 'You bitch. You evil whore. You – '

'The third thing,' she continues, ignoring Dawson and addressing Webster, 'and the most interesting one, is a taped exchange between yourself and Peter Dawson in his office on the tenth of March – just four days ago – in which you instructed him to murder DCI Burnside.' Webster is ashen. Burnside is smiling. Pauline turns to Gary Hedges. 'He's all yours.'

Hedges is looking punch-drunk. He still can't quite believe it. Neither can the other officers. Webster makes a play for time.

'This is total rubbish and I utterly refute it. I don't know who you are, but you're obviously in league with Burnside. I will not stand here and have these wicked allegations thrown at me.' He turns to Hedges. 'Call ACC Lee, head of the Pepper squad, and tell him I want to speak to him personally, right away. I want to get this sorted out once and for all.'

Hedges nods curtly and gets on the radio. Burnside, catching Pauline's beaming face, hisses, 'I wouldn't start celebrating yet. This means he's gonna do a deal.'

EXTRACT FROM TAPED INTERVIEW WITH DS GARY HEDGES,
TAPE 84A/92, 27.06.00

CHAMBERS: 'It was a tough call for you to make, wasn't it, deciding whether to believe Burnside or Webster. What was going through your mind?'

HEDGES: 'To be honest, I was all over the place. I mean, I trusted the guvnor and everything, and I believed what he'd told me when we met up at Whiteleys, but then old Webster really started messing with my mind. This was when I got hauled back in after that do on the Heath. I was in his office for about three hours. He was telling me all this crap – well, I know it's crap now – about Burnside's past. Then he said I'd have to do as he said, co-operate with the enquiry or he'd investigate me an' all for being an accessory. I can't afford to lose me job, I've got three little ones and the wife doesn't work. So it was tough, yeah. I tell yer, I sweated more that night in Silks than I did running the bleedin' marathon.'

CHAMBERS: 'So what swung it for you?'

HEDGES: [*laughing*]: 'I could see the whites of his eyes.'

CHAMBERS: 'Webster?'

HEDGES: 'Duh. Yeah, Webster. I could tell he was panicking. Trying to keep his cool and paddling like crazy underneath.

CHAMBERS: 'What did ACC Lee say when you phoned him?'

HEDGES: 'Apart from being narked I'd disturbed his dinner? He believed Webster. I mean, why wouldn't he, the bloke appointed him to run Pepper. Not that we went over all the ins and outs on the phone, but I could tell he thought Burnside had cooked up those tapes. Gawd knows how. Talk about suspending disbelief. But that's the old handshake business, innit? If you're one of the boys, you've gotta be OK.'

CHAMBERS: 'You must have felt pretty despondent.'

HEDGES: 'Yeah, well, it was obvious Webster was gonna do a whitewash on Lee 'til you two produced the goods.'

CHAMBERS: 'What happened next?'

HEDGES: 'I could hardly throw him in chains, could I? Not with Lee giving him a character reference. I had to let him go.'

CHAMBERS: 'Why didn't you arrest Burnside then, if Webster still had the upper hand?'

HEDGES: 'Webster shot off straight after I phoned Lee. He was too busy covering his arse to care.'

CHAMBERS: 'What about Dawson?'

HEDGES: 'I told Charlie Pitson and Jude Aldinger to take him back to the factory. Course, by this time the natives was getting restless so I got the other uniforms taking statements, and me and Burnside went with the paramedics to see his brother.'

CHAMBERS: 'Did Burnside still have the gun?'

HEDGES: 'Nah, he gave it to Charlie and told him to take it back with him and get it to ballistics.'

CHAMBERS: 'You also had an important piece of news that Burnside wasn't aware of, didn't you?'

HEDGES: 'News?'

CHAMBERS: 'About Mal Burnside.'

HEDGES: 'Oh! Yeah. I got a call on the radio that day about six o'clock. Kent Police. We'd got an APW out on Burnside Haulage.

They'd stopped one of his lorries at Dover. All kitted out for stowaways. Had a false ceiling and everything.'

CHAMBERS: 'Confirming what Frank had suspected.'

HEDGES: 'Spot on. Turns out Mal ain't the charitable type he pretended. Frank says he's got these plaques and awards 'n' stuff for trucking aid lorries out to Romanian orphans and Bosnian refugees. His wife showed him a pile of newspaper cuttings, pictures of all these grinning, gap-toothed urchins hanging round his neck. "Uncle Mal" they call him over there, like he's bleedin' Father Christmas. Nobody realised it was a cover for bringing back illegals.'

CHAMBERS: 'A very successful scam, by all accounts.'

HEDGES: 'Oh, yeah, he'd been running it for years. All the time Warwick Chamber of Commerce was awarding him – what was it, Citizen of the Year, I think he got – there he was, literally farming these children. It turns me stomach just to think of it, even now. Little kiddies with no mums and dads, no one to care about 'em. He used to wait 'til they was thirteen or fourteen and load 'em on his lorries like livestock.'

CHAMBERS: 'Boys too?'

HEDGES: 'Apparently. He had other outlets, besides Dawson.'

CHAMBERS: 'Awful.'

HEDGES: 'Too right. You know, I felt sorry for him when I walked in the office and saw him lying on the floor. He was in a right state. The paramedics was strapping him on a stretcher, giving him oxygen, putting him on a drip and all that. You saw him, didn't you?'

CHAMBERS: 'I did. He was in a pretty bad way. He'd lost a fair bit of blood.'

HEDGES: 'Still conscious, though, wasn't he? Still evil.'

CHAMBERS: 'What do you mean by that, "still evil"? It's an emotive phrase for a police officer to use, surely?'

HEDGES: 'You think we don't feel nothing? You know, sometimes I think you journalists are more callous than us coppers. Let me tell you, I feel it all the time, especially since I've had kids of me own. You gotta bury it down deep inside, or you wouldn't last ten minutes in the job. But I tell yer, when I heard what that bastard said about those youngsters they'd kidnapped, it made my blood run cold.'

CHAMBERS: 'We've got it on tape. Let's play an extract now.'

[*A click as she presses a button. Then:*]

MAL [*whispering hoarsely*]: 'You think you're so clever, don't you, Frank? Reckon you got this one wrapped up now, eh?'

FEMALE PARAMEDIC: 'Put the mask back on please, sir.'

MAL: 'I ain't finished with him, yet. There's something I gotta say.'

BURNSIDE: 'What's that?'

MAL [*pausing*]: 'You're full of shit, brother.'

BURNSIDE: 'That it?'

MAL: 'yeah.' [*His breath rasps noisily*] 'Unless there's something you want to ask?'

BURNSIDE: 'Don't piss me about.'

MALE PARAMEDIC: 'Mr Burnside. We're ready to go now.'

BURNSIDE [*ignoring him*]: 'I ain't playing Twenty Questions here, Mal. Spill it.'

MAL: [*wheezing*] 'I'd rather watch you sweat.'

BURNSIDE: 'You –'

CHAMBERS: 'It's the girls, Frank! Remember earlier, outside Dawson's office, we overheard a row? Mal said something like he hadn't planned to kidnap Kristina and Katie Watson, just Sanja. He knows where they are!'

BURNSIDE: 'Christ I forgot all about that. She's right, ain't she, Mal?'

MAL: 'Wouldn't you like to know?'

CHAMBERS: 'Dawson said something about a depot.'

FRANK: 'That would be your depot, wouldn't it, Mal?'

MAL: 'You think I'm gonna answer that? [*He laughs, then starts caughing violently. The paramedics confer in low voices.*]

FEMALE PARAMEDIC: 'Right, we're off. No more talking. Ready, Arthur? On my count: one, two, three…' [*They lift the stretcher and begin walking. Sound of their footsteps tramping down the corridor. Burnside, Hedges and Pauline follow.*]

BURNSIDE: 'The bastard knows where those girls are.'

HEDGES: 'He's playing with you, Guv.'

BURNSIDE [*striding rapidly*]: 'You don't need to tell me that, Gazza. He's been doing it all his bleedin' life.'

MALE PARAMEDIC: 'Would someone get the door for us, please?'

CHAMBERS: 'I'll do it.'

[*Mal is still coughing. He sounds rough. There's a low, steady hum of voices – they're obviously progressing through the club.*]

HEDGES: 'Don't sound like he's up to doing any more talking, Guv.'

BURNSIDE [*grim*]: 'There's still breath in his body. He might as well use it for some good. I'll have a go outside.'

[*Tape cuts to outside Silks. Sounds of the West End at night: the roar of traffic, people hailing taxis, horns honking, revellers laughing, drunks shouting.*]

BURNSIDE [*shouting over the noise*]: 'What the hell is that film crew doing here? Get out of the way!' [*Sound of scuffling, someone being shoved.*]

IAN DI MICHELE: 'Ow!'

BURNSIDE: 'Stay out of it, unless you want some more. And get that bleedin' light out of my eyes. ' [*Aside, to Pauline*] 'I'll speak to you later.' [*To Mal*] 'Mal! Can you hear me?' [*Mal groans*] 'You've got to tell me where those girls are. That kid you snatched is asthmatic. She needs to use an inhaler. She could die without it.'

MAL [*struggling*]: 'She's ... gonna ... die ... anyway.'

BURNSIDE: 'What do you mean?'

MAL: 'Jonno's ... got ... his ... orders.'

BURNSIDE: 'Who's Jonno?'

CHAMBERS: 'One of Dawson's henchmen. I've heard him mention him once or twice. Ex-Paras or something.'

BURNSIDE: 'I remember. Petrol-bombed my house.' [*To Mal, shouting*] 'Where's the bleedin' depot?'

MAL: 'Secret.' [*He makes a gurgling noise. It's impossible to tell if he's laughing or choking. The paramedics obviously think it's the latter.*]

FEMALE PARAMEDIC: 'I need suction!'

MALE PARAMEDIC: 'I've got it.' [*There's a high-pitched hissing noise.*]

FEMALE PARAMEDIC: 'Clear?'

MALE PARAMEDIC: 'Yup. Let's get him inside. Stand back, make room please.'

HEDGES: 'Guv, give it up. He's out of it.'

FEMALE PARAMEDIC [*to Burnside*]: 'Do you want to come with your brother?'

BURNSIDE: 'He won't last the ride if I do.'

HEDGES: 'I'll get one of the button mob.' [*To the paramedic*] 'Hang on, mate, he needs an escort. He's under police guard, this one.' [*The tape clicks off.*]

HEDGES: 'He wasn't too happy about your lot turning up, was he?'

CHAMBERS [*short*]: 'No.'

HEDGES: 'I thought he was gonna deck that bloke. And the look he gave you...'

CHAMBERS: 'Let's move on, shall we?'

BURNSIDE: 'Debbie?'

DEBBIE: 'Yes. Who's this?'

BURNSIDE: 'It's Frank. Burnside.'

DEBBIE: 'Oh! Mal's not here.'

BURNSIDE: 'I know that. He's with me. Or he was.'

DEBBIE: 'What – where is he now?'

BURNSIDE: 'On his way to casualty.'

DEBBIE [*screeching*]: 'Oh my God! Is he alright?'

BURNSIDE: 'No. But then he never has been.'

DEBBIE: 'I don't understand. It's not something... terminal?'

BURNSIDE: 'If there's any justice in the world.'

DEBBIE: 'Frank! Just tell me what's happened to him.'

BURNSIDE: 'He got shot.'

DEBBIE [*screams*]: 'Oh my God. Is he – how bad is it?'

BURNSIDE: 'He'll live. Probably. Which is more than can be said for those girls he kidnapped if we can't find them. Know anything about that, do you?'

DEBBIE: 'No. I swear to God.'

BURNSIDE: 'You're lying.'

DEBBIE: 'I'm not. Honestly. Mal doesn't tell me anything. I don't know where he is or what he's doing half the time.'

BURNSIDE: 'I don't believe you, Debbie. You set me up yesterday. That stuff about your husband not understanding you was all an act. You and Mal cooked that up to keep me off his tail. So don't come the innocent with me. You're in this up to your neck.'

DEBBIE: 'I – it's not true, Frank. I really fancied you.'

BURNSIDE [*harsh*]: 'Shut it, Debbie. Mal's under arrest. It's all over. We know what he does and we know how he does it. So if you want to save your skin, you'd better start talking, and fast. Now, where's the depot? We think he took them there.'

DEBBIE: 'This has nothing to do with me, Frank. I'm not getting involved.'

BURNSIDE: 'There's a four-year-old girl holed up somewhere, frightened out of her wits. Have you thought about that? She was holding on to Kristina's hand, too scared to let go, so your husband kidnapped her as well. A job lot. That's how careless he is with human lives. They mean nothing to him. Is that what you're like, Debbie? Or is there a shred of decency left in you?'

DEBBIE [*breaking down*]: 'It was a mistake. It all went wrong. He phoned me. He didn't know what to do. He – he was only supposed to get one girl.'

BURNSIDE [*shouting*]: 'Is that supposed to be some kind of excuse? For Christ's sake! I know all that. What I don't know is, where he took them. [*Silence*] 'Look, Debbie, you ain't going anywhere. There's a squad car on its way as I speak and they're going to take you in for questioning. Now, I don't know what the charges will be yet, but you tell us where the depot is and you'll have something we might be able to negotiate with. Am I speaking your language?'

DEBBIE [*sniffing*]: 'It's on the Woolwich industrial estate in Plumstead. There's a sign outside the warehouse that says "Children in Peril". It's the name of Mal's charity.'

EXTRACT FROM ARTICLE, 'MY DEADLY DOUBLE LIFE' BY PAULINE CHAMBERS,

REPRODUCED WITH KIND PERMISSION FROM *REAL LIVES* MAGAZINE (JULY 2000).

By the time Firebrand Productions get to Plumstead, the two police cars we are chasing are some way ahead. It's impossible to keep up with them, but we ride their tail as best we can, taking advantage of the slipstream the flashing blue lights and wailing sirens create to shoot past drivers who have pulled over. I've lost count of how many laws we've broken between the West End and Woolwich. Tony, the director, is driving while Dave, the cameraman, hangs out of the window, filming, and Ian, the assistant director, holds on to his legs. I am map-reading from a battered A–Z. I am travelling with the crew because Frank won't take me in the squad car. It may be my punishment for tipping off Tony about the showdown at Silks, or it may be police protocol. Being a girl and paranoid, I suspect the former, until Ian points out I'm not a paid-up member of CID yet, no matter that I've been behaving like one.

We're pumping adrenalin as we screech into Woolwich industrial estate. It looks like a ghost town at this hour of the night. 'Slow down,' I tell Tony as he jolts over a pothole. I open my window and lean out, listening. I can't hear anything. The air is chill and carries an odorous whiff of sewage. 'It'll be off the main drag. Probably at the far end,' I guess. It seems unlikely Mal would choose premises that are overlooked.

I'm right. We're saved from making a wrong turn by the sight of the cop cars reversing at high speed out of a side road, so we latch on behind and follow. They dive down the next side road off to the left, the last before the road comes to a dead end. There are only two warehouses along this stretch. The first is derelict. The second, separated by a stretch of scrubby wasteland, bears the sign 'Children in Peril'. Unlike the other warehouses, the forecourt has a high fence around it topped by barbed wire. It also displays prominent warnings about security cameras and guard dogs. These have obviously failed to deter, for the heavy metal gates are standing open. We roll through them in convoy and stop well back from the police. The yard is illuminated by security lights, but the warehouse itself is in darkness. Two huge container lorries are parked up in a loading area. In front of the warehouse, the staff parking spaces are occupied by two cars, a silver Mercedes and a blue Peugeot estate.

Dave leaps out and continues filming, panning round the yard and then zooming in on Burnside and Hedges. They're conferring about something, so I go over. I've been a part of things this far, and I don't see why I should be excluded now. The uniforms give me the once-over with mocking grins – I've forgotten I'm still in my tart's gear – but since Frank doesn't challenge me, they say nothing. One of them is on the radio, checking the cars' number plates. It is Dave who spots the body.

He comes panting over to us. 'The Merc. There's someone in it. They look sort of slumped forward. As if they're… '

'Stay here,' Frank barks. He and Hedges start to run towards the car.

'…dead,' finishes Dave. He and I look at each other. I've never seen a dead person before. Not in the flesh, as it were. Not real guts, real brains, real blood. I don't think Dave has, either. He came to us from Children's BBC. Suddenly, this is all too horribly real.

Tony and Ian join us. 'What's up?'

Dave's eyes are popping. 'I was going in tight, shooting from over there' – he points to the far side of the yard by the fence – 'and I realised the driver was still in the car. They've gone to take a look.'

'So why aren't you sodding well filming over their shoulders?' Tony snaps. 'Go on!'

We approach cautiously. Burnside is wrapping a handkerchief around the door handle. He opens the door and peers in, then retreats quickly. Even he can barely disguise his revulsion. 'It's Clare Miller,' he says to Hedges. 'Though there ain't much of her left to identify.' He spots me hanging back and beckons me over.

'Go on, then, take a look. You know the woman. I could do with a second opinion.' His voice is hard. I know he's getting his own back at me. I shake my head. I feel sick. Dave is braver, but then he's got Tony and Ray to answer to. He circles the car, filming from every angle. Then he throws up into a dustbin.

'She's been shot at close range, probably several times. Tell 'em we need an ARV here. And where's the other backup?'

'On it's way, Guv,' the officer with the radio replies. 'Control says the Peugeot's a hired car. The Merc's registered to a Clare Miller.'

'*Miss* Clare Miller,' Burnside corrects him, with only a touch of irony. 'She was very particular about that.'

'D'you reckon it was this Jonno character? Must've been someone she knew, to get that close,' Hedges says.

'Seems likely.' Burnside's face is inscrutable. Is he thinking what I'm thinking, remembering Dawson bearing down on us with his shotgun? I get a flashback, see Dawson's fixed eyes, the long barrel levelled at me. I shudder. I could have ended up like Clare Miller. I still might. The other car must be Jonno's, which means he's still here. As for what we might find inside the warehouse... I am not allowing myself to think about that. And then I hear a cry.

At first I think I've imagined it. No one else seems to hear it. I recall reading that women are supposed to have sharper ears than men, and strain to listen. Yes, it's definitely a cry. A thin, wailing child's cry. 'Listen!' I hold up my hand. 'I can hear something.' Everyone falls quiet. The cry is louder this time.

'Katie Watson,' Hedges says. 'What do you want to do, Guv?' He glances behind. 'Where's that armed response unit?'

'We can't afford to wait for them. I'm going in.'

'Guv –'

'If it was your kid, you'd be in there.'

'True. But – '

'I've got no family. No one's going to miss me. Meanwhile there's a four-year-old kid, two teenage girls and a maniac with a shooter in there. It ain't a hard decision.'

His eyes avoid mine. I swallow hard. 'I'd miss you,' I whisper, so softly that he doesn't hear. Tony does, though, and shoots a suspicious look at me. Frank turns away abruptly and walks towards the warehouse. This time, Tony doesn't have the nerve to send Dave after him. I watch, my heart in my mouth, as Frank stands with his back to the wall and reaches for the side door. He turns the handle and pushes it open, keeping his body well clear.

'This is Detective Chief Inspector Frank Burnside. I'm unarmed and I'm alone. Can you hear me in there?' No answer. The girl's crying is pitiful. Silent tears trickle down my cheeks. I brush them away with the back of my hand, and catch Ian doing the same. Hedges and the other officers are motionless, their faces rigid.

Frank tries again. 'Jonno. It's Frank Burnside. I know you're in there; Mal's told us the entire story. I just want to talk to you, make sure the girls are safe.'

Still no answer.

He glances at Hedges. Hedges shrugs. Frank has one last attempt. 'I'm coming in, Jonno. Just me, alright? I'm not carrying a piece. I'm coming in now.' Holding his hands aloft, he steps inside. Instantly, he is swallowed up by the dark. We can't see or hear anything except Katie's gulping sobs. I feel as if I can't breathe.

The clamour of sirens diverts our attention and we all swivel round. It's the armed response unit, closely followed by not one but two ambulances and two more police cars. Police officers in bulletproof jackets jump out of the van carrying rifles and immediately fan out across the forecourt, taking up vantage points. Hedges confers with the officer in charge. They glance anxiously at the warehouse. Dave, silently directed by a mouthing Tony, gets all this on film.

Frank's voice rings out, clear and steady, from inside. 'Hear that, Jonno? We've got company. Armed backup. Which means you're completely surrounded. You know, and I know that you ain't going to get out of here alive unless you co-operate. The game's up, Jonno.'

Silence. Even the child is quiet. It's more ominous than the crying.

'I'm gonna switch on the light, Jonno. See what's what. Don't do anything stupid, now.' Through two high windows we see the flicker of fluorescent lights coming on, one after another, so that a pool of bright light seeps out from under the main doors.

'Jonno? Where are you? Where are the girls?'

'Over here, you wanker.' The voice is harsh, deep, mocking. There's a gasp, followed by a squeal. A girl calls out something in a foreign tongue.

'Kristina!'

It's impossible to tell who is shouting. The officer in charge sends men in through the side door. Another team has already gone round the back. The rest are lined up, rifles cocked, waiting for the main doors to be pulled open.

A shot rings out, followed by two more in rapid succession. There is a man's cry – ghastly and gut-churning. Immediately, the air is rent with screams and hysterical crying. Two armed officers yank back the main doors. We stare at the tableau in front of us. It does not make any sense.

BBC Breakfast News, 15 March, 7.00 am.
'... A man and a woman have died after a siege involving three kidnapped children came to a dramatic end late last night with a

shoot-out between members of an international criminal gang.
'The children, four-year-old Katie Watson and teenagers Kristina
Tomasic and Sanja Gregovic, who were snatched earlier
yesterday on Hampstead Heath, were being held in a South-East
London warehouse by an armed gunman. They were discovered
alive and well after police, following a tip-off, raced to the scene
and surrounded the building.

'An unarmed senior detective entered the warehouse to
negotiate with the gunman, a trained killer, who was reportedly
under orders to execute the hostages. However, when the police
officer challenged him, a third man intervened and shot the
gunman himself. He was later revealed to be Davor Tomasic, the
father of one of the hostages, who is wanted by the National
Crime Intelligence Service.

An independent television company, which used an
undercover reporter to infiltrate the gang, filmed this exclusive
footage of the tense final minutes of the siege.' [*Cut to the scene
outside the warehouse*].

Armed police are lined up, ready to storm in. All eyes are on
the closed doors. The illuminated interior is glimpsed through the
top windows, frustratingly, too high to see in through. We hear
Burnside challenge Jonno; Jonno's sneering reply; Kristina's
warning to Davor; Davor shouting her name. The three shots:
bang, bang, bang. The dying man's hideous yell. The girls
screaming and crying.

Too late, the officer in charge issues a command and the doors
are pulled back. For a split second, nobody moves. In that freeze-
frame moment, the floodlit scene looks like the finale of a play:
Jonno's body on the floor, centre-stage; Sanja, behind him,
shielding little Katie's face in her skirt; a kneeling Davor cradling
Kristina, the pistol still dangling from one hand; Burnside, stage
right, half-hunched, one arm held protectively across his face.

Then, action: the armed police shout brusque commands. Davor drops the gun, making no attempt to resist. He hugs Kristina tight, then releases her and gets slowly to his feet, holding his hands in the air. Several police officers rush in and arrest him. Three others point guns at Jonno, until it's obvious he's dead.

Burnside steps over to Sanja and Katie. Silently, he takes their hands and leads them out of the warehouse towards the onlookers. The camera zooms in on the girls' tear-stained, filthy faces, Burnside's grim, grizzled visage. Behind them, a sobbing Kristina is having to be physically dragged away from her father, who is being led away in handcuffs. The last image we see is of Kristina's distressed face and outstretched arms. [*Cut back to newsreader*]

'Davor Tomasic, who runs an employment agency in Zagreb, is also thought to responsible for killing forty-one-year-old Clare Miller, who was found dead at the scene. Miss Miller, who ran a promotions agency in London's Bayswater, was an associate of Tomasic's and is said to have played a crucial role in the kidnapping.

'Rumours have been circulating all day about the motive for the kidnapping, but it now appears that the two older girls, who are both Croatian, are key witnesses to an international smuggling operation involving illegal immigrants from Eastern Europe. Kristina Tomasic was working as an au pair for the Watson family and was out walking with their daughter, Katie, and her friend, Sanja Gregovic, when the attackers struck. Miss Gregovic, an illegal immigrant, is now claiming political asylum.

'Katie Watson was reunited with her parents, Marie and Gerald, at Hampstead police station in the early hours of the morning. [*Cut to police station*].

Marie Watson is embracing her daughter, speechless with

relief. She strokes Katie's hair, her face running with tears. Gerald Watson, more aware of the TV cameras – or perhaps more afraid of breaking down in public – stands stiffly next to them. He kisses Katie on the cheek only when urged to do so by baying photographers.

Katie, clearly a robust child, seems remarkably unfazed by her ordeal. Bouncing in Marie's arms, she catches a tear on her finger and licks it. 'It's salty, mummy. Have you been eating crisps?' The assembled police officers fall about laughing. The press pounce on the soundbite with glee. There is no sign of Kristina. [*Cut back to newsreader*]

'Firebrand Productions, which has been secretly filming members of the crime syndicate for a TV documentary, used a female reporter to win access to the gang's inner circle. Pauline Chambers, twenty-five, posed as a nightclub hostess, living a double life for several weeks to observe the operation first-hand. [*Cut to outside the warehouse*].

Pauline is standing there, still in hostess guise, and has Burnside's leather jacket over her bare shoulders. (The 'interview' is obviously being conducted by Tony Dillon, off-camera, who clearly had the foresight to set up the package before biking it to the BBC, thus scoring a major publicity coup.)

CHAMBERS: 'As a journalist, I've always considered it my mission to bring the truth to people. I never imagined that would entail wearing a corset concealing a hidden camera –', she looks down at her front and almost corpses, 'and it's got me into some frightening situations at times – but the results speak for themselves.' [*She gestures behind her, where police and forensic teams are hard at work.*]

DILLON [*out of view*]: 'What influence do you think you've had on the police investigation into this operation?'

CHAMBERS: 'We can't reveal too much at this stage because

charges are still pending, but I think it's safe to say the evidence I recorded has helped catch at least three gang members, as well as exposing this shameful and illegal sex-smuggling trade, which exploits vulnerable young girls from Eastern Europe and closer to home.'

DILLON: 'Are you saying that, without your contacts and secret cameras, the police might still be clutching at straws?'

CHAMBERS: 'That might be overstating the case a little,' she looks beadily at the unseen Tony, 'but certainly I have been working closely with one senior detective, DCI Frank Burnside, who was the courageous unarmed officer who went in to rescue the young girls. I was able to provide him with some really very shocking evidence about what was going on in the hostess club which could indeed have implications that go far beyond this current investigation.'

DILLON: 'Are you able to tell us any more about that aspect of it, yet?'

CHAMBERS: 'What I can say is that this operation – Operation Playmates, as the police dubbed it – appears to be part of a bigger picture that suggests police corruption on a massive scale. The Metropolitan Police has its own, highly publicised, anti-corruption enquiry going on, Operation Pepper, which, in the light of the material I've gathered, now looks as if it might be implicated itself.' [*Cut back to newsreader*].

'A spokesperson for the Metropolitan Police press office has refused to comment on the allegations concerning corruption made by Miss Chambers. They did, however, confirm that they are holding three men in connection with Operation Playmates. Two of them were arrested following a raid on Silks Hostess Club in Piccadilly, central London. One of the two men is under police guard at St Thomas's Hospital after being shot in the leg. His condition is said to be serious, but stable.

'In a further development, it's been revealed that Detective Chief Inspector Frank Burnside, who led the investigation, had been suspended from duty prior to the arrests being made. Although his participation has been pivotal throughout, it's unclear as what the future may hold for the sometimes controversial detective, who is himself expected to have to answer to an enquiry panel as part of Operation Pepper's on-going internal anti-corruption drive.'

Diary, 15 March

I'm a star! Frank and I are all over the news this morning – shame it happened too late for the papers, but I'm giving the *Sun* an exclusive later and the phone's been going non-stop since the story broke. I've done five radio interviews already (from bed – very Paula Yates) and I've had to resort to putting on the answering machine just so I can catch up on some shut-eye before my TV appearances later. Sam's fielding calls at the office and setting up my schedule: I'm doing a piece with Sky News, an interview for ITN, plus I'm taking part in a debate on the role of undercover journalists for the BBC (prerecorded, not live, thank goodness). Oh, yes, and three magazines – no, four, I think she said – are bidding for my 'true-life experience', some writer wants to turn my story into a screenplay (we can't decide if he's for real or a nutter) and a company manufacturing rubber corsets wants me to model for them. I said no way! Frank suggested I ought to investigate the possibilities of a computer game – 'Journo Cop' he called it – but I think he was joking. Still, it's an idea. I quite fancy reinventing myself along the lines of Lara Croft.

Frank left half an hour ago; he said he had to see Roger Sutton and get things 'straightened out'. Actually, I think he was relieved to get out of here. He looked pretty hacked off about me gabbing to reporters. He accepts it's my job, but he doesn't like it much. I've been careful not to talk about him too much, beyond the obvious stuff, but inevitably we're both in the spotlight so he's not best pleased. As it was, I had to do a lot of making up to him over the business with the Firebrand crew when we got home last night! Not that I minded...

It was 3.30 in the morning when we finally got back. I was still up on the adrenalin, so I opened a bottle of champagne to celebrate. Frank was being really moody and said he didn't feel like partying. When I asked why, he said, 'It's not every day you shoot your own brother'.

I said, 'It's not every day your own brother tries to kill you', but he said that wasn't the point. When I asked him what was the point, he said he'd never worked that way and it wasn't his style; he'd always prided himself on using his wits, not a gun.

I got a bit exasperated – well, we had a row, actually – because I don't see how he's to blame. I mean, according to Frank, the gun went off when they were struggling, which makes it an accident, pure and simple. When I said that, his face went bleak and he didn't answer. It made me wonder: did he shoot Mal deliberately? They were out of the range of the camera, so I guess no one will never know. I didn't dare ask; his expression was too intimidating.

When we'd both calmed down, Frank agreed to have a drink 'to keep me company', as he put it. I think it was more to drown his sorrows than celebrate, but he didn't actually say that. I was so elated and buoyed up with champagne – Frank didn't have any, he drank my Scotch – that everything else went over my head. I feel pretty rotten now about being so insensitive. All the time I was banging on about landing the scoop of the century, he didn't know whether he'd got a job to go back to or not.

By the time I'd finished the champagne and Frank had drunk

me out of Scotch, we were fairly mellow and much friendlier. We were cuddled up on the sofa listening to Bob Dylan (the only recording artist we can agree on) and I was nodding off on Frank's shoulder when he whispered in my ear, 'I heard what you said, you know. About missing me.' Then he pulled me into his arms and kissed me; a lingering, soft, tender kiss. One thing led to another and we made love.

It wasn't like yesterday: that had been rough and ravenous and raw but, in a way, it was almost a game, each challenging the other to see how far they'd go. Then, we'd been building up to it since that first night at Silks and when we finally took our clothes off and I felt his skin against mine, I wanted him so badly I was practically begging, a total slut. He made me wait, the bastard, holding himself over me, teasing me, nudging me. Then, just as I thought I was about to explode, he screwed me senseless. Shameless. Fantastic. But selfish, too. We were both gratifying ourselves. They were essentially solo performances. Whatever inhibitions we cast aside, neither of us let down our emotional guards.

This time it was different. It wasn't shagging. There was no second-guessing. It was serious, adult lovemaking; two people giving and sharing, taking pleasure in each other's pleasure. Frank was incredibly intense, staring into my eyes the whole time as if he was trying to read meaning into every flicker of my face. If I'm honest, it was a little disconcerting. His openness demanded the same from me and I found it hard to meet his gaze, knowing what I've done to him. I felt more of a whore having loving sex in the missionary position than I ever did yesterday demonstrating my knowledge of the *Kamasutra*.

The dawn was beginning to break by the time we'd finished. We sprawled on the sofa, our legs interlocked, our cooling bodies striped with the bars of pale light pouring in through the blinds. It's a moment I'll always remember.

I made a pot of tea and brought in a duvet and we stayed on the sofa, scoffing biscuits and drinking tea and talking. Really talking. I told Frank about my father, how close we'd been and how it had affected my relationships with men ever since. He reciprocated by opening up about his childhood, telling me what it had been like growing up in Mile End and what happened to make him join the police and how he very nearly went the other way, like Mal. I don't think he's used to talking about himself like that; I get the feeling his relationships with women don't usually get to the confessional stage. I felt very privileged and special.

Neither of us slept. There wasn't time. We switched on the television at 7.00 am and saw the story on the news, and from then on things became a whirl of phonecalls and messages. It wasn't until just now, after Frank had gone, that I remembered I'd switched the hidden camera on when we first came in, out of force of habit as much as anything else. I'd forgotten about it almost immediately, but the tape's got a running time of three hours, so Frank's life story (not to mention our lovemaking) must be on it. I don't want to know. I put it away in a drawer without looking at it.

I've come to a decision. I'm not going to use it, the stuff about Frank. None of it. It's too personal. It's also fascinating and totally gripping and would make brilliant television, but I wouldn't feel right, broadcasting it. Not any more. Tony and Ray have got their story, and it's bigger and better than anything we thought it would be. Firebrand Productions is on the map; Pauline Chambers is on her way up and Frank Burnside's secrets will stay secret, which is how it should be.

EXTRACT FROM TAPED INTERVIEW WITH
SUPERINTENDENT ROGER SUTTON,
TAPE 86A/92, 19.07.00

CHAMBERS: 'Superintendent Sutton, you are – were – Frank Burnside's superior officer, yet you seem to have wavered a great deal in your opinion of him. One minute you were leading what, to all intents and purposes, was a witch-hunt against him; the next, he was being welcomed back as a conquering hero. Where did you personally stand, and why was your position so inconsistent?'

SUTTON: 'I'd always thought Frank Burnside was trustworthy; he wouldn't have held such a responsible position in Crime OCU if he wasn't. However, when Commander Webster approached me about him, I was bound to take the allegations he raised very seriously, whatever my personal consideration; anything less would have been failing in my duty. As has been proven,' [*he coughs delicately*] 'people aren't always what they seem, even police officers.'

CHAMBERS: '*Especially* police officers.'

SUTTON [*stiffly*]: 'Precisely.'

CHAMBERS: 'Are you saying that Webster effectively came in and took control?'

SUTTON: 'I'm saying that, from that point onwards, it was the Pepper squad that set the agenda concerning Burnside; not me.'

CHAMBERS: 'So, to go back to my original question, what was it that changed your mind about Burnside? It was still his word against Webster's at that stage; the tapes hadn't been authenticated.'

SUTTON: 'I was extremely pleased to see Frank Burnside apparently vindicated after the arrests at Silks nightclub, although saying he was "welcomed back like a conquering hero" is an exaggeration that's been put about by the media. I remained cautious, naturally – how could I not when the implications were so grave? – but I listened to what he had to say, and I viewed the tapes he showed me, and my first impression was that they were genuine and that his story, incredible as it sounded, was true.'

CHAMBERS: 'So it was just copper's instinct that swung it for you? That's a rather slender basis for detecting the truth, isn't it? I thought modern policing used scientific methods.'

SUTTON: 'I had, just that morning, received forensic evidence which, at least in part, verified Burnside's story. That helped.'

CHAMBERS: 'This was Dawson's gun?'

SUTTON: 'Yes. Ballistics matched it to the one used to kill the solicitor, Keith Gaughan. Unfortunately, it also had Frank's prints on it, and of course those of his brother, Malcolm, so it wasn't a complete get-out, but the tape from Dawson's office showed how the gun ended up in Frank's hands.

We also had a description of Gaughan's last client from his secretary, Gladys May. Apparently, Gaughan had told her she could finish early, but she returned to the office to fetch something and spotted this man leaving. She described him as looking like Richard Harris and said he wore boots.'

CHAMBERS: 'Richard Harris the actor? Do you know, I hadn't thought of that before, but now you mention it, he's Dawson – before the face-lift.'

SUTTON: 'Certainly not Frank Burnside.'

CHAMBERS: 'No. Can't think who I'd cast as him.'

SUTTON [briskly]: 'The point is, there was evidence to suggest that Burnside had been framed, certainly for the murder of Keith Gaughan, which made me much more inclined to believe his version of events than I might otherwise have done.'

CHAMBERS: 'What about the cassette that Dawson had? The one incriminating Webster in the diamond robbery? That was incredible.'

SUTTON: 'Webster was still sticking to his story about it being a fit-up. The cassette was requisitioned by the Pepper squad.'

CHAMBERS: 'But where did Dawson get it from? He didn't make it, did he?'

SUTTON: 'No, Keith Gaughan made it. Actually, we have you and your bugging devices to thank for finding out about that.'

CHAMBERS: 'The one in Dawson's phone?'

SUTTON: 'SOCO found it the next day when they were doing a sweep of Dawson's office. It recorded a call from Webster on 14th March. He said Gaughan had been on to him, panicking about Burnside's surprise visit. Apparently, Gaughan was drunk and raving and saying that, if he went down, he had proof and would take "everybody else" with him.'

CHAMBERS: 'And this "proof" was the tape.'

SUTTON: 'Gaughan must have recorded it secretly at the time, as some sort of personal insurance. As a solicitor, he knew how crucial such evidence would be. Unfortunately, it didn't protect him; it got him killed.'

CHAMBERS: 'By Dawson.'

SUTTON: 'By Dawson. Webster's instructions were for him to go and see Gaughan and find out exactly what he had up his sleeve. He didn't tell Dawson to silence him, but I should think that was tacitly understood. Webster knew how trigger-happy Dawson was.'

CHAMBERS: 'But what I don't understand is, why was Webster so shocked when Dawson produced the tape? Surely he knew all about it?'

SUTTON: 'Oh, I think the shock was absolutely genuine. It looks as if Dawson double-crossed him, hoping to save his own neck. That tape became his insurance; something to do a deal with. He'd probably lied to Webster that he couldn't find anything, which would have given him the excuse for murdering Gaughan, not that he really needed it. Both of them were vulnerable with Gaughan shooting his mouth off.'

CHAMBERS: 'But you didn't know any of this at the time you met with Burnside.'

SUTTON: 'No. At that point everything was still very much up in the air and no one knew where the balls were going to drop. To coin a phrase.'

CHAMBERS: 'So how did you find Burnside at that interview?'

SUTTON: 'Understandably, he was very angry at the way he'd been treated, and he was particularly upset by my failure to support him, as he saw it.'

CHAMBERS: 'It went a bit further than that, surely?'

SUTTON: 'Frank did make some rather wild accusations, yes.'

CHAMBERS: 'Against you?'

SUTTON: 'He had just uncovered a web of corruption. He didn't know how far it had spread. Yes, he suspected me.'

CHAMBERS: 'I believe he called you "Webster's whipping boy"?'

SUTTON: 'Did he? I don't remember. It sounds like Frank. He's not a man to mince his words.'

CHAMBERS: 'How did you convince him you weren't?'

SUTTON [*chuckling suddenly*]: 'By doing him one hell of a favour.'

CHAMBERS: 'What's so funny?'

SUTTON: 'Because I've never bent the rules in my life, but I did so for Frank Burnside – to prove I wasn't bent! There's got to be logic in that somewhere.'

DICTAPHONE TRANSCRIPT, TAPE 91A/92.
15.03.00; 14.30

BURNSIDE [*in car*]: 'The truth is out there. That's *The X Files*, isn't it? Never did rate the show myself: it's all conspiracy theories, classified documents, secret agents and aliens. Now I'm practically living it. Minus the aliens. Then again, nothing would surprise me after the last couple of weeks. I could get beamed up between Catford and Cranbrook. If Wilkins appears smoking a cigarette, I'll know I'm in trouble.

'I'll say the name for you again, shall I, Webster? Just in case you didn't quite catch it. Wilkins. Dick Wilkins. That's the bloke I'm going to see. Ring any bells? Yeah, I bet it does; I bet they're clamouring like crazy. They're tolling for you, Webster. With a bit of luck.' [*Burnside sounds upbeat, optimistic. He switches on the radio, keeping the volume low, and taps his fingers on the wheel in time to the music. He even whistles. Apparently he's musing about the case, for he returns to recording his thoughts a minute or so later.*]

'See, Sutton was telling me there was nothing he could do, it was all in the hands of the Pepper squad. And, for some strange reason, I don't trust your boys. It strikes me that Operation Pepper, which sounds so fine and principled in theory, was actually set up to protect sharks like you and throw fishes like me to the public. That way, the Met. is shown to be accountable, you get the press and the politicians off your back and your lot can get on with running the firm. Hedges told me what Lee said. As far as I'm concerned, it ain't an investigation into police corruption; it's a bleeding protection racket.

'So you can see why I ain't putting my faith in the criminal justice system. The evidence we've got ought to be more than enough, but "ought" don't cut it these days. For all I know, you've got someone to bury the tapes and experts on the payroll to swear they're fakes. Slap an injunction on that documentary and you're almost home and dry. Of course, Dawson would have to meet a nasty accident inside, but I'm sure that ain't beyond your scope. You could buy off Mal with a couple of grand and he'd pop me for free. QED.

'Call me paranoid, but I'll go that extra mile to make sure I nail you. An extra hundred miles or so, actually, there and back, but who's counting? It's a sunny day, I've had spectacular sex with a gorgeous girl and I'm in the mood for a blast down the A21. A blast from the past, in your case, Webster. Should be very interesting to hear what your old OPPO has to say. I've got the secret camera kit on in case he's shy, and no bugger from Pepper's getting his mitts on that tape.'[*He hums along with The Levellers; not terribly well.*]

'I gotta say, I wasn't feeling quite this chipper when I went to see Superintendent Sutton this morning. Frankly, I was feeling a bit let down, a bit cheesed off about things. I mean, I crack a crime ring, nick two blaggers, save three kids and expose police corruption – and nearly get myself killed in the process – and he has the gall to tell me that I ain't off the hook yet. It's a bit steep. Especially since I'm innocent and the geezer who framed me is so bent he can see up his own arse. Enough to make any man feel bitter.

'So I said to him, "I ain't having my career rest on the say-so of this bastard", and he said, "I'm sorry, pal, but what can I do?", or words to that effect. And I said, "Here's a suggestion for you, sir, off the top of my head. Get hold of that tape Dawson had and let me listen to it again." Because I knew the clues were on it. I remembered hearing this other bloke talking; some name I ain't come across before. I thought, well, he's either dead or keeping a very low profile, considering the shit that's been flying around. So let's find out.

'And you know what, Webster? Sutton came through. I didn't think he was going to, at first. He was bleating on about the tape being property of the Pepper squad and how he couldn't intervene in an official enquiry, all the usual codswallop. So I reminded him that, if I went down, as my boss he wouldn't come out of it smelling too sweet, neither. No more promotion boards. Off the cocktail circuit. He'd be lucky to hang on to his own job. Whereas, if he helped me expose you for the crook that you are... Well, you can see the logic, can't you? So did Sutton. He's a jobsworth but he ain't a fool. He got the tape copied and sent over within the hour.

'When I left him, he was calling up the file for Graham Underwood, the young PC that got shot. I should've told him not to hold his breath; it's probably gone the same way as Dawson's. I'm right, aren't I? He was getting quite excited about the idea of putting one over on the Pepper squad, so I didn't put a damper on it. Gave me special dispensation to go and find your mate Wilkins, the monosyllabic geezer on the tape, even though officially I'm still on suspension. He even helped me track him down. Bet you didn't think we'd manage that, eh?'

[*Burnside joins in with the song again*] 'What a beautiful day...'

TRANSCRIPT OF FILM, TAPE 57V/404, 15.03.00, 16.00

Dick Wilkins does not look surprised when Burnside introduces himself. A frail-looking man with papery skin and white, wispy hair, he appears older than his sixty-five years. The hand that he extends has a discernible tremor. He stands aside to let Burnside in. 'I've been expecting a visit.'

Burnside follows him through the large, well-kept house. Someone is vacuuming the living room. He gestures towards the door. 'Housekeeper – well, I call her that. She comes in every day. Invaluable. Let's go through to my study.' A black poodle gets out of its basket in the hallway and trots at Wilkins's heels, its claws clicking on the tiled floor. 'I saw the news,' Wilkins throws over his shoulder. 'I must say I was intrigued at what that reporter girl said. I thought to myself, "There's a lot more to this than meets the eye".' He opens a door, revealing a book-lined room with a knee-hole desk and a couple of armchairs. Turning to Burnside he continues, 'I assume that's why you're here.'

'Got it in one,' Burnside drawls.

The study has French windows opening out onto an impressive garden. The little dog paws them, whining. 'Oh, all right, Freda. Wait a minute.' Wilkins produces a key from a desk drawer and lets the dog out. 'She needs a run. Been cooped up all day. Want a look outside? Marvellous views. Though developers...' He waves a hand. 'It's a matter of time, I suppose. But I'll be long gone by then.'

He leads Burnside out into the garden. Burnside swivels, panning the secret camera round, taking in the extensive lawns, the well-tended flower beds, an ornate pond, an arbour with a seat. Most of the beds are devoted to rose bushes. 'Not much to see in March, but it looks stunning by July,' Wilkins announces, following Burnside's gaze. He ambles over to a rose bush and plucks a withered deadhead. 'Time to get the secateurs out soon. Before the sap rises.' He falls silent, twirling the rose by its stem. Burnside seems in no hurry to question him; it's obvious Wilkins is prepared to talk.

'This was Audrey's favourite. She was very fond of roses. Well, she loved the garden. Used to be out here at all day. I used to say to her, "What do you do out there, all that time?", and she'd say, "Just pottering, Dick. Just pottering." Never did understand what that meant. But since she went, God bless her, I've learned. That's what I do, these days. I just... potter.'

His eyes are moist. He blows his nose on large cotton handkerchief, unashamed of showing emotion. 'It's a bit nippy out here. Let's go back in. Freda's done her business. Come on!'

The shout is to the dog. They troop inside. Wilkins installs Burnside in an armchair, orders a large pot of tea from the housekeeper, then says, 'Out of curiosity, how did you find me? I find it hard to believe David would have told you where I was.'

'I got onto Stafford Row nick. They had a Richard Wilkins there, same time as Webster. It had to be you,' Burnside replies. 'We knew you were retired because they gave us your DOB. My guvnor pulled a few strings with the old pensions department, and hey presto.'

'Co-operative guvnor.'

'He's got his reasons.'

'Haven't we all.' Wilkins sighs. 'And they always seem such good ones at the time.' He sighs heavily and folds his hands in his lap. 'So: how much do you know?'

'I know this is important enough for David Webster to try and silence me any way he can. I know it involves a diamond robbery my brother and a slag called Dawson was doing. I know you and Webster was going to get a cut of the proceeds. I know there was a bent MPS solicitor involved called Keith Gaughan. And I know it went seriously wrong and a police officer got killed. I've got other names floating around, but I need you to put it all together.'

'Hmmn.' Wilkins gets up from his armchair, with an effort. 'David called me up the other day. Suggested a round of golf.' He snorts. 'Well, look at me, I can't swing a golf club, not these days. I used to be quite fit, when he and I worked together. Shows how long it's been since he last saw me.

'I humoured him; met up with him at the clubhouse. We went out on the course; he hit, I watched. Eventually he got to the point. Told me things were heating up and that you were asking questions. He said he wasn't going to let it go any further but he wanted me to be prepared, just in case.'

'Did he make any suggestions?'

Wilkins laughs rather wildly. 'He asked if I still had my old pistol – we kept a few, from a raid once.'

'And do you?'

Wilkins goes over to the bookcase and reaches behind a copy of a Collins *Dictionary of Quotations*. 'Yes.' He pulls out a shoebox, lifts the lid, and retrieves the weapon. Burnside gets up smartly, so smartly it makes the dog jump and commence yapping.

'Put that down.'

'It's all right, Burnside,' Wilkins says, almost skittishly. 'She's not for you.' He polishes the barrel with a soft cloth. 'I look after her, keep her clean, oiled, primed. One day, she's going to look after me. When I've made my peace with my Maker.' He holds the gun aloft, examining the gleaming barrel, then puts it back in the box. Returning the box to its hiding place, he continues, 'I am not a well man, Burnside. I have cancer. My wife died six months ago – a pulmonary embolism, following a fall – and I find living without her intolerable. But I have not been able to... finish things while my past haunts me so.' He gives Burnside a smile. 'Perhaps you are to be my deliverance.'

'You need a priest for that, not a police officer.'

'Oh, I've got one. He can grant me forgiveness, but you – you can make a real difference. You can see the truth is told.'

'So, tell me then,' says Burnside.

Wilkins sits down again, facing Burnside. The dog jumps on his lap. Stroking the animal meditatively, he begins.

'Peter Dawson used to be David Webster's snout when he was a sergeant at Stafford Row. It was an expedient relationship: Dawson used to give him tip-offs; Webster used to turn a blind eye if Dawson had something going down. I knew about this and went along with it and, I suspect, there were quite a few others at

Stafford Row who did, too. I suppose we regarded it as being "broad-minded" rather than being bent – it was often simply the best way of catching the real, hardened criminals.

'Increasingly, though, it began to go further than simply turning a blind eye. David was becoming disenchanted with the police and started accepting bribes, then taking a cut... it was still fairly minor league, but he'd stepped over the line. He used to get tanked up, start bragging about his unofficial "income", tell me I was missing out, it was all there for the taking. I had private school fees to cover, Audrey wasn't working, so in the end I thought, "why not?". I was never comfortable doing it, but that's no excuse, I'm aware of that. However, David got quite blasé about it. I think he harboured fantasies about running the Stafford Row manor himself.

'Then, in July 1980, Dawson came to David, desperate for help, and asked him to get himself and a mate – your brother Mal – off a burglary charge. They were both on bail at the time. I think David must have swung that for them originally because Dawson, at least, would normally have had his application for bail refused, given his record. Their court case had been pending for some months, but it had suddenly been brought forward and this was going to scotch their chances of pulling off a robbery they'd been planning to execute before the trial. And this wasn't a house-breaking, which was Dawson's usual bag, it was much more ambitious. It involved intercepting a consignment of smuggled diamonds off a particular flight from Amsterdam. Obviously they were only going to get one shot at it, and if they were found guilty on the burglary charge, which was more than likely, they'd be sent to prison before the diamonds even arrived in the country.

'Prior to then, they had both been quite happy at the prospect of receiving a few months in custody. It would have worked in their favour; no one would have suspected them of the diamond heist and they could have kept a low profile until the heat had died down. But now, they had to ensure they got off, which was why Dawson offered to cut David and me in for a percentage if we could swing the trial.

'Well, I found out that the officer in charge was a very straight sergeant called Parry. We knew he wouldn't be swayed, so we didn't even try to – '

'Pity I didn't know that; I wouldn't have tried, either,' Burnside interrupts. 'From what I've heard, you and Webster exploited my little blunder to great advantage.'

'I didn't have anything to do with that; it was all David's doing,' Wilkins replies. 'But yes, he was delighted that you'd offered them the opportunity to cover their tracks, as it were.'

'I bet.' Burnside's tone is sour.

'For what it's worth, I am sorry,' Wilkins says. His eyes are bright, almost feverish. 'This is why I'm so glad you've come, Burnside. I feel I owe you, greatly, for what they did. I want to make amends personally.'

'Go on,' Burnside says grudgingly.

'Once we'd realised Parry was no-go, David suggested we try a different tack, see who was prosecuting the case. As luck would have it, it turned out to be Keith Gaughan, a solicitor David had arrested once for importuning in a public lavatory. He'd let him off the charge, I can't remember why – probably because he thought he'd be useful some day. Which, indeed, he was.

'Gaughan was very nervy, not what I'd call reliable for doing this sort of thing. He had a drink problem, he was in debt and his personal life was a mess. But we didn't have much choice so we decided to approach him. To give him credit, he wasn't keen, but David reminded him about the favour he owed, and we offered to cut him in on the deal, and he was persuaded to throw the case. I think a degree of blackmail was probably used, but I wasn't party to that.

'Anyway, Gaughan did his job alright and managed to make a pretty good show of bungling things. I believe he arranged for the wrong witnesses to turn up on the wrong days, and then failed to deliver a key continuity of evidence statement. The magistrate was, of course, deeply unimpressed with his inefficiency and the defence exploited it to the hilt, which was Gaughan's intention. He called for an adjournment to sort things out, the defence objected and the magistrate threw it out. Peter Dawson and Malcolm Burnside walked free.'

'And that was when I stuck my oar in and gave Mal an ear-bashing for fraternising with Dawson in the first place.'

'Yes.' Wilkins laughs. 'That put the wind up everyone, I can tell you. We were fine-tuning the details of the robbery outside the magistrate's court when you came over. No one was sure what you'd heard, or how much you'd registered about what was going on. Actually, Dawson was quite keen on getting you taken out of the picture right then. In retrospect, we should have realised what a trigger-happy psychotic he was. Of course, we said no.'

'Big of you. I'd better warn you, Webster's a lot less squeamish about ordering killings these days.'

'Oh, I'm not scared of David,' Wilkins chuckles. 'Not in the slightest. More tea?'

'I think I need something stronger.'

'Right you are' Wilkins gets up and opens a heavy wooden sideboard. He pulls out a bottle of single malt. 'How about a drop of this?'

'Nice one.'

Wilkins pours them both a generous measure and hands a glass to Burnside. Burnside drinks, exhales. 'Ahhh...'

'You sound like you need this.'

'It's been a corker of a week. And I didn't get any sleep last night.'

'Well, you look good on it.'

'Do I?' Burnside sounds amused. 'Cheers.'

Wilkins lifts his glass in salute.

'So who did these diamonds belong to?' Burnside asks.

Wilkins settles himself back down. 'Quite a lot of people thought they owned them. Which is not to say that they did. As I understood it, the gems were being smuggled by some faction of the European mafia. A big East-End firm, run by a notorious gangster called Neil Cook, had agreed to launder them over here, for a percentage. The consignment was coming in from Amsterdam with a courier, a woman. Dawson got to hear about it on the grapevine, realised there was a window of time when she would be unprotected, and decided to rob her.'

'Ambitious.'

'Very, considering the number of people who would be out to get him, if he succeeded. Which he did.'

'So that's why he's lit up like the Christmas fairy.'

Wilkins looks confused. Burnside waves his hand. 'Likes to wear his wealth, does Dawson.' He takes another sip of whisky. 'So how did they pull it off then?'

'Pretty much as arranged. The plane landed, Malcolm tailed her from the airport and Dawson was ready waiting outside the hotel where the handover was due to take place. The courier was having an affair with Cook's second-in-command, a chap called Stuart Bell, hence the hotel. They were planning to seal the deal and have a bit on the side at the same time. He was waiting for her in the hotel room, which was why he didn't see what went on outside.'

'And this was when Mal and Dawson nobbled her?'

'Correct. They held her up as she got out of her taxi. Malcolm snatched the diamonds – two million pounds' worth, it's rumoured – while Dawson waved his gun around. Unfortunately, a young PC happened to come around the corner at that point, saw what was happening, and tried to apprehend them. So Dawson shot him.'

'There must have been some fallout from that.'

'There was. Huge public outcry. The police officer was very young, fresh-faced – a lovely lad. He left a teenage wife, pregnant. Press made him out to be a hero. Which he was.' Wilkins looks away, out into the garden. 'I felt sick to my stomach at being involved in the whole bloody thing. I baled out, as soon as I heard. Didn't want any more to do with it. I told David, he could have my cut. Or better still, give it to the poor blighter's widow. I don't expect he did for one minute.'

'And Dawson and Mal came out of it without a scratch.'

'Amazingly, yes. David packed them both off out of the way for a long time, let things cool down. They both did well out of that, too. Dawson went to South Africa, got involved with diamond dealing, doubled the profits from what I heard. Malcolm did pretty well, too, I gather.'

'If you like living in a purpose-built palace with a prostitute.'

'Ah. Money doesn't buy taste, does it?'

'Didn't Cook's lot come after them? What happened to Bell and the courier?'

'She skipped the country. Wisely. Cook had Bell take the rap with the mafia; set him up for a hit. Bell got a knife in the guts in a club one night. Cook didn't escape, though. He was jumped coming out of his local. He was tortured, killed, dismembered and packed into little plastic parcels. They found his head down by the Thames flood barrier.'

Burnside whistles. 'Well that tape of Gaughan's makes a whole lot more sense now.'

'What tape is that?'

'Keith Gaughan secretly recorded the inquest you lot had after the robbery. It was his way of buying a bit of insurance. It failed, by the way.'

'I wasn't aware of any meeting. But as I told you, I washed my hands of it as soon as I heard about...' He pauses, struggling to remember the PC. 'Underwood. Graham Underwood. Yes, that was the lad's name.'

'But you're on this tape. You're at the meeting. Webster talks to you.'

'Not me. I'm sorry, Burnside, but you're mistaken.'

'I've got the tape here.' Burnside takes it out of his jacket pocket. 'Got a cassette player?'

'Over there.' Wilkins points to a small hi-fi system on a shelf. 'Never use it much. It was for Audrey's music, mainly.'

Burnside puts the tape on. They listen in silence. Webster's voice booms out, 'I don't recall Wilkins or myself agreeing to that. Did you?'

'No,' comes the reply. It does not sound like Wilkins. Neither do the other three clipped responses from the same speaker.

'Well I'll be damned.' Wilkins looks baffled. 'He had someone else in on it the whole time.'

'Do you recognise the voice?'

'I don't think so,' says Wilkins, shaking his head. 'No, I can't say that I do.'

TRANSCRIPT OF VOICEMAIL, TAPE 4T/998, 16.03.00, 10.00

TONY DILLON: 'Pauline, are you there? Pick up the phone! I need to speak to you at once. I've been reviewing those tapes you biked over. Pauline!... Well, if you're not there, then ring me as soon as you get this. I want to know just what you've been up to.

There's reams and reams of stuff here about Burnside. You didn't tell me you had all this. You told me that angle wasn't worth pursuing any more. I trusted your judgement, Pauline. You're a great reporter, girl; you've proved that. But I think you've got too close to the subject to be objective – up close and very personal indeed, from what I've just seen. This stuff is dynamite. It changes the whole perspective. In fact, I think we need to go at this from a completely different angle. So get your very fetching arse over here, pronto. I want to film a new wrap and we need to get working on it right away. Love you, Babe. You're a star. See you soon. By the way, you were great on the news. Ray's thrilled. Publicity's going through the roof. Me-ga!'

Diary, 16 March

Oh, God. I'm in the most awful, awful mess. Everything was going so brilliantly and now – now I just don't know which way to turn. And it's all my own fault.

I should never have set Frank up like that. I mean, he was fair game to start with, but after he and I got together I basically knew he was OK. If I'd had any sense, I'd have stopped filming him then, but I didn't. I kidded myself there might be something more going on and kept the cameras rolling. And now Tony's got his grubby mitts on the tapes and wants to redo the entire documentary. I was so taken up with all the interviews and media attention, and when he requested the tapes I biked the whole lot over without thinking. Frank is going to totally kill me.

I've tried everything I can think of to try and dissuade Tony, but he won't listen. His argument is that we're a victim of our own success: because we pulled off such a coup with the coverage of the arrests at Silks and the kidnapping at the warehouse, people won't want to hear the same story twice, especially as it'll be really out of date by the time the documentary is transmitted. Hence the need to put a new spin on the material. He's thinking of calling it *Burnside: Confidential* and billing it as a profile of a flawed, real-life detective with a past that comes back to haunt him. That way he gets to focus on Frank and draw in the two linked investigations and present it as some sort of film-noir style story.

Strictly in terms of television, I have to say it's a great concept, but knowing how much it would hurt Frank, I'm holding out against it. The trouble is, having made the blasted tapes, I'm on very weak ground. I told Ray it would be construed as 'dumbing down', to which he replied, 'I leave the cant to the critics; it's the ratings that count'. When I pointed out that, in any case, the story's not over yet, it's barely begun, Tony rolled his eyes and said in a patronising voice, 'And how does that preclude this approach, Pauline?'. Then he repeated his acid remark about me being too close to the subject to be objective and said perhaps this would teach me to be more professional in the future. And that from a man who slobbered down my neck. If Ray hadn't been there, I would have chucked my coffee over him again.

Quite apart from the fact that Tony came on to me, it's really hypocritical of him to say that, because the sexual chemistry between me and Frank is what they really like. Ray reckons we 'crackle' on screen. They wouldn't have got that if I'd kept my distance. In fact, they wouldn't have got anything if I'd kept my distance. Still, crackling's one thing, snogging's another. I told them they're not showing any scenes of me being intimate with Frank. I did overstep professional etiquette, yes, but let's not broadcast that. I'd get into a lot of trouble, plus it would ruin the credibility of the documentary.

They took my point – reluctantly – but it's not stopped them getting carried away. Ray wants to portray us as this mismatched, crime-fighting duo. I don't remember delivering any snappy one-liners; that must be Frank's role. I'm the one that gets to run around in a corset showing my cleavage. Apparently it's all in the edit. They called Ian in and he was waxing lyrical about grainy images, smash cuts, slo-mo and cool urban music. I had to laugh, because he obviously fancies Frank rotten. He described him as being 'mean, moody and magnificent – the archetypal troubled cop'. I said, 'That's all very well, but I'm not being cast as a dumb broad to satisfy you guys and your Raymond Chandler fixation'.

I'm still working on them, but they seem determined to make the programme this way (whatever happened to *Hidden Chambers?*). I don't know what else do to, short of refusing to co-operate. And that would be stupid, after all I've been through. I've put my life on the line for this show. When I think what Dawson put me through – not just the awful fondling and creepy threats and the porn video, but almost shooting me in the street – it makes me go hot and cold all over. I've gone into territory that no other reporter's dared to, no other female reporter anyway, and I've got fantastic results. I have to keep reminding myself of that. I've nailed my colours to the mast with this. Pauline Chambers is somebody, and somebody to be reckoned with. If I pull out, I'm nobody, a failed hack who didn't ultimately have the courage of her convictions. Can I live with that either?

I keep telling myself it's early days, yet. I don't have to make a decision now. They won't be able to do anything until after the cases go to court, which will be months. Sometimes these things can drag on for years. The Met. is still denying the corruption allegations, but all that could change. Commander Webster has finally been suspended, pending a full enquiry (Wilkins's confession was the icing on the cake), so who knows what the fallout will be?

At least Frank's been reinstated. I get the feeling his heart's not really in it, though. Having been let down so badly by the system has made him more cynical and disillusioned than he was to start with. When he got back yesterday after going to see Wilkins, he was looking really grim. He played me the tape, which was incredible, and when I asked why he was so fed up – I mean, he should have been jumping for joy – he said, 'I joined the force to get out of gangs and street fights; not to join a bigger gang and carry on fighting.' He said joining the police had been a deliberate act to cut himself off from the lifestyle he'd had as a youth. It had forced him to change. It was drastic, but it worked. 'I drew a line: Mal was on one side of it, I went the other. Or I thought I had. Now I ain't so sure.'

To cheer him up, I suggested we go out to dinner, which we did. I know this great pub in Hammersmith where they serve proper Thai food and good English beer, so we went there. After a couple of pints, Frank started to unwind and we ended up having a nice evening – low key, nothing special, just the chance to relax and chat. It's the first time we've gone out together on a proper 'date', which was a bit of a novelty for both of us. He held my hand on the way home – we walked back to the flat – which was really romantic. When we went to bed, he held me very tight and said he hadn't felt as close to anyone in years. We slept curled up like spoons and I woke up cocooned in happiness.

Frank's gone now. He went back to his flat this morning to get more clothes and sort the place out – he hasn't been there since the night Dawson tried to shoot him. I'm glad he wasn't here when Tony rang. I don't know what I'd have done. I've been at Firebrand all morning, so don't know what Frank's up to now. He left me a weird message on my mobile an hour or so; something about being summoned to meet a senior police officer that he hadn't seen for twenty years. It was a bit cryptic. I hope he's OK.

HEDGES: 'Hedges.'

BURNSIDE: 'Gazza. How you doing?'

HEDGES: 'Guvnor? I'm fine. How's life as a celeb? Saw you in the *Sun* today. Very touching.'

BURNSIDE: '"Touching"? Now there's an adjective that ain't often used to describe me.'

HEDGES: 'Picture showed you walking out the warehouse holding those two girlies by the hand. My wife went all gooey when she saw it. It's on the front page.'

BURNSIDE: 'And there's me hoping I'd made page three.'

HEDGES: 'Dream on. That's for your little reporter girlfriend.'

BURNSIDE: 'She ain't my girlfriend. We just… '

HEDGES: ' …sleep together? Gets better and better.'

BURNSIDE: ' …worked together, I was going to say.'

HEDGES: 'More fool you then. No offence, Guv.'

BURNSIDE: 'I'm not saying it didn't have its perks.'

HEDGES: 'I should bloody hope not. Phwoar!'

BURNSIDE: 'But it wouldn't be fair to imply we were anything more than… good friends. At this stage. If you get my drift.'

HEDGES [*pissing himself laughing*]: 'Yeah, yeah, whatever you say…'

BURNSIDE: 'Anyway, I didn't ring to discuss Miss Chambers. Can you talk to Sutton for me? I can't get hold of him.'

HEDGES: 'He's in a meeting with Vice. We found Dawson's gaff this morning. They're angling to take over.'

BURNSIDE: 'They were making noises right from the start. If they'd been doing their bleeding job properly they'd've found those premises months ago. Could've saved us all a load of grief.'

HEDGES: 'I think that's what Sutton's telling him.'

BURNSIDE [*snorting*]: 'How'd you find the place?'

HEDGES: 'Tomasic gave it up. He's singing like a bird. Anything to drop Dawson in it.'

BURNSIDE: 'Yeah, well Dawson's got off light compared with Clare Miller.'

HEDGES: 'You know Dawson's behind Xsecs, too? Cal Wright's boys have been over there. Found the real books. Miller just ran the place for him.'

BURNSIDE: 'Nothing would surprise me. Dawson's main racket's porn and prostitution. Silks is a cover, that's why he keeps it upmarket, doesn't bother with nude table dancers and laser light shows. His punters are regulars, very loyal. Or they're recommended. He doesn't advertise. Doesn't need to. It's all word of mouth. They know what he offers behind the scenes.'

HEDGES: 'Pretty specialised stuff, judging by the reports that've been coming in this morning.'

BURNSIDE: 'So where is this outfit?'

HEDGES: 'Notting Hill, like you said. Bloody great mansion all kitted out like proper studios. Permanent sets, the lot. Neighbours thought it was a foreign language institute.' [*He chortles*] 'So what do you want me to tell Sutton?'

BURNSIDE: 'I'm gonna need backup. In about an hour.'

HEDGES: 'Sure, boss. What's going on? Thought the high jinks was over.'

BURNSIDE: 'Maybe. Maybe not. I ain't taking any chances.'

HEDGES: 'What's the job?'

BURNSIDE: 'I went back to my place this morning, found a message on my answering machine. It was from a bloke called Wishart. Andrew Wishart. He was my old inspector from '77–82. Dunno what happened to him after I joined the Flying Squad. I ain't heard his name in donkey's years. Said he was ringing to congratulate me on my achievements. He also said he had a proposal that might interest me.'

HEDGES: 'I don't get it, Guv. Why's that so bad?'

BURNSIDE: 'Ain't you seen Wilkins's confession?'

HEDGES: 'Wilkins? Name rings a bell. Yeah, I heard it this morning. Retired copper, topped himself. Sutton was in a bit of a stew.'

BURNSIDE: 'Jesus.'

HEDGES: 'You alright, Guv?'

BURNSIDE [*wearily*]: 'Yeah, Gazza. I'll live.'

HEDGES: 'So what did he confess to?'

BURNSIDE: 'Everything. Told me the entire story. I'll fill you in later. But the one thing he did say was, he weren't in that meeting Gaughan recorded.'

HEDGES [*mystified*]: 'Wasn't he?'

BURNSIDE: 'No. It was someone else. I checked. They *refer* to Wilkins, but he ain't there himself.'

HEDGES: 'You lost me, I'm afraid Guv. I ain't heard that tape, neither.'

BURNSIDE: 'Sutton's sitting on 'em?'

HEDGES: 'So tight you'd think they was stuffed up his arse.'

BURNSIDE: 'Urggh.'

HEDGES: 'What you're saying is, you don't know who this mystery bloke on the tape is, that right? And you're thinking it could be Wishart?'

BURNSIDE: 'I knew you'd made DS for a reason.'

HEDGES: 'But you're gonna meet him anyway?'

BURNSIDE: 'Last piece of the jigsaw. I sincerely hope.'

HEDGES: 'You ain't meeting him by a canal, are yer?'

BURNSIDE: 'We're having lunch. Somewhere snazzy in Soho. Silvio's. Berwick Street.'

HEDGES: 'Italian?'

BURNSIDE: 'Give me a break.'

HEDGES: 'You said there was a mafia connection. "Silvio's" sounds Italian to me. That's all I'm saying.'

BURNSIDE: 'Well if he's carrying a violin case, I'll skip the starter and get on the radio to you lot, OK?'

TRANSCRIPT OF FILM, TAPE 402V/404. SILVIO'S, BERWICK STREET.

16.03.00, 13.00

The restaurant is modern but not minimalist; formal without being overbearing. The prices, we see from the menu displayed outside, are astronomical. The patrons, we see when Burnside steps inside, confirm the reason why: a British film director dines with a Hollywood actress; a stand-up comedian with a leading political pundit; the editor of a satirical magazine with a foreign correspondent; an art collector with a style guru. The linen, the silverware, the wall hangings, the waiters, all spell exclusivity. It does not look the sort of restaurant where one could conceal a sub-machine gun beneath the table; neither does it look the sort of place where police officers – even senior police officers – would (or could) normally dine.

Burnside gives Wishart's name and is led to a table towards the back of the room where a balding, middle-aged man is sitting. The man stands up and extends his hand, beaming. 'Burnside! Good to see you!' He pumps Burnside's hand vigorously.

'Inspector Wishart.'

'ACC now, Frank.'

'ACC Wishart. Congratulations, sir. What division?'

'National Crime Squad.' Wishart resumes his seat, rubbing his hands. 'Jolly good. I must say, this menu looks intriguing. Have you been here before?'

'No.'

'Ah. You're in for a treat, then. Excellent. Shall we order? The mussels are good. What about a drink?'

'If you don't mind, sir, I'd like to know what this is all about.'

Wishart mouths 'water' at the hovering maitre d' and dismisses him with a discreet signal. He leans forward. 'Word has got around.'

'About – ?'

'You, of course.'

Burnside sighs. 'With respect, sir, the grapevine to the NCS must be running a bit slow. I've been reinstated at Crime OCU and the investigation by the Pepper squad has been dropped pending a full enquiry into Commander Webster. Who framed me. Obviously that bit of gossip hasn't reached you yet.'

'Oh, yes, I've heard all about that. That is what I was referring to, actually.'

'Yeah?'

'Don't glare at me like that, Frank. We've covered a lot of ground, you and me.'

'As far as I remember, you didn't have much faith in me as a sergeant.'

Wishart looks uncomfortable. 'I admit, there were times when your reputation, and your behaviour, gave me cause for concern, yes.'

'You believed the rumour-mill then, too. Thought I was bent, didn't you? You and half the nick. That was Webster's doing, an' all. Him and someone else.'

'Superintendent Sutton briefed me comprehensively this morning. I know all about Webster's dealings. Clearly he's a very cunning man.' Wishart pours himself and Burnside a glass of Pellegrino. He says, without looking up, 'I have to admit to a sneaking regard for the fellow. Keeping up such a deceit for so long is quite an achievement. And actually getting himself selected for an anti-corruption operation... that's a stroke of genius.'

Burnside snorts in disgust.

'Though of course, being on the receiving end of Webster's machinations, I would expect you to have a different perspective.' He drinks, observing Burnside over the rim of his glass of fizzing water.

'If you're so bleedin' impressed with Webster, what do you want to see me for?' Burnside's voice rises. Several of the diners glance round. He ignores the looks. 'Come to do his dirty work, have you? Gonna do a deal with me on his behalf? Get your old pal out of schtook?'

Wishart's easy-going expression refuses to alter. Carefully, he puts down his glass. 'It's natural for you to feel sensitive about this, Frank. I don't blame you. If I'd been through what you've been through, I'd jump to conclusions, too. But you're wrong. The man I really admire is you. Webster's clever, yes. But you've proved yourself even more clever. He's been playing us for fools all this time and no one saw it. Except you. You've more than exonerated yourself. You've excelled yourself.' He leans back in his seat, genial. 'So, in answer to your question, I asked you here to thank you, on behalf of the Metropolitan Police. And to make you a proposal.'

Burnside's voice is wary. 'Which is?'

'I've got a job for you, if you want it.'

'Doing what?'

'Running your own syndicate at the National Crime Squad.'

'Is this a sop?'

'Flowers are for funerals, Frank. Pay-offs are for victims. You know how the Met. hates apologising.' He leans forward again, smiling. 'We can't afford to lose good coppers, Frank. A man of your ability should be in the top league. I know a genuine thief-taker when I see one. I need you in the NCS.'

'I – ' For once, Burnside appears lost for words.

'Bit of a bombshell, I realise that, but what do you say? Will you think about it?'

Burnside reaches into his jacket and pulls out his radio. 'Gazza?'

The radio crackles loudly, startling the wealthy art collector, who is sitting nearby. 'Yes, Guv.'

'I'm going to have the … ' Burnside studies the menu. 'Pâté, for starters. I'll see you lot down the pub.'

CONFIDENTIAL MEMO
TO: Ray Dunthorne
FROM: Tony Dillon
DATE: 16 March
RE: *Burnside: Confidential*
Love the wrap you suggested but can't see Pauline going
for it as things stand. She's obviously besotted with
Burnside, which is clouding her professional judgement.
If we want her to 'come out' to him, expose the story-
within-the-story, we're going to need a much bigger
carrot. My suggestion is, give her her own series, call it
Hidden Chambers, as per our original intention, and set
her up with, say, half a dozen separate investigations to
do over the course of a year, maybe two (sponsorship?)
Some fancy foreign locations, additional journalists if
necessary. Make her executive producer! If *Burnside:
Confidential* is the smash we think it's going to be, it's a
win-win situation all round. Let me know soonest.

Tone

The pub is noisy, smoky, boisterous. Burnside is with his Crime OCU colleagues at the bar – Sutton, Hedges, Terri and a bunch of others we don't recognise. There is much back-slapping and laughing going on. We see them from Pauline's point of view as she enters the pub, looks about and then goes over to Burnside. 'Here I am.' She kisses him. Much cheering from the assembled company. 'What's up? Everyone seems very excited.'

Burnside is grinning broadly. He's clearly drunk. He puts an arm around her shoulders and whispers something into her ear, too soft for the mike to pick up. Hedges wolf-whistles loudly. Pauline pulls Frank to one side. 'Did you say what I thought you just said?'

'I don't know, do I?'

'I thought you said – ' She leans over and whispers in his ear, cupping her mouth with her hand.

He looks at her, eyes glowing. 'I did.'

'You're pissed. Men always say that when they're pissed. When you're sober, you'll deny it completely.'

'Better get it on tape, then.' He makes a grab for her.

She pulls away. 'Talking of which, did you wear my equipment on your lunch date?'

'Yeah. Turned out I needn't have bothered, but better safe than sorry, eh? Want a drink?'

'I'll have a beer. Thanks.'

Burnside shouts to Hedges, who is getting a round in, ordering two more beers.

'So he wasn't your mystery man, then?'

'Don't think so.'

'But you're not absolutely sure.'

'I'm pretty sure. One thing I've learned recently, Pauline. You can't be absolutely sure of anything in this life. Sometimes,' – he drops a kiss on the top of her head – 'you've just gotta follow your instincts and hope for the best.'

'Yes,' she says quietly.

'Aren't you going to ask me what Andrew Wishart wanted, then?'

'What did he want?'

'To offer me a job. National Crime Squad.'

'Is that good?'

'Good? It's better than good. The NCS is – well, they're top dogs. It's the British equivalent of the FBI. I get to head my own syndicate, choose my own investigations, work proactively. I get to call the shots. It's what I've always wanted.'

'That's fantastic.'

Gary Hedges brings their drinks over. 'Here you are, Guv.' He grins at Pauline. 'Great news, innit? I'm Gazza. We never got properly introduced the other day.' He holds out a sticky hand.

'Leave off, Gazza, you've got your own,' Burnside says, but good-naturedly.

'Just wanted to meet the famous Miss Chambers. You can go undercover with me any time, love.' Hedges, still ogling, lurches away.

'That's the other thing,' Burnside continues. 'A lot of it's undercover work. What I do best.'

'I thought that – incident – with Kim Hyde put you off that.'

'Nah. It's like falling off a horse. You've gotta get back on again. I did one up in Newcastle earlier; got a result there. It all came back. It's a real buzz.'

'Probably because you got a result with that policewoman, Liz whatsername.'

'You're jealous, Pauline.' Burnside looks tickled.

'No. Yes. A bit. But you're mine, now. Aren't you?'

'Well… alright. If you say so.' He bends to kiss her again. All of a sudden, she buries her head in his shirt. 'Come on. We're supposed to be celebrating.' He lifts her chin, looks puzzled. 'Why the tears?'

'Because… because it's so hard sometimes, with my job, and your job. They're bound to clash…'

'Not to mention my age and your age.' He gives her a squeeze. 'Let's not look at the long term, sweetheart. You know and I know it can't last. Let's just enjoy it while it's good. Yeah?'

'Yeah,' she sniffs. 'Sorry. I'm not really in the mood for celebrating. I don't want to be a party pooper. I'll go, catch you later.'

'I'll come with you, then. I've had a skinful, anyway.'

'Sure?'

'Yeah. We can crack open a bottle from the offie, just you and me.'

'That would be nice.' She glances at her watch. 'Your place or mine?'

'Mine. I never did get round to sorting out my gear. I'll just say goodbye to the lads.'

'OK.'

As soon as Burnside's back is turned, Pauline gets out a mobile and presses a memory button. 'Tony. It's me. Frank's house, thirty mins, tops. Right. I'll see you there. Bye.'

TRANSCRIPT OF FILM, TAPE 404V/404. BURNSIDE'S HOUSE, SOUTH LAMBETH.
16.03.00, 18.45

The Firebrand Productions crew is parked up in their van outside Burnside's house. Dave, the cameraman, takes some shots of the exterior, while Ian fends off nosy neighbours, telling them there's nothing to see. Catching a whiff of excitement, they pay no attention to this and a gaggle of onlookers forms across the street.

Eventually, a black cab turns into the road and chugs towards them. The door opens and Burnside gets out, followed by Pauline, dressed in combat trousers and a T-shirt, with a quilted jacket hanging open. Dave points the camera at them. Burnside's face darkens. He starts to walk towards him, clenching his fist. 'What the hell do you think you're playing at? Haven't you bloody well seen enough? This is finished now. It's all over. Get out of here.'

Dave stands his ground. Tony, foreseeing that an expensive video camera is about to be pulverised, intervenes. 'Look, Frank, we just want – umfff.' The ever-resourceful Dave swings around to show his director on the floor, spitting blood and teeth. A second later, the camera goes skywards, there's a loud crash and Dave joins him on the deck.

We know this from Pauline's secret camera, worn under her baggy clothing. Burnside, though, does not make the connection straight away. 'For Christ's sake, Pauline. Tell them to get lost. Don't your lot know when to stop? They've got the scoop or whatever you call it. They've got their documentary. What more do they want? Blood?' This last word is hurled at Tony, who is being helped to his feet by Ian. 'Well, they've got that, too!' He takes her by the arm. 'Come on, let's get inside. I'm sick of all this.'

Pauline does not move.

'Don't tell me you're feeling sorry for that slimeball Tony. He's had it coming for a long time.'

'No.'

'So why are you standing here? Come on.'

Pauline takes a deep breath. 'You don't mind, do you, Frank? A piece to camera, on the record? The end of a brilliant story?

Just to wrap?' Her voice is over-bright, her presenter's voice.

'What are you on about? The frigging camera's had it.'

'Please, Frank. Just tell us how you feel, now you've got your life back again. And a new life in the National Crime Squad to look forward to. You must be a happy man.'

Burnside's eyes widen. His mouth drops. He lunges at Pauline. She screams. Burnside grabs hold of her T-shirt and yanks it up. The onlookers gasp. He sees the recording gear taped to her chest and lets go, turning his back on her in disgust. Pauline stifles a sob and runs after him. 'Frank! I had to do it this way. I knew you wouldn't co-operate if I asked you. I'm sorry... look, we can set it up another time, do it properly, not like this.'

He turns to her, face livid. 'There won't be another time, Pauline. So let's say goodbye now.'

'Frank... '

'What beats me is, you know how I feel about this. My privacy being invaded. I don't want my life being made into some sort of a soap.'

'I'm sorry... I'm really sorry.'

He stares at her, realisation dawning. 'You've been filming me all along, haven't you?'

'Yes.' It comes out as a whisper.

'You little bitch.' Burnside takes her by the shoulders and shakes her.

'Leave her alone!' Ian tries to pull him off. Burnside swats him away like a fly. Ian staggers backwards, holding his nose. 'I'm going to call the police.'

'I am the bleeding police.'

'Yes and you're acting like a typical thug. That's one aspect of the police we'd love to catch on camera.' Ian is panting and his voice sounds odd, but he carries on. 'You're doing your reputation no end of good, Burnside.'

Burnside lets Pauline go. She collapses in a heap, sobbing. We can't see him any more, just the road. He says, quietly, 'You don't get it, do you, Pauline? It's not just that I feel personally betrayed by you. It ain't even that I'm camera-shy. How do you think I'm going to do my new job, working undercover, when every crook from here to kingdom come's seen my mug on the television screen? Have you thought about that? No. Of course you ain't.'

He starts to walk away, then stops. 'I'd like to say it was nice knowing you. But I don't think I can.' We hear his footsteps retreat and fade. The door being unlocked. The door being slammed.

Pauline stands, unsteadily. Dave comes over to her, holding another camera. 'I always keep a spare for emergencies. I think this counts as one.' He zooms around, taking in Tony, Ian and Pauline, all of whom look either bruised, bloody or bedraggled. 'Come on, do a piece to camera yourself.'

'What's the point?'

'Perfect wrap. Burnside wreaks havoc. Raging bull lashes out. Heroic cop decks crew. Take your pick.'

'Don't be stupid. Looking like this?'

'That's the whole point.'

Tony, who can't talk, nods, holding his jaw. Ian puts an arm around her. 'Dave's right. It's a fantastic way to end it. Superb footage.'

Pauline blows her nose. 'How's my mascara?'

'Smudged, but appealing. Leave it,' Ian instructs.

She squares her shoulders and rakes her hair with her fingers, standing with her back to Burnside's house. Dave frames the shot. Over Pauline's shoulder, we see Burnside looking out of the living-room window. For a second, his gaze meets ours. Then he draws the curtains.